P9-AEU-479

"You can't marry every woman who needs a husband, Matt,"

Charlotte said. "You can't always take responsibility for the mess other people have gotten into.... You try so hard to make everything right, but you're only human."

Matt thought of how he'd reacted to her earlier. "I think I've proven that."

"I think we both have," Charlotte said.

"I suppose you want me to apologize."

"Not necessarily. Do you want me to?"

"For what?"

"For kissing you back."

"Damn it, I'm the one who initiated the kiss. I'm the one who'll apologize." He slammed the metal first-aid kit so hard it made Charlotte wince. "I'm sorry. It won't happen again."

"Oh? How are you going to guarantee that? Do you think you can control my emotions, too? Or didn't you notice that I was just as involved as you were?"

"I won't let things get out of hand again," he insisted.

"See? There you go trying to take on everyone else's responsibilities. What if I want it to happen again?"

Dear Reader,

From a most traditional marriage of convenience to a futuristic matchmaking robot, from a dusty dude ranch to glistening Pearl Harbor, from international adventure to an inner struggle with disturbing memories, this month's sensational Silhouette **Special Edition** authors pull out all the stops to honor your quest for a range of deeply satisfying novels of living and loving in today's world.

Those of you who've written in requesting that Ginna Gray tell dashing David Blaine's story, and those of you who waved the flag for Debbie Macomber's "Navy" novels, please take note that your patience is finally being rewarded with *Once in a Lifetime* and *Navy Brat*. For the rest of you, now's the time to discover what all the excitement is about! Naturally, each novel stands solidly alone as, you might say, an extra special Silhouette **Special Edition**.

Don't miss the other special offerings in store for you: four more wonderful novels by talented, talked about writers Nikki Benjamin, Arlene James, Bevlyn Marshall and Christina Dair. Each author brings you a memorable novel packed with stirring emotions and the riches of love: in the tradition of Silhouette **Special Edition**, romance to believe in . . . and to remember.

From all the authors and editors of Silhouette **Special Edition**,

Warmest wishes.

CHRISTINA DAIR
A Will of
Her Own

Silhouette Special Edition

Published by Silhouette Books New York

America's Publisher of Contemporary Romance

To my mother,
who taught me the joy
of reading, the value of love
and the meaning of courage.

SILHOUETTE BOOKS
300 East 42nd St., New York, N.Y. 10017

A WILL OF HER OWN

Copyright © 1991 by Louzana Kaku

All rights reserved. Except for use in any review, the reproduction or utilization of this work in whole or in part in any form by any electronic, mechanical or other means, now known or hereafter invented, including xerography, photocopying and recording, or in any information storage or retrieval system, is forbidden without the permission of Silhouette Books, 300 E. 42nd St., New York, N.Y. 10017

ISBN: 0-373-09666-6

First Silhouette Books printing April 1991

All the characters in this book are fictitious. Any resemblance to actual persons, living or dead, is purely coincidental.

®: Trademark used under license and registered in the United States Patent and Trademark Office and in other countries.

Printed in the U.S.A.

CHRISTINA DAIR

comes from a long line of romance readers and grew up on romantic classics such as *Sleeping Beauty, Jane Eyre* and *Gone With the Wind*. After majoring in literature in college, she taught high school English.

Now that she has two young daughters and has "retired" from teaching, Christina has discovered still another career that allows her to indulge her passion for writing and reading: romance novelist. Her first book was published in 1984, and two others followed in 1986 and 1987. *A Will of Her Own* marks her debut in the Silhouette Special Edition line.

Christina resides with her husband and their daughters in Cerritos, California. She is active in school and community groups and has served as Special Events Coordinator, Treasurer, Vice President and Co-president of the Orange County Chapter of Romance Writers of America.

VASSAR

(Voice Activated Security System and Robot)

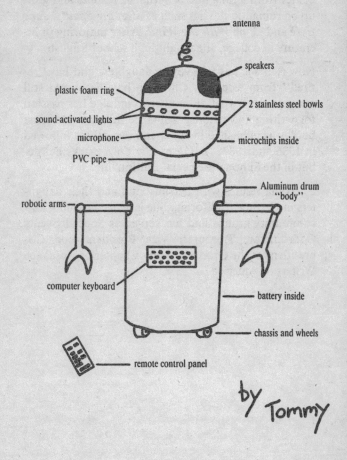

- antenna
- speakers
- plastic foam ring
- 2 stainless steel bowls
- sound-activated lights
- microphone
- microchips inside
- PVC pipe
- Aluminum drum "body"
- robotic arms
- computer keyboard
- battery inside
- chassis and wheels
- remote control panel

by Tommy

Chapter One

"Is that a no?" Matt Oliver asked politely.

Pushing the tortoiseshell glasses down as far as the subtle angling of his nose would allow, Matt drilled Charlotte Lambert with a gaze that belied his casual question. On the mahogany desk between them, stacks of legal briefs were lined up like soldiers.

"An absolute, definite, unequivocal no!" She crossed her arms as she stared back at him. "You know, I wouldn't believe it if I hadn't seen it, but I think Matthew Oliver, brilliant young attorney, has finally flipped. Don't worry, though. Given enough time, you'll be grateful I kept my wits about me."

Matt merely nodded. It was impossible to take offense when Charlotte Lambert's mouth, which was curved in a generous smile, took the sting out of her words, as did her green eyes, which gleamed with barely suppressed amusement. As usual, Charlotte's short dark hair was brushed back from her face, showing off her long neck and elegant cheekbones. She was the only person Matt knew who could give the impression of cruising at just below the speed of sound even when she was sitting still.

Steepling his hands, Matt settled back in his leather chair and gave her a few minutes to reconsider. After all, he'd never proposed marriage to a woman before; he couldn't believe such a momentous decision could be made in less time than it took him to snap his fingers.

"Would you like a little more time to think it over?" he asked after several silent moments.

"If I had a year—"

"Which you don't."

"My answer would still be no. And don't try to intimidate me by peering over your glasses. Take those preppy things off and look me in the eye."

"They aren't preppy," Matt protested, though he tossed them onto his desk. "I need them for paperwork."

"Well, I'm not made of paper," Charlotte informed him with a dismissive wave of her hand. "Just tell me what my relatives and their assorted attorneys have done to drive you to this act of desperation?"

Matt shifted in his chair as he tried to think of a convincing way to sum up the situation. "Nothing new. Just more of the same old stuff. But time's running out." He sat forward and drilled her with a look that had been known to make even the most seasoned attorney wish his client had settled out of court. "You have exactly eighteen days to come up with a husband, or forfeit controlling interest in a company worth roughly twenty million dollars. I happen to think it's asinine to sit back and let those piranhas you call relatives sink their teeth into the majority of a company you've put the last six years of your life into—and all because of some crazy clause your father put in his will five years ago.

"More importantly, I don't think it's what your father wanted. He'd made an appointment with me, and he'd told you he was going to make some changes in his will. If he'd lived another week, he would have left Rutherford Packaging to you, lock, stock and barrel. You know it, and I know it. Unfortunately, that won't hold water in court. So you have two options: find a husband or contest the will. I'm ready to file a motion to have the will ruled invalid as soon as you give me the word."

Charlotte released a long-suffering sigh that Matt made a point of ignoring. When she spoke, her voice was low but steady.

"I will not testify that my father was incapacitated, however briefly. There isn't anything you can say that would persuade me to drag his name through the courts—not even if I thought we had a prayer of convincing the judge that a man who was a partner in one of the most lucrative land development companies in Southern California was anything but lucid every moment of his life."

The way she said it, with not the least glimmer of amusement in her eyes, made Matt realize that she was dead serious.

"As for that other option," she added. "It might interest you to know that I called Husbands R Us just this morning. Unfortunately, they're fresh out this month, but suggested I call back after the first. I told them that would be too late. Besides, I think I've come up with a third alternative: Do you have any idea where I could hire a hit man?" Picking an imaginary piece of lint off the slacks of her tailored navy-and-white pantsuit, Charlotte settled back with a grin.

Matthew successfully fought the urge to laugh; it would only encourage her outrageous attitude. He wondered if it would be more effective if he walked around the desk and shook some sense into that gorgeous head of hers. How the hell had she survived thirty-one years with this damned Pollyanna attitude of hers?

When she asked, "You don't happen to know if the cost of eliminating the other heirs would be tax deductible as estate planning, do you?" Matthew barely controlled the urge to hurdle the desk and throttle her.

"Interesting idea. I'll have one of the clerks research that possibility," was all he said as he made a note on a yellow legal pad. He refused to give her the satisfaction of knowing it was one of the most preposterous suggestions he'd ever heard, or that her two uncles were such greedy bastards that he too had considered a hit man on several occasions. "However, since I don't have adequate time to research that rather unorthodox strategy, what do *you* suggest I do with you?"

"Not marry me, that's for sure. Besides, don't you think my relatives would be suspicious if I suddenly up and married three weeks before the estate is to be settled? To my attorney, no less?"

"They'd probably just consider me a money-grubbing bastard. They're well acquainted with that subspecies."

Charlotte gave an unladylike snort.

"Bear in mind that I don't have to be the groom. I'm perfectly willing to step aside if you know someone else with the patience of three saints, who'd put up with you on a temporary basis. It could save you a lot of grief. Not to mention a great deal of money."

"Matt, we've gone around and around about this for the last few months."

"Just over seventeen months, to be exact."

Charlotte nodded; she'd come to terms with Matt's exacting nature. "I thought I'd made myself clear on the subject. I'm not willing to get married just to satisfy my father's rather eccentric will. Now why the sudden panic on your part?"

"I always assumed you'd come to your senses in the nick of time. In case you haven't looked at your calendar lately, this *is* the nick of time."

Unable to sit still any longer, Charlotte rose and walked to the windows that met at right angles behind Matt's desk. She heard the creak of his chair and knew he'd turned to watch her, but she continued to study the vast sprawl of Los Angeles thirty-three stories below. The June fog had finally lifted, leaving behind the kind of day Southern Californians rarely enjoyed, for today she could see all the way from the San Gabriel Mountains to the island of Catalina. On a day this perfect it was hard to believe that her father was gone. Or that he'd left the kind of will worthy of Machiavelli.

Yet here she was, actually entertaining the idea of marrying Matthew Oliver, an attorney with the prestigious law firm of Russell and Winslow, so that she could gain sole ownership of Rutherford Packaging.

The company, which had been passed down from her maternal grandfather, had been on the verge of bankruptcy six years ago when she'd bet her father she could turn it around. He'd called her bluff, and two years later she'd not only dragged the company out of the red but into a policy of expansion. At the same time, she'd allowed her marriage to disintegrate until divorce was the only possible course open to her. She'd happily returned to the use of her maiden name, but the divorce had been harder on her father. No, if she was honest, she'd admit that it had been the lack of grandchildren that had really bothered him.

It was then that her father, fearful his only child would become a workaholic old maid and convinced that he and Rutherford Packaging had contributed to the breakup of her marriage, had drawn up a will that required she be married in order to inherit RP. If not married at the time of his death, she had eighteen months to come to her senses and find a suitable husband. If she wasn't a sensible married woman by that time, only forty percent of the company would pass to her, and the remaining sixty percent would be divided between her late mother's two brothers and a sister. It was a classic case of damned if you do and damned if you don't.

But Charlotte wasn't willing to marry because it was convenient. She'd made that mistake already. If she married again, it would be for love, and she was smart enough to know that you couldn't go shopping for love as you could for the perfect little black dress. She'd watched her father search unsuccessfully ever since her mother's death twenty-eight years before; he'd never found it. And she'd watched Aunty Rhue pursue it through four marriages and almost into the fifth; reality never lived up to Rhue's expectations. No, she wasn't willing to go out and beat the bushes for a husband, not even if it meant losing control of the company she'd practically resurrected from the grave.

When Matt said quietly, "I was serious about that marriage business," she took a deep breath and turned to face him.

"I appreciate the offer. Really I do. But I'm not sure it's worth all the effort. After all, I'll still be chief executive officer of RP. It'll still be a family-owned company, and I'll still be making the decisions."

"Maybe."

"Maybe? What do you mean 'maybe'?"

"Given controlling interest, your relatives could always vote to replace you as CEO."

"They wouldn't! At least not as long as I'm showing a profit!"

"Or they could sell off their shares of the company."

"To whom?"

"Anyone who wanted to buy them. And since you've turned RP into such a profitable venture, it shouldn't be too difficult to find someone willing to buy in."

That was a new wrinkle! Something she hadn't even thought about. The one thing she'd assumed during all the legal haggling over the will was that no one would willingly relinquish interest in a business that had been in the family since its founding at the turn of the century.

Not for the first time during the past seventeen months, Charlotte studied Matthew Oliver very carefully. From his brown hair, lightened by the sun, to his steady brown eyes and squared chin, Matt exuded determination and rock-solid dependability. It was only the dangerous glint in his brown eyes that ever gave her pause. During the first few months, she'd been haunted by the image of herself as a helpless deer foolishly walking into the territory of a hungry mountain lion. Not that that had ever stopped her; the word *discretion* rarely crept into her vocabulary. Then she'd learned about Matt's steely control and she'd relaxed a bit . . . not completely, mind you, but enough to sit easily in the glare of his dark gaze.

Added to all that was the slight angling of his nose, undoubtedly the result of a physical altercation, body language that fairly screamed he was not a man to be messed with, and the kind of physique usually associated with professional athletes—he was the sort of man who turned women's heads when he entered a room.

Yet that wasn't what intrigued her—or at least she wouldn't have thought so before Matt's unusual proposal of marriage had prompted some very strange flip-flops in her stomach. What she admired most was his mind and his ability to cut through all the legal mumbo jumbo to the heart of the matter. And the bottom line, for her at least, was what would happen to the company she'd poured her life's blood into.

Leaning back on the edge of Matt's credenza, she crossed her arms and stared straight into his dark eyes. "You're just saying that to scare me."

"Is it working?"

Charlotte nodded.

"Good. Because I want you to consider all the possibilities before you give me your final answer."

"How do you know my answer wasn't final?"

Matt grinned and settled back comfortably. "The first answer out of your mouth is rarely your final one. I've gotten used to ignoring it and waiting for the one you've given some thought to."

Charlotte smiled. "Oh, yeah?"

"Yeah," he responded softly.

His smile, coupled with the fact that he knew her so well, created an unexpected sensation of warmth. Who would have thought that this controlled, precise man would learn to tolerate her impulsive nature? Or that she would come to depend on him?

Not that she needed someone to depend on, she reminded herself. It was just that his shoulders were so wide, so perfect for leaning on. And she'd become used to them being there for her.

"I'm not greedy, Matt."

He nodded. "I know that."

"I don't have to have Rutherford Packaging to survive."

Matt nodded again, but kept his silence in the way of most sage counselors.

"I've got Dad's interest in Buena Vista Land Development."

"That's tied up," he reminded her.

"It won't be forever. And I've got the house and everything in it."

"Which you wouldn't sell if you were down to your last penny."

"But I don't need money. I've got enough to keep me comfortably for quite a few years."

Spoken like a woman who's never wanted for anything, Matt thought, and felt his anger rising. Maybe he shouldn't worry about her. Maybe he should just let her go on as she was.

But, dammit, this wasn't about money! It was about justice. It was about arranging a settlement that would keep Charles Lambert from turning over and over in his grave. It was about Charlotte getting what she'd earned, even if he didn't understand how anyone who could shrug off several million dollars had hauled a floundering company back on course.

"It's up to you," he said simply. "I'm the attorney for your father's estate; you're his executor. Ultimately, I'm charged with carrying out the intent of his will just as you're charged with executing the court's decisions. Just promise me you'll think about it."

"Okay. I'll think about it. Anything else?"

"No."

"Then I'm out of here," Charlotte informed him as she scooped her purse from the chair she'd occupied earlier and headed for the door. Looking back over her shoulder, she said, "Try not to propose to anyone else on the rebound, will you? I'd hate to have your fate on my conscience." Then she was gone.

Matt found himself alone, staring at the empty doorway and wondering if she'd ever said anything as prosaic as "goodbye." If she had, he'd never heard it.

After a moment, he flipped open one of the folders and began sorting through the legal documents. Well, he'd made the effort, he assured himself. Offered the bachelor's ultimate sacrifice. And she'd turned him down flat. Now he could quit worrying about her.

She's a big girl, he told himself. She'll have to take her lumps like everyone else. He should be relieved at being let off the hook. Hell, he *was* relieved at being let off the hook.

Wasn't he?

Charlotte hung up the phone in her office and eyed the stacks of paper that covered her desk. It wasn't really messy; it just had that lived-in look. Thank God, there was still room to prop her feet up on the edge of it, she thought as she eased out of her shoes and stuck her stockinged feet up for a minute.

Upon her return from Matt's office, she'd discovered that the manager of Rutherford's Riverside facility had phoned four times and that the Atlanta facility was unable to purchase enough raw paper product from its usual source. In the past two hours she'd managed not only to calm down her Riverside manager, but to round up enough material for the Atlanta outfit to meet its present contractual obligations. She was weary but exhilarated. If she could drop by the club and play a couple games of tennis after work, she'd feel like tackling her neglected paperwork at home tonight. Charlotte had the phone in her hand, ready to call her housekeeper and let her know she'd be late for dinner, when there was a knock on her door.

"Come in."

When John Everling, the senior accountant, stuck his head around the door, she cradled the phone.

"How's my favorite boss?" John asked with a deceptively boyish grin. "Another one of those days with nothing to do but sit around with your feet on the desk, I see."

Charlotte laughed as John eased his lanky frame into the chair opposite her. Only a few years older than her thirty-one years, John was the first person she'd hired after her appointment as CEO of Rutherford Packaging. Behind his horn-rimmed glasses and computer-sharp mind beat the heart of a gambler. He'd burned the midnight oil with her many times and backed her on some of her more daring decisions. There was no doubt he recognized exhaustion when he saw it.

"What's new in the numbers game?" she asked, without bothering to slip her feet back into her shoes.

"The numbers look good," he assured her. "But I've had a few strange phone calls I thought you should know about."

Charlotte's feet dropped back to the floor. "Oh?"

"A friend of mine called from Waldheim last week." There was no reason for him to mention that Waldheim was one of their toughest competitors. "Said he just wanted to chat. See how the wife and kids are, that kind of stuff. Before he hung up, he asked how the company was doing. I didn't think much of it at the time.

"Then yesterday I got a call from a fellow over at Forester's. Pretty much the same stuff."

Charlotte nodded. RP had surpassed Forester's production during the previous quarter.

"Today someone called from National Paper Products."

"The conglomerate National? The New York Stock Exchange National?" When John nodded his answer to both questions, Charlotte sat back in her chair and let out a little whistle.

"Charlotte, are you planning to sell RP? Because if you are, I think you ought to inform your employees. Some of the older folks are close to retirement. They might want to take early retirement rather than get the boot when the new owners take over. And some of us may not want to work for a big, impersonal conglomerate."

"Me? Sell? You must be out of your mind!"

"The men who called must have a reason to think RP is on the market. If the word wasn't put out by you, then it must have been those money-grubbing relatives of yours." John rose and paced around the small office, all the while massaging the back of his neck as though he could rub the problem away.

"RP is successful because of your leadership. You don't sit around considering a move until the opportunity's been lost. You go with your gut instincts. But if one of these other companies gets involved..." Shrugging, John looked over at her. "I just thought you should know. That's all. See you tomorrow."

"Yeah. Tomorrow," Charlotte murmured as John departed. Then she was reaching for the phone again. This time she punched in Howard Rutherford's number.

"Hello."

"Uncle Howie," she said without preamble, "I want to know if you're planning to sell your share of RP?"

"Why, Charlotte, how nice to hear from you, honey." She heard him take a puff on the cigar that was never far from his hand. "How're you doing?"

Knowing Howard Rutherford as she did, Charlotte realized that his evasion was as good as an admission of guilt.

"How could you?" she demanded. "Your father founded the company."

"Along with a haberdashery and millinery. Both of those went out of business long ago," he said with another puff. "You must learn not to be so sentimental over a simple business."

"I'm not talking about sentiment. RP has increased its value almost three hundred percent over the last four years. Where else could you get that kind of return?"

"And what about the next three years? There's no telling where your unorthodox business practices might lead?" Puff. She could picture him leaning back, with his feet propped up on a table. "These are my sunset years. I shouldn't have to worry about where my next meal is coming from. I'm sure you can see how several million in the bank is preferable to a company that makes cardboard boxes."

Charlotte gritted her teeth and refrained from pointing out that it wouldn't hurt him to forego a few meals, that RP produced sophisticated packaging as well as plain brown boxes, and that just because he and his brother, Walter, had bankrupted several businesses over the years didn't mean that she couldn't keep Rutherford Packaging solvent.

Instead, she asked as sweetly as possible, "But if you and Uncle Walter wanted to sell, why didn't you come to me first?"

"We thought about that." Puff. Puff. "Sure we did. But then Walt and I decided that we didn't want to see our favorite niece get in over her head."

Charlotte gritted hard enough to make her jaw hurt and spoke through her teeth. "And just how did you figure I'd get in over my head?"

"We weren't sure you could come up with that kind of cash."

"I can sell Dad's share of Buena Vista Land Development."

"I was under the impression that was tied up at the moment," he murmured, but Charlotte could tell that he wasn't nearly as disinterested as he'd been the moment before.

"Yeah," she said with a sigh, and wondered what form of idiocy had ever prompted her to discuss her financial situation with Uncle Howie. Overwhelming grief, she decided, could certainly do a number on a person's gray matter.

"I can put up my forty percent of Rutherford as collateral for a loan."

"Maybe. But then you'd still have to finance the other twenty percent."

"The other twenty percent! You mean Aunty Rhue is in this with you?"

"You didn't think we'd leave our little sister out in the cold, did you?"

"You have before."

Howie laughed and took a few puffs on his cigar. "You know, I think that high-powered lawyer of your dad's undervalued RP for the estate. Either that, or sixty percent of the business is worth damn near as much as a hundred percent."

"What's the best price you've been offered?" Charlotte demanded. Subtlety was wasted on Uncle Howie.

"Seventeen five," he informed her after taking another dramatic puff on the cigar.

Charlotte felt a sinking sensation in her stomach and suddenly hoped Uncle Howie choked on his cigar. Even if she took out a mortgage on the house and a loan on her share of RP, she wouldn't be able to raise that kind of money. And she'd promised her dad's partners in Buena Vista Land Development that she wouldn't do anything, including selling her interest or taking out a loan on it, to make waves. They were in the middle of a multimillion-dollar land deal with a Japanese firm. The least little ripple on their financial pool might cause the Japanese to back out.

Damn! Her relatives certainly had her over the proverbial barrel. The one she'd like to stuff her uncles into and send over Niagara Falls.

"Let me get to work on these numbers," she said. "I'll get back to you."

"You do that, Charlotte," her uncle said with a laugh. "You just do that, honey."

A quick phone call to Dorothy, Matt's secretary, was all that was necessary to arrange Charlotte's entry to the offices of Russell and Winslow after the usual business hours. Matt was in conference when she called, but Dorothy assured her that he would be burning the midnight oil tonight.

The business district had closed shop, and the street people had taken up their positions in doorways by the time Charlotte made it downtown, but at least she had no trouble finding a parking place. Once inside the first-floor lobby, she waited impatiently as the security guard verified her identity and escorted her to the thirty-third floor. After letting her into the offices of Russell and Winslow, he left.

To her surprise, Charlotte discovered it wasn't necessary to turn on the overhead light, for moonlight filtered
in through the floor-to-ceiling windows, creating shadows
that gave even the most insubstantial items the illusion of
bulky importance. Making her way quietly down the hall
toward the light spilling from Matt's office, Charlotte
wondered again why she hadn't just phoned him. Why had
she needed to come face-to-face with him for this?

Her first glimpse of him at his desk, where several large
volumes lay open as he made rapid notes on a yellow legal
pad, almost caused Charlotte to turn back. This man—
with his shirt open at the collar, his tie hanging loose and
his sleeves rolled up—seemed quite different from the
Matthew Oliver she was used to. He wasn't simply a legal
mind but a flesh-and-blood man. That thought made her
uneasy.

Then she remembered the men and women at Rutherford Packaging. Remembered the people who depended on
their wages in order to clothe and feed their own flesh-and-
blood families. She thought of Zeb Tibbens, who could
neither read nor write but who'd been the most diligent
worker at her facility for the past forty years. Of Miguel
Ortez, who'd progressed to a managerial position on the
strength of his brains and determination, despite the fact
that he'd never graduated from high school. Of Melinda
Johnson, who, after five years as RP's best sales rep, had
confessed to Charlotte that she'd falsified her résumé, for
she'd never even attended, let alone graduated from,
Stanford University. But when Melinda had applied for the
position, she'd been desperate to support herself and four
kids after her husband abandoned them—and she'd
known she could handle the job. What would happen to
these and others who'd helped to make RP the company
it was today? There were too many lives depending on her

for Charlotte to allow her uncles to turn Rutherford Packaging into a subsidiary of a by-the-book corporation.

Stepping into the office, Charlotte watched as Matt's head came up.

"How'd you get in here?" he asked, after removing his glasses and blinking owlishly several times. "What time is it?"

"Almost ten," Charlotte responded. "Security let me in."

He tossed his glasses onto the desk. "Why?"

"I needed to give you an address," Charlotte said as she began to rummage in her purse. "I know it's here . . . here it is," she proclaimed as she removed a business card from her bag and set it facedown on the desk in front of Matt.

Matt put his glasses back on and studied the card.

"Ten a.m." he read, and then looked questioningly at her.

Charlotte nodded. "Your secretary said you were free all morning tomorrow. The name and address are on the other side."

"Dr. Steven Harris," Matt read aloud. Obviously puzzled, he looked up at her. "Are you sick or something?"

"I'm healthy as a horse. *You're* the one having the blood test in the morning."

"Blood test?"

"You aren't squeamish, are you?"

"Squeamish?"

"You know, the big macho type who runs at the sight of a needle or faints at the sight of blood."

"I've never fainted. Now tell me why I'm having a blood test," he demanded as he pushed his glasses down and peered over them. This time Charlotte let him get away with his blatant attempt to intimidate her.

"The state of California requires it."

"Requires it? For what?"

Charlotte smiled. "For a marriage license, of course."

Chapter Two

"Marriage license?"

Leaning against the doorway, Charlotte nodded slowly and tried to gauge his reaction. "You asked me to marry you this morning. You haven't forgotten, have you?"

"Yes. No." He raked a hand through his hair. "I mean, yes, I asked you and no, I haven't forgotten."

"Are you officially withdrawing the offer?"

"No. Of course not. It's just that . . . I wasn't expecting . . . you caught me by surprise, that's all."

"I like having the element of surprise on my side," she told him at the same time she decided he looked . . . cute . . . when he was surprised. More boyish. Less controlled. She realized she'd never caught him completely off guard before, and she was enjoying it.

Charlotte watched as he removed his glasses, closed his eyes and ran a hand over his face. The furrow between his brows refused to be swept away, and the whisper of his hand passing across a day's growth of beard made a sound so intimate that Charlotte felt her pulse quicken. When Matt opened his eyes, they were dark and somber. He was in control again.

He took a drink from the cup of cold coffee on his desk and grimaced. "Mind telling me what changed your mind?"

And so she told him what she'd learned from John Everling's strange phone calls and of her conversation with Uncle Howie. She told him about Zeb and Miguel and Melinda and how they depended on Rutherford Packaging. She even tried to explain that money wasn't the issue; it was the people she cared about.

But some things she didn't tell him. She didn't mention the fact that it had taken her a very long time to get her anger under control or that once the anger had crystallized into dogged determination, she'd had only one thought in mind: to keep RP out of her uncles' hands. That was when she'd begun to seriously consider Matt's offer of marriage. It seemed like the perfect solution at the time, but now that she was face-to-face with him in an office where moonlight spilled through the window, she wasn't sure it was such a good idea.

That's why she finished by stuffing her hands into her pockets and saying, "You don't have to go through with this if you don't want to, you know."

Clasping his hands behind his head, Matt leaned back in his chair and smiled. "I'm considered a fairly decent catch. You're not trying to weasel out, are you?"

"I'm not a weaseler," she said as she came away from the doorjamb. "Besides, you're the one who's doing the sacrificing."

"Charlotte, I'm hardly the sacrificial lamb type. Have you considered the fact that *I* might be after you for your money?"

She laughed. "Have you thought that *I* might be trying to save on legal fees?"

"Wouldn't do you any good. Once we're married, legal ethics will preclude my handling the estate. We'll have to turn it over to another attorney. You'd be better off if you were after me for my body— It's not *that* funny," he informed her as she let out a whoop of laughter and settled into a chair. "Want some coffee?"

While he stood in the conference room, pouring two cups of strong, hot coffee, Matt gave himself a stern lecture. This was business, pure and simple, he told himself. A merger. Period. It wasn't about how pleased he'd been to see Charlotte standing in his office. It wasn't about how her presence lit up a room or how her laughter turned an ordinary day into an extraordinary one. It was about keeping her greedy relatives from taking what should, by rights, be hers. He reminded himself of that one more time when she turned her trusting smile up to him and thanked him for the coffee.

"So when do you want to tie the knot?" Matt asked once he was seated again. The desk reminded him of the distance that needed to be maintained. "The rest of this week is pretty full," he told her as he glanced through his calendar. "Next Monday or Tuesday looks good."

"Let's make it Tuesday. I have a tennis game scheduled for Monday."

"Wouldn't want to interfere with that. But try not to mention to anyone that a tennis game took precedence over our marriage. Okay?"

"It won't look good if I cancel," she explained. "I've beat Debbie four times straight. The only thing worse than a poor loser is a winner who won't give you another chance."

"It's nice to know you have your priorities in order," he murmured as he scribbled a note on his calendar. "How about a morning wedding? We could schedule a meeting with your relatives after that."

"I don't want them at the wedding."

Matt nodded. The less contact he had with them, the better. "I'll try to arrange for a wedding in judge's chambers around 9:00 a.m. and a meeting with your relatives late that afternoon. That way we can come back here, have a short meeting with the attorney taking over the estate, and still have lunch before we spring the news on your relatives. How does that sound?"

"Talk about priorities!"

Matt glanced up and flashed her a predatory smile. "I never go into battle on an empty stomach."

"Sounds great," she responded, but thought, what do we do after that? It wasn't like her to avoid a question, but this was one she'd danced around long enough. "Then what?"

"The attorney asks the court to settle the estate as your father instructed and you keep controlling interest of RP."

Exasperated with herself as much as with his obtuseness, she asked, "What about us? What kind of...marriage do we have?"

"A friendly one, I hope. After all, we have to give the impression that we're married in more than name only."

"But we won't be, right?"

He drilled her with his dark brown gaze, but instead of making her squirm, it straightened her spine and brought her chin up.

"Well?" she demanded.

"I think it's best if the truth of this marriage is kept between the two of us since the judge might not take an en-
lightened view of our arrangement. As far as the rest of the
world is concerned, we're madly, passionately in love. We
can't live without one another. That means we'll have to be
seen together. We'll have to live under the same roof. That
doesn't mean we have to share the same bed. Any more
questions?"

"Just one—your place or mine?" she asked with an
impudent grin. When Matt raised one brow in mute question, she added, "To live at, I mean."

"Yours I'd imagine. I have a one-bedroom condo at the
beach. That would make the separate-bedrooms part difficult."

Though Charlotte smiled, she decided that one bedroom would be tempting the Fates just a little too much.
Not to mention her own feminine curiosity.

Charlotte waited until Tuesday morning while she was
dropping oranges into the juicer and Mrs. Nguyen, her
housekeeper, was frying eggs, to inform the woman that
she'd be bringing home a husband that night.

"You getting married again?" the usually imperturba-
ble woman demanded. "About time!"

"You don't even know who the bridegroom is," Charlotte pointed out.

"Doesn't matter. You need a husband. You're a smart
girl. I'll bet you chose a good man. Right?"

A good man? Charlotte wondered. "Yes. He's a good
man," she answered truthfully.

Mrs. Nguyen gave the egg an expert flip. "Someone I
know?"

"Matt Oliver, the attorney for the estate."

The housekeeper set the frying pan off the stove and turned to Charlotte with a grin. "You have more than a good head. You have..." She stood a moment, searching for the right words. After eleven years in America, she still had trouble with English when she became excited. Finally she grinned. "You will wake up smiling in the mornings, yes?"

Charlotte nearly choked on her freshly squeezed orange juice. After dabbing her mouth with the back of her hand, she informed her housekeeper, "I always wake up smiling."

Mrs. Nguyen snorted in disbelief before scowling at Charlotte's dress.

"Did I spill something?"

"You getting married this morning? That's no dress to get married in. You go upstairs and find something pretty for your wedding day. Go on now," the older woman insisted when Charlotte would have protested. "Something soft and romantic," she advised as Charlotte headed out of the kitchen.

Looking in her bedroom mirror, Charlotte decided she'd been thinking more about the meeting with her relatives than the wedding. It probably wouldn't do to show up for her marriage in her going-into-battle dress, as she thought of the gray outfit. It was what she wore to meet hard-sell clients. Mrs. Nguyen was right; it wasn't appropriate for a wedding, especially her own.

She finally settled on a pale pink silk blouse with long, full sleeves and a high, soft collar. With it she wore a silk skirt in shades of pink and mauve, with a coordinating scarf folded into a triangle and draped over her right shoulder. She tucked the ends of the scarf into a pink belt that accented her trim waist. It was soft and romantic enough for a wedding yet tailored enough for the meeting in the attorney's office.

Satisfied that she would pass muster with her house-keeper, Charlotte descended the curving oak staircase to find Mrs. Nguyen nodding her head in approval. She smiled back at the woman, refusing to acknowledge the knot that was forming where her stomach used to be. Last-minute nerves were for *real* brides.

"Flowers?" Charlotte asked as she gazed at the arrangement Matt held out to her. "For me?"

"You should have flowers for your wedding day," he said softly. "No matter what the circumstances."

Charlotte knew she should feel foolish standing in the hallway of the municipal court building, accepting a bouquet of flowers, but she didn't. She was touched by Matt's kindness and surprised to find tears clogging her throat.

Around them, men in somber suits huddled in conferences with their clients while others paced or smoked to pass the time until court was called into session. Still she stood rooted to the spot, gazing up into the brown eyes of the man she was going to marry.

"So should you," she said when she could finally trust her voice.

With trembling fingers she plucked a single rose from her bridal bouquet. Handing the arrangement back to Matt, she broke the stem off short and then stood on tiptoe in an effort to place the blossom in the buttonhole of his lapel.

"Can you bend down just a little?" she asked in a voice that was too faint to be her own.

Even in a room full of strangers, this was an oddly intimate thing to do, she realized as he bent his knees to accommodate her height. Beneath her hand she could feel his heart pounding, and against her cheek his breath felt like a warm caress. Her fingers refused to cooperate. It had to be the tangy masculine scent of his cologne mingling with the sweet bouquet of the blossoms that made her feel light-headed, Charlotte told herself.

"There," she murmured, almost relieved to have the rose in place.

Standing back to admire her handiwork, Charlotte was suddenly all too aware of the way the silk clung to her figure and of how devastating Matt looked in his gray suit.

How must they seem to the people around them, she wondered? Like lovers? She caught the eye of a woman across the hall. How romantic, the woman's look seemed to say. How poetic!

How foolish, Charlotte reminded herself. For they weren't lovers at all. They were business partners.

"I just guessed about the colors of the flowers," Matt said as he handed the bouquet back to Charlotte.

"They're perfect."

"The florist said I couldn't go wrong with pastels. Especially this time of year. But I didn't think of the boutonniere."

Don't run off at the mouth, Matt admonished himself. But he'd been nervous all morning. No, it had started yesterday. He'd been unable to concentrate all afternoon. He'd left work early and stopped by the florist on impulse. Then, with the flowers stashed in his refrigerator, he'd packed some clothes in a suitcase and discovered he couldn't sleep. That's why he was acting strangely, he told himself. Not enough sleep. He wondered if he would get any more sleep tonight or would he lie alone in his bed, conjuring up images of what his wedding night should be like?

"Judge Dorn is expecting us at nine," Matt said as he glanced at his watch. "I think we can go in now."

With his hand at her back, Matt guided Charlotte down the hall to a door marked Private. He'd barely knocked when the door was opened by a tall, thin man in his sixties.

"Judge Dorn," Matt said as he shook hands.

"Matt, my boy. I was beginning to think you'd turned coward at the last minute. You must be the bride," the older man said as he pulled Charlotte into the room and closed the door. "I can see why you've finally decided to take the plunge, my boy. Just let me get our witnesses and we can get on with the ceremony."

While the judge went out through another door that opened into the courtroom, Matt glanced down at Charlotte. She was pale beneath her tan, and her eyes, when she looked up at him, seemed bigger than usual.

"Are you okay?" he whispered when he bent down to her.

Giving her best impression of a reassuring smile, Charlotte nodded.

"Your hands are like ice," he said when his fingers grazed hers. "Are you sure you're all right?"

"I'm fine," she whispered as the door opened once more. From the indulgent look on the judge's face, she realized that once again they were playing the part of a loving couple. When the two women behind him exchanged knowing looks, Charlotte wondered why she'd ever worried that this charade was going to be tough to pull off.

Then Judge Dorn began giving instructions, and she found herself standing shoulder to shoulder with Matt and uttering "I do" in a voice that was barely audible. The ceremony was blessedly brief and free of well-intentioned lectures on the meaning of marriage or the importance of love in our modern world. Before she knew it, the judge had pronounced them man and wife and given Matt permission to kiss her.

Matt stared down into the large green eyes of his wife. *His wife.* Why did that sound so natural? And why did Judge Dorn's words have the blood pounding in his veins? It's just a kiss, he told himself. He'd kissed hundreds of women. Why should the idea of kissing Charlotte have him tied in knots? He stood for several seconds, wondering how she could still be an enigma to him after all the hours they'd spent together since her father's death. Then he realized that in all the time they'd been together, he'd never really seen the woman. He'd seen the grieving daughter and the tough businesswoman and even the ghost of the little hellion she must have been, but he'd never—until this moment—really considered the woman.

Perhaps his desire to find the sensual woman who lurked behind the brash and blithe facade was what had him taking her in his arms. Perhaps that was why he was so aware of each curve of the surprisingly pliant body that filled his arms and why he savored the first tentative touch of his lips on hers. Perhaps. But he was honest enough with himself to admit that it was need that had him deepening the kiss. And hunger. A hunger that surprised him and, if the trembling of Charlotte's body was any indication, frightened her.

"We need to sign the official papers before you two run off," Judge Dorn said when Matt finally pulled his lips free of Charlotte's and held her at arm's length.

Matt wasn't sure what he'd expected to see in Charlotte's eyes, but it certainly wasn't laughter. Yet that was exactly what he discovered. That and the fact that the trembling hadn't been from fright or passion. It was laughter causing the quaking of his bride's limbs. Matt hurried everyone through the signing of the official papers and managed to hustle his bride out of the office and onto the elevator before she gave in to the laughter that was bubbling within her.

"Do you think you've settled down enough to go to the office?" Matt asked as he backed into his parking space and turned off the engine.

"Quit scowling," Charlotte admonished. "Brides are supposed to be happy."

"Happy. Not demented. We're not going up to the office until you're capable of accepting people's best wishes without howling with laughter."

"I never howl. Besides, I wouldn't mind if you smiled just a bit. A groom isn't supposed to look like he wants to strangle the bride."

"This is the way I am. I'm not some young, besotted fool, you know."

"Besotted?" Charlotte repeated in a strangled voice. "No one will ever mistake you for 'besotted.' Though I'd really appreciate 'friendly' if you think you can manage that." When she received what could best be described as a scowl, she shrugged her shoulders and reached for the doorknob. "Have it your way. But if you can't look a little happier when my relatives arrive, we're never going to pull this off."

"We pulled it off back at the courthouse, didn't we?"

Charlotte nodded, remembering the way she'd found herself caught up in the fantasy they were spinning for everyone else. She'd been surprised to find herself putting her hand in his. Surprised to find herself smiling up into his eyes. And most surprised of all to discover that she liked the feel of his lips on hers. She'd practically melted in his arms right then and there, until the logical part of her brain had reminded her that this was all a charade. A play in an unspecified number of acts. If she was this susceptible to him in act one, there was no telling what condition she might be in by the time her father's will was settled.

Luckily her sense of humor had come to the rescue. In her experience, laughter was always the best line of defense. She just wished Matt wasn't so serious about the whole thing. That wasn't true. She also wished he wasn't so good-looking and that his kiss hadn't set off fireworks. Just her luck, she thought, that she'd avoided romantic entanglements since her divorce only to discover that the man she'd agreed to marry for business reasons could make her pulse accelerate with a look. She was going to have to keep Matt at arm's length during the days ahead. And she had the awful feeling she was going to be forced to rely heavily on her sense of humor, demented though it might be.

Tossing aside the magazine she'd been thumbing through, Charlotte rose to pace Matt's office. With the chairs set up to accommodate her relatives, as well as Matt and herself, she found the space too small to allow a good prowl. Small spaces and enforced quiet always drove her a little crazy.

"You can use the hallway if you'd like," Matt told her, looking up from the papers on his desk.

"I'll go outside if I'm bothering you," Charlotte told him as she checked her watch. "I could always check the reception area."

"No. I don't want you to meet with your relatives without Alice or myself present."

"Okay. You don't suppose they're in Alice's office, do you?"

"No, I don't. They're late. And not for the first time, I might add. If they'd arrived, Alice would have buzzed us."

Charlotte nodded and began to pace again. She knew what Matt said was true. She had great faith in Alice Kelsey, the attorney who would be handling her father's estate from now on. She not only came highly recommended, but Charlotte had liked her the moment they'd met. Initially she'd been surprised to find that a senior partner was taking over the estate. But when Matt explained that Alice had been his mentor at Russell and Winslow, Charlotte realized that the older woman's involvement was really a personal favor to Matt.

Still she'd been impressed with the woman. She'd liked the fact that Alice was older, probably in her fifties, with an air of calm that was almost contagious. She'd liked the woman's golden hair shot through with silver and the kindness in her pale blue eyes. But most of all, Charlotte had respected the steel that she'd glimpsed beneath the soft exterior. Dealing with the Rutherford clan required a great deal of steel.

Charlotte jumped when the phone rang. Matt slanted her a quick look, then answered it before it could ring again.

"Matt Oliver speaking . . . okay . . . give us two minutes, then bring them in. They've all arrived," he informed Charlotte after hanging up the phone. He rose and came out from behind the desk. "Are you all right?" he asked. Then, before she could answer, he said, "You don't have to be present when Alice informs them of our marriage if you don't want to."

"You're joking, right?" she asked with a grin. "I wouldn't miss this for the world."

"You're sure?"

Charlotte nodded. "It's only the waiting that drives me crazy. Once things are rolling, I'll be fine." She watched as he shrugged into the suit coat he'd hung on the back of the door. "You're going to let Alice break the news to them, are you? Somehow I thought you'd want to do that yourself."

"I'd like to," he admitted as he slid into the seat closest to her and gently pulled her down beside him. "But Alice is your attorney now. It's best if your relatives realize that right away. Just relax and enjoy this," he whispered when he heard voices on the other side of the door. "I know I intend to."

But it wasn't easy to relax with Matt's arm draped across the back of her chair or with his thigh grazing hers. Nervously she plucked her bouquet from the corner of the desk and set it on her lap.

"Charlotte, darling," exclaimed the first woman through the door as she rushed forward and touched her cheek to Charlotte's. "How are you, my dear?"

"Just fine, Aunt Rhue. You look wonderful," she said as the older woman straightened and Charlotte got a good look at the brightly flowered dress she wore. Subtlety was not a Rutherford characteristic. "Your engagement seems to agree with you."

"Yes, it does, doesn't it?" Rhue asked with a laugh.

"Hello, Carver," Charlotte said in acknowledgment of the small, quiet man behind her aunt.

Like everyone else, Charlotte had been surprised when her aunt had agreed to take the colorless man as her fifth husband. However, this was the first time Charlotte had seen her aunt's soft features retain that blissful, loving look for six months. Her aunt was romantic but fickle.

"Charlotte," Uncle Howie said from across the room as he slid into the seat closest to the door. He rarely bothered with the social amenities.

"Uncle Howie," Charlotte murmured. "Uncle Walter," she said as the quiet member of the family took a seat beside his older brother.

Once everyone was settled, Alice Kelsey crossed the room and took her seat behind the desk.

"As Charlotte's new attorney, I'd like to thank you all for coming on such short notice," Alice began.

Four heads swiveled as one to look first at Charlotte then at Matt. As they swung back toward Alice, Charlotte forced herself to breathe.

"I know you're all wondering why Mr. Oliver is no longer handling the Lambert estate, so let's get that detail out of the way before we continue. Legal ethics aren't hard and clear on the subject, but they do discourage a husband handling the affairs of his wife in a situation like this one. Since Charlotte and Matt were married earlier today, they've asked me to take over as attorney for the Lambert estate."

As four pairs of eyes swung back in her direction, Charlotte felt Matt's arm slip around her shoulders. Pulling her close, he smiled at the gaping assembly. If the ridiculously dumbfounded looks on her relatives' faces were any indication, they hadn't expected the announcement. Charlotte wondered fleetingly if she was being unfair to them, but just the thought of what her uncles had planned for RP and its employees quickly dispelled that notion.

Aunt Rhue was the first to come back to life. "Why, darling, how wonderful!" Bobbing up from her chair, she rushed over to throw her arms around her niece. "Who would have thought you'd find your true love in a court of law?"

Chapter Three

"True love, my foot!" Uncle Howie bellowed from his position by the door. "Can't you see this is just a trick? She's trying to cheat us out of our inheritance!"

"Actually, Mr. Rutherford," Alice interjected calmly, "none of the property in question has been transferred to you. You were entitled to it only if Charlotte remained unmarried. The details of the will are very specific on that point."

"I don't give a damn about the details," Howie continued as he hauled himself to his feet. "All I know is that I'm being cheated by my niece and some shyster lawyer. If your father knew," he shouted as he stabbed his cigar in Charlotte's direction, "he'd be spinning in his grave."

Matt came to his feet. "I think that's enough," he said softly.

"Like hell it's enough! Oh, wait a minute," Howie said slowly as he gave Matt a speculative glance. "Maybe

Charlotte really is the innocent in all this. Maybe it's you, Oliver. Maybe you've gotten greedy. Isn't your cut as attorney enough? Or do you want more? Maybe you won't be satisfied with less than half of everything my niece stands to inherit. Is that it?"

"I think you'd better stop while you still can," Matt informed him.

"I hit a sore spot, did I? You see that, Charlotte, honey? He's only using you. Trying to get your money. You've got to learn to be a better judge of men. That first guy you married was a real jerk and now this . . ." He gave Matt a slow up-and-down appraisal. "I never figured you for the type who'd fall for bulging biceps and a smooth line. Maybe you're not as bright as everyone thinks if—"

Whatever else Uncle Howie intended to say was lost in a squawk of outrage when Matt grabbed a handful of his shirt and raised him up until only the tips of the older man's toes were touching the ground. Matt kept Howie there so that they were eye to eye, and when he spoke, his voice proved all the more menacing for its icy control.

"I put up with your sniveling and whining while I was attorney for the estate. I even tolerated your obnoxious personality. I had no choice. But now that Charlotte's my wife, I won't stand for you harassing or insulting her. Is that understood? Well, is it?" he demanded with a vicious shake when Howie didn't answer.

"Yeah," Howie breathed. "I understand."

With a nod of approval for the older man's sudden grasp of the situation, Matt lowered him gently to the floor, then took the time to brush the wrinkles from his jacket.

"Good, because I really hate it when I lose my temper."

"Yeah," Uncle Howie muttered as he backed toward his chair and slumped into it. "So do I."

Matt merely smiled as he took the time to straighten his tie and adjust his cuffs before resuming his seat beside Charlotte.

Shocked by this new aspect of Matt—an aspect she'd never dreamed existed—Charlotte sat mutely as her husband put his arm around her shoulder and pulled her closer to his side. Sitting there, she was forced to acknowledge the truth of what Matt had told her earlier: he wasn't the sacrificial lamb type. Truth was, she'd seen flashes of ferocity in him before, but until now she hadn't realized that a barely civilized jungle cat lay beneath that cool, controlled exterior. She'd never been an advocate of the whip-and-chair approach to life. She wondered if there was any other way to keep a wild cat from turning deadly.

"In his will," Alice continued in her calm, soothing voice, "Mr. Lambert made provisions for each of his late wife's relatives, should Charlotte be married when the estate is settled. Unless someone else has questions concerning the validity of Miss La—Mrs. Oliver's marriage, I have copies of pages twelve through fourteen of Charles Lambert's will for each of you." When none of the other relatives showed any inclination to protest their niece's marriage, Alice handed each of them several photocopied pages.

"Please look at item eight at the bottom of the first page," Alice Kelsey proceeded in her dignified fashion. "It's headed 'Provision in the Event that My Daughter Has Come to Her Senses and Married.' You will note that it continues onto the next two pages, and you will find that each of you has been adequately, though not lavishly, provided for by Mr. Lambert."

Charlotte took the pages from Alice and stared at them as though she were reading, all the while praying that she wouldn't have to answer any questions. Concentration was impossible after the encounter between Uncle Howie and Matt, and what really amazed her was the fact that Alice continued as though she hadn't just witnessed one of her colleagues pick up and shake a man like a cat with a rodent in his teeth. Perhaps estate lawyers were used to seeing the less civilized side of people.

The rest of the meeting continued in icy silence. Few questions were asked, and Charlotte's relatives showed no inclination to hang around after the meeting. Led by Uncle Howie's unusually quick strides, they departed more quietly than they had arrived.

When Matt went in search of some files he needed to take home, Charlotte found herself alone with Alice Kelsey.

"I thought the meeting went quite well," Alice said as she began packing papers into her briefcase.

"You mean other than the fact that my uncle got ugly and Matt—my husband manhandled him?"

Alice smiled and reached out to pat Charlotte's hand. "I've seen worse. Why, I once handled the estate of a world-renowned gun collector. Turned out that every member of the family was as nuts about firearms as he was, and they all arrived carrying their own small, deadly weapons—with permits. After the first angry meeting, I handled everything through conference calls. The phone bills were hefty, but at least I didn't have to keep ducking under the desk," she finished with a laugh.

"I've never seen Matt like that," Charlotte murmured.

"Neither have I, but I've always suspected that there was fire beneath that cool facade of his. There's a great deal more to that boy than is seen on the surface. Although," she said with a surprisingly girlish wink, "what we see on the surface isn't so bad, is it?"

"No, it isn't," Charlotte mumbled as she told herself that thirty-one-year-old divorcées do not blush. Unfortunately, she was developing an acute appreciation of the muscle and sinew that lay beneath the conservative suits Matt favored.

"I suppose every young female employee—and some who aren't so young—has tried to hook Matt at one time or another. I'm sure there are some broken hearts in the office today."

Charlotte turned to stare at the older woman. Was she trying to say that there was someone special—a significant other, as people said—who'd be sitting home alone tonight?

"Don't worry," Alice assured her as she snapped her briefcase shut. "Matt never dated anyone with the firm. He has hard and fast rules about mixing business and pleasure." She smiled. "At least they've been hard and fast until now. But rules and regulations can't stop love, can they?"

"No," Charlotte said when the silence lengthened. "I suppose they can't."

Alice glanced at her watch. "I've got another appointment this evening. Tell your husband that I'll keep you both informed as things move along." She started toward the door, then paused and turned back. "Try not to let this meeting upset you. I realize that it wasn't the wedding day most young women dream of, but you two were right not to wait. There's nothing wrong with mixing a little practicality with the passion."

"Especially when that practicality can save me twenty million dollars, right?"

"That's right," Alice agreed as she took several hesitant steps back in Charlotte's direction. "I've been married to the same wonderful, exasperating man for twenty-seven years, and his practicality probably has as much to do with that fact as the passion. Don't be angry with Matt because he's practical—and don't believe a word of what your uncle said. I've known Matt since he began clerking here, and there's not a dishonest bone in his body. If Matt Oliver says he married you for love, then you can bet that's exactly what he means. Put today behind you. Go home and create the kind of wedding night that dreams are made of."

Looking into Alice's worried blue eyes, Charlotte felt guilty at deceiving the woman. She was on the verge of confessing that Matt had never claimed to love her, that there was no passion to find and that the marriage was nothing but a scheme to help her gain sole ownership of Rutherford Packaging, when the door opened.

"I thought you'd be gone," Matt said when he saw Alice.

Though he said it with studied nonchalance, every nerve in his body responded to the haunted look in Charlotte's eyes. Where was the smile he was used to? Why did she turn to look out the window, leaving him to guess at her mood?

"Perkins was looking for you," Matt continued as he dragged his gaze back to Alice. "But I told him you'd left for the day. You can probably catch him at the elevators if you hurry."

"I'd better run then. Perkins is the office marathoner," Alice said in explanation to Charlotte. "Congratulations again," she called over her shoulder as she rushed down the hall, leaving Matt to study Charlotte's profile in silence.

When Charlotte continued to gaze out the window, Matt went to his desk and began sorting through his papers. He was a man who lived alone; he was used to silence.

But he discovered he wasn't used to Charlotte's silence. What was she thinking? Was she sorry she'd ever agreed to this plan of his? She was undoubtedly embarrassed by the way he'd lost his temper today. God knows he was. He should never have let Howard Rutherford get to him. A snake didn't suddenly grow feet and learn to walk like a man; he shouldn't have expected Howard Rutherford to act like anything but the cynical, avaricious reptile that he was.

Matt shook his head. He hadn't resorted to physical force in almost twenty years. Not since Vietnam. In fact, he was surprised to find that the young hothead he'd been still existed beneath his crisply tailored business suit; Matt would have sworn that he'd put that part of himself to rest long ago.

He was even more surprised to realize that he wanted to explain himself to Charlotte. He wanted to tell her about the rough-and-tumble youth he'd led. About the violence of war that had almost cost him his life. He wanted to explain how he'd carefully and systematically put that part of his life behind him. He wanted to pull her into his arms and feel her head resting on his shoulder while he promised that he'd never pull a stunt like that again. He was probably losing his mind.

"I've got a few more things to clear up on my desk before I can leave," he finally told her. "Why don't you go on home. I'll pick up my things and meet you there."

Charlotte turned back to him. "I need to swing by RP and check on a few things."

"Sure. You might want to inform them of our marriage while you're at it."

She gave a nervous little laugh. "I hadn't even thought about that."

"You should," he said curtly, surprised to find himself annoyed by her comment. "Because if you don't mention it, people will begin to wonder. We can't have that, can we?"

"No, I suppose not. Although it should all be smooth sledding after dealing with Uncle Howie. I'll see you this evening," she said as she left.

Matt only nodded. He kept busy until he heard the door shut behind her, then he found himself drawn toward the window. Waiting for her to emerge on the street below, he wondered what it was about Charlotte Lambert—no, Charlotte Oliver—that could make a sane, practical man fantasize about swimming oceans and slaying dragons. What had she done to stir his long-dormant protective instincts? And how had she managed to shatter his hard-won self-control without so much as one seductive, come-hither glance? He was still wondering when she reached the parking lot where he'd arranged for her to leave her car before taking a taxi to the courthouse.

"What have I gotten myself into?" he asked aloud as he watched her turn out of the parking lot and speed down Wilshire Boulevard in her red Corvette.

Turning off Sunset Boulevard and heading up winding Los Feliz Boulevard into the high-priced foothill area of North Hollywood, Charlotte couldn't help shaking her head. She was still reeling from the reaction her staff had exhibited to her marriage. She'd never even guessed so many people still believed a woman's life was unfulfilled unless it was filled with a man. The whole attitude was as outdated as the Edsel. *That* was why she'd been irritated by her staff's effusive congratulations. That, and the fact she was discovering that "The Big Lie," as she was coming to think of her marriage, was leading to so many little lies.

She was never going to take up espionage as a profession, she decided as she negotiated a sharp curve and made a quick turn onto her street. In agreeing to this marriage, she'd never even considered how difficult it would be to lie to her friends and co-workers.

She cut into her driveway and eased past the side door where she usually parked. She didn't stop until she had reached the garages that sat beside the tennis court.

Mrs. Nguyen and her teenage son, Tommy, lived in the apartment above the garages. Now she was going to have to continue "The Big Lie" in front of them. Charlotte cut the engine and sat gripping the steering wheel. She didn't know if she could go through with it.

"Of course you can," she informed the worried woman staring back at her from the rear-view mirror. "Just think of what would happen to RP if Uncle Howie got his hands on it."

After that spine-straightening pep talk, she got out of her car and started toward the house just as Matt's black Jaguar turned into the driveway and came to a halt by the side door.

"You just getting home?" Matt asked as he stepped out of the car.

Charlotte nodded and kept walking toward him. "It took longer at RP than I'd expected."

"Everything go all right?"

"Sure. Everyone was overjoyed." She stopped just in front of him. The car door was still open, forming a barrier between them. "I feel awful," she whispered. "I'm not good at telling lies."

When Matt saw the pain in her eyes, he felt something twist inside him.

"Just think of the alternative," he murmured as he reached out to brush a strand of hair off her forehead. "And remember it's only temporary."

Charlotte nodded then glanced over her shoulder at the sprawling Tudor home she'd lived in all her life.

"This is going to be the toughest. Mrs. Nguyen and Tommy are more like family than anyone I'm related to by blood. When I told her about our marriage this morning, she was so excited. I don't know how long I can keep up the pretense in front of them."

"I'll be right beside you," he promised, unable to pull his gaze from hers.

He watched as she moistened her lips with her tongue and managed a tremulous smile. Her lips were suddenly so tempting that he had to turn away before he kissed them. Grabbing his suitcase from the back seat, Matt wondered why he'd never noticed how enticing her mouth was before. He wondered how he could have worked with her during the past year and a half without noticing she had skin that begged a man to touch it and eyes that would tempt a saint. He suddenly wondered how he would ever endure the next few weeks or, God help him, months.

With his suitcase in one hand and his briefcase in the other, Matt followed Charlotte through the front door.

"Mrs. Nguyen," she called as she dropped her purse onto the small table in the foyer. Absently she draped her silk scarf over the newel post of the staircase that spiraled into the entryway.

"She's probably fixing dinner," Charlotte explained as she crossed to the living room.

She stepped out of her shoes and left them beside the sofa before disappearing into the hallway that led to the kitchen. Matt dropped his stuff beside the stairs and followed her. After all, he'd promised to back her up. He found her standing beside the desk that was just off the kitchen.

"Mrs. Nguyen isn't here," Charlotte informed him as she removed her earrings and lay them beside the phone. "But she left us a note."

"And dinner, if my sense of smell is any judge. What does the note say?"

Charlotte shrugged. "I don't know."

"Well, read it."

"I can't."

"What do you mean, you 'can't'?"

"Mrs. Nguyen's handwriting is atrocious. I always have trouble deciphering it. Usually I just wait until she gets home."

"You just wait? But it's beside the phone. What if it's an important phone call?"

Charlotte slanted him an exasperated look. "It's been my experience that if it's really important, people call back. Either that or Mrs. Nguyen comes home."

"But she left you a note. It *needs* to be read."

Her brows drawn together in a frown, Charlotte gazed up at him. "Are you always this logical?"

"Yes."

"I was afraid of that. Here," she said as she handed him the note. "You try."

"Cag-reg-a-put-elm."

"Cagregaputelm?"

Matt took his glasses out of his breast pocket and put them on. "That's what it looks like. Or maybe it's 'car-gaputlems.' The only thing I'm sure of is that there is an exclamation mark at the end."

"Congratulations!"

He lifted one brow and stared at her. "I don't see you doing any better."

Charlotte laughed. "Not congratulations on finding the exclamation point. The word is 'congratulations.'"

Matt squinted at the paper. "How can you tell?"

"What else would she put an exclamation mark after?"

He studied the word a few more seconds before shrugging. "It's as good as anything I can come up with."

"What else does she say?"

"'Luck in kissin','" he read slowly. "Is that a traditional Vietnamese saying?" he asked after an awkward moment.

Stepping closer, Charlotte studied the paper Matt still held. "'Look in kitchen,'" she read.

Charlotte led the way around the corner and into the spacious kitchen. On the counter was a large pan covered with foil. Beside it was another of Mrs. Nguyen's famous notes.

"Lasagna," Matt said after one whiff. His mouth watered when he looked under the foil to confirm his judgment. "How did you know that's my favorite?"

Charlotte looked up from the note she was studying. "I didn't. I'm as surprised by this as you are." Looking back at the scrap of paper, she was forced to admit, "I can't tell if we should put it in the oven at three hundred fifty degrees for four hours or at four hundred degrees for thirty-five minutes."

"Four hundred degrees," Matt said promptly, then put his hands to the side of the pan to gauge how warm the dish was. "For about forty minutes."

Charlotte was still studying the note. "How can you tell?"

"I'm a bachelor, remember? I know how to cook."

Charlotte glanced up in time to see him set the oven thermostat and slide the pan onto the rack.

"You'll make some woman very happy someday," she retorted, then realized she was the woman and this was the day. She coughed to cover her embarrassment and turned her attention back to the note. " 'Sled infrigmentum. Tall insect,' " she read aloud. "There must be one of Mrs. Nguyen's famous grasshopper pies in the refrigerator," Charlotte informed Matt as she opened the refrigerator door.

Instead she found a tossed salad and a cheesecake, both of which she set on the counter. Without further comment she dipped her finger into the cheesecake and took a big bite.

"Mmm, chocolate chip."

Matt took the note from her. "It says 'Salad in 'frigerator.' "

"Not fair," Charlotte mumbled around another stolen bite of cheesecake as she waggled her finger toward the salad. "You had a clue."

"But I don't see how you could possibly get 'grasshopper pie' out of this."

"I didn't say that it said 'grasshopper pie.' I read 'Tall insect.' A grasshopper is a tall insect."

"Sure," Matt affirmed. "Just like a dachshund is a tall dog."

"Picky, picky," Charlotte complained as she stood on tiptoe to peer over Matt's shoulder. " 'Table,' " she read after several moments of concentration.

"Table is set," they read in unison.

"It makes a lot more sense than a 'tall insect.' "

"We'll see," Charlotte said as she led the way to the dining room.

However, the scene she found set in the dining room had her stopping before she crossed the threshold. When Matt bumped into her, she stumbled forward and only his steadying hands on her shoulders kept her from pitching headfirst into the room.

As she stood there with her back pressed against Matt's chest, Charlotte was surprised to discover that his hands on her arms made her feel safe and cared for while the solid length of him pressed against her back made her aware of the vulnerability she rarely acknowledged. She wasn't sure how the two emotions had become so suddenly juxtaposed within her, she only knew that she didn't like the feeling. She especially didn't like the fact that the man she'd married as a matter of expediency could cause these unsettling emotions. When, she wondered, had she stopped seeing Matt as her attorney and begun to see him as a man? More importantly, how was she ever going to backtrack to that safe professional relationship?

As she gazed into the dining room, Charlotte decided that her housekeeper was not going to be of any help. The romantic scene that she'd set for the new bride and groom would do justice to a Hollywood movie. At one end of the thirty-foot table, two places had been set opposite each other. The good china and silver had been brought out, as well as the antique crystal that was kept for special occasions. The silver champagne bucket sat beside the table, and a bottle of champagne was on ice. As if all that wasn't enough, Mrs. Nguyen had placed candles not only on the table but on the buffet and servers. Charlotte decided there were enough candles to set off the fire alarm if they were all lit at once. When she stepped across the threshold, violins began to play.

"What the hell is that?" Matt muttered as the violins rose to a crescendo.

"Music."

"I know that. Where did it come from?" Matt asked, his gaze sweeping the room as if he expected to see a hundred and one strings hiding in the shadows.

"Probably one of Tommy's gadgets. He's what the school counselors call 'mechanically inclined.' They suggested we encourage him, so he's constantly rigging up surprises."

"How do you suppose he rigged this one up?"

"Probably an electronic eye," Charlotte said with a shrug. "I've given up trying to understand the technical details. I figure I can deal with anything as long as he abides by his promise not to attempt a miniature space shuttle."

"Space shuttle?"

Charlotte turned around in time to see the horrified expression on Matt's face. "He's promised," she assured him. Then, to take his mind off the nightmare of becoming embroiled in a matter of national security, she added, "He's great with cars. He's adjusted mine so that I can actually cruise at one hundred and twenty miles per hour...if the need ever arrives. You'll have to let him work on yours."

"A hundred and twenty?" Matt raised one eyebrow. "I didn't know you planned to enter the Indy 500 this year." Without raising his voice, he added, "I don't want him to touch my car without permission."

Charlotte nodded agreement as she decided there'd be icicles hanging in Satan's kitchen before that happened. The man obviously had no appreciation for adventure...or speed.

"Why don't you pour the champagne while I dish up the salad?" she asked before he could launch into a lecture on the dangers of speeding.

* * *

"So you worked your way through college and law school?" Charlotte asked as she placed a piece of cheesecake and a cup of coffee in front of Matt.

"I had my veteran's benefits and a couple of small scholarships. They helped out, but law school's expensive. So, yeah, I put myself through school. Didn't have much choice," he said around his first bite. "Mmm, that's delicious."

"Why didn't you have a choice?" Charlotte asked.

"My dad died when I was thirteen. Mom had enough trouble just keeping food on the table and clothes on our backs. Anything extra I wanted, I had to work for. We can't all be born with a silver spoon."

Though Matt's voice held no bitterness, Charlotte looked up from stirring her coffee.

"Silver spoons aren't all they're cracked up to be, you know."

Matt took a sip of his coffee and leaned back in his chair. "No, I don't know. Why don't you tell me," he invited, wondering how he'd come to feel so relaxed with a woman who usually exasperated him beyond belief. He was certain the champagne had something to do with it.

"First of all, it makes it tough to talk."

"A problem you obviously overcame."

Charlotte smiled at him. "Yeah, but it wasn't easy."

Matt smiled back, content for the moment just to gaze at her in the flickering candlelight. Charlotte had insisted they light the candles so Mrs. Nguyen's feelings wouldn't be hurt; he'd agreed in order that the housekeeper wouldn't become suspicious. Now he found all he wanted to do was study the way Charlotte's skin took on the rich color of honey and how her hair reflected the mellow glow of candlelight. But it was her eyes that intrigued him the most. He was fascinated by the way the color could turn from subtle jade to deep emerald; he'd never known eyes as expressive as hers. He wondered again how she survived in the business world.

"More importantly," she continued, "it kept me from seeing what I really wanted out of life—and it made it too easy for me to drift into things that didn't make me happy."

"Like your marriage?"

She took a sip of champagne and ran her finger around the rim of the glass before looking up at him. "Exactly like my marriage."

Chapter Four

She'd guessed at the start that Matt was a man of patience. The way he sat looking at her proved it. He was curious; it was there in his eyes. But she knew he'd wait until she was ready to talk. If she didn't tell him tonight, it would just happen some other time. It might as well be now, Charlotte decided.

She wasn't sensitive about the subject. She'd always thought a person should learn from her mistakes, and her marriage had been a mistake that had taught her a great deal.

"Brent and I grew up together. In high school he was most popular, most athletic, most likely to succeed. Everyone liked him. I was not the exception." Charlotte took another sip of coffee and looked Matt squarely in the eye. "Actually, I still like him. He's a lot of fun. That's the problem, though. He doesn't understand there are serious moments in life. He doesn't understand that there are responsibilities and people who depend on us.''

"He couldn't hold a job, huh?"

Charlotte shook her head. "Worse than that, he didn't need to. His parents left him a trust fund that takes lavish care of him. He doesn't have to work . . . even has an accountant to pay his bills. *They* at least had the good sense to realize he would never grow up.''

"Rough life," Matt commented without conviction.

Yes, she could see how a man who'd had to fight for everything he had would underestimate the hazards of that sort of life-style. She could even see how a man with Matt's drive might overcome them. But Brent had been weak. If her marriage had taught her nothing else, it had taught her that.

Despite her hard-won knowledge, Charlotte couldn't resist a smile when she remembered her own girlish naiveté. "He treated my insistence on getting an M.B.A. as a whim. He thought it was a stage that would pass. When I went to work with Dad, he was appalled. He couldn't understand why anyone would *want* to work. When I took over Rutherford Packaging, our marriage was all but finished. I was at work trying to avoid corporate bankruptcy while he was sunning in Hawaii or skiing in Vail.''

She stopped and hoped Matt would draw his own conclusions. She still hated the thought of the other women, because that she saw as a personal failure. She hadn't been able to keep Brent from straying even when he was at home.

"One day he returned from Rio and found my things missing. I think he actually called to find out which laundry I'd left his shirts at, but Dad assumed he wanted me back.'' She'd come to realize that had been the worst moment of the whole fiasco: the moment she told her father she'd failed at her marriage. "Dad couldn't understand how I could just walk away from him."

"Charles actually wanted you to go back to this guy?"

"I told you Brent was likable," Charlotte reminded him. But honesty forced her to add, "But mostly Dad hated that there were no grandchildren to spoil. He loved kids. His one regret was that he didn't have a dozen."

"He told me once that he wouldn't trade you for a whole baseball team."

"Really?"

He nodded, and the smile she turned on him had his heart hammering beneath his white dress shirt. He'd had no idea at the time that Charles's simple comment would mean so much to his daughter. But it had struck a chord with Matt because Charles was a die-hard baseball fanatic. Matt had been certain, then, that his client intended to change the ridiculous marriage clause in his will. When he'd received word of Charles's death, Matt had regretted not only the loss of a rare man but the fact that Charles had left such injustice behind.

The injustice had sharpened Matt's grief over the man's passing, and it had twisted in his gut like a dull knife ever since. He told himself this was the reason he'd proposed marriage to Charlotte. But he knew as he looked into green eyes reflecting the dancing candle flames, that it wasn't injustice that would keep him tossing in his lonely bed tonight. He'd be at least that honest with himself.

Charlotte sat forward and rested her chin on her hand. "Now it's your turn."

"I've never been married. Never even came close."

"Until now."

Matt smiled. "Until now," he agreed.

Charlotte waited only a few seconds before prodding. "Details," she told him. "I want details."

"There's not much to tell." Matt shifted in his chair and tried to decide how to sum up his checkered past. "When I was younger, I wasn't into structured institutions like marriage. Once I grew up, I didn't have the time."

"You were a rebel, were you?"

Matt shook his head. "A rebel is someone who believes in something other than the status quo. I was simply a hotheaded troublemaker."

"I don't believe it."

"It happened so long ago that sometimes I can't believe it either." But the violence was still there, buried deep beneath the layers of the life he'd created for himself. "I grew up not far from here. Down in San Pedro on the wrong side of the tracks. My dad—my old man, I would've said in those days—worked on the docks. My mom worked in houses like this. Cooking and cleaning for other folks." He eyed her sharply. "There was a time you wouldn't have let me near your door, let alone in your house."

One of his sharper memories was of coming to a house like this one. A big house with a huge Christmas tree in the front window and several teenage girls lounging out back by the pool. He'd come to tell his mom that he was leaving. Joining the Marines. Her employer hadn't wanted to let him in the kitchen, but she'd been afraid to have him linger anywhere near her daughters. Oddly enough, it was an image that had stayed with him through a harsh winter boot camp: Christmas tinsel and balmy Southern California sunshine. He'd promised himself that someday he'd live like that. And that he and his mother would be a real family. He'd come close to fulfilling the first promise, but he'd been too late for the second.

"How does one go from young troublemaker to adult icon of law and order?"

"With a stopover in the war in Southeast Asia."

He watched the frown of confusion pucker her forehead. "What does the war have to do with it?"

"It demonstrated, as nothing else had, that fighting and hatred lead to death. I decided I wouldn't let death win."

Charlotte smiled at the way the young hothead had set his goal. He'd been a man of logic, even then, she decided.

"I'll bet your parents were proud of you."

"Dad died when I was thirteen," he said with a shrug. "Mom died when I was in my last year of law school."

"I'm sorry," she murmured, and was on the verge of placing her hand on his when he pulled it away. Charlotte decided the woman had died proud of her son. What woman wouldn't be proud of a child who had turned his life around that way? "What about afterward? No military romance? No stolen moments in the law library?"

Matt smiled. "There was no time for those things. I was too busy studying and working. I had so much lost time to make up for."

"And once you started practicing law?"

"I've dated some, but most of my energy has been channeled into my work. There wasn't anything left over to spend on any long-term relationships."

In the foyer, the grandfather clock began to chime. Matt was silent as it tolled eleven.

"Speaking of lost time," he said as he checked his watch. "I think we'd better get things cleaned up here. I have an early court date tomorrow."

"I'll just take these things into the kitchen. Mrs. Nguyen will wash them in the morning. You can go on up if you want. It's the first door to the left at the head of the stairs."

Matt stood and stacked his dishes. "I'll help," he told her. "Remember, I've been a bachelor a long time. I'm used to doing these things for myself."

"A truly liberated male," Charlotte said by way of a compliment.

"You can have Dad's room," Charlotte informed him as she lead the way up the stairs. The gentle sway of her hips beneath the demure pink skirt had Matt's pulse racing, and the sway of the hem against her shapely calves made him wonder about all the leg hidden from view. This marriage stuff was going to his head, he decided.

At the top of the steps was an old-fashioned library with bookshelves lining the walls. Matt had met with Charles Lambert in that room on several occasions. He followed as Charlotte led the way toward the left side of the U-shaped walkway that overlooked the large formal entryway. Stopping before the first set of double doors, she turned to face him.

"This was Dad's room. I think you'll find it comfortable enough, but if you want anything changed, just let me know."

"I'm sure it'll be fine," he told her. He was surprised to find a pucker of worry between her brows. "I don't want to cause any household upheavals. After all, I'll only be here a short time."

Charlotte nodded. "My room is across the way. If you need anything..."

"I travel light," Matt said as he nodded toward the suitcase he was carrying. "But I think I have everything I need."

"Well then... good night."

"Night."

Matt watched as she took a few steps away then turned back. "I haven't really thanked you," she said quickly. "There aren't many men who'd be willing to make this kind of sacrifice, especially for people you don't even know. I can only tell you they're good people. Good employees, too. If they knew what you're doing, they'd thank you. As it is—" she shrugged "—I guess I'll have to thank you for them."

"I'm doing it for Charles," he said, and watched the tension ease from her shoulders.

"For Dad?"

Matt nodded. "I don't think he'll rest easy if your relatives take over RP. I liked him. Admired him even more than that. I think this would make him happy."

Matt was surprised at how quickly she moved. He was almost immobilized by the quick, impulsive kiss she planted on his cheek. He would have given in to the urge to hold her close if his hands hadn't been filled. As it was, she pulled back too quickly and had already turned to leave.

"I still appreciate it," she called over her shoulder just before she disappeared into her room.

Matt knew he was in trouble the minute he walked into the bedroom. The feeling had nothing to do with the huge four-poster bed or the obvious expense of the other furnishings. It was due to the work of the indomitable and evidently romantic Mrs. Nguyen. Champagne nestled in a silver ice bucket on the dresser. Crystal goblets sat on a matching tray nearby. Candles were all over the place: on the bedside table, on the massive dresser, even on the hearth. Music played, softly this time, and the bed was turned back revealing what looked like satin sheets in a luxurious shade of ivory. Draped across the foot of the bed was a lacy pink nightgown that Matt knew instinctively would hide just enough from a man's sight to drive him crazy. The thought of the lace molding itself to Charlotte's willowy body had blood rushing to a certain part of his anatomy—and it wasn't his brain. Muttering an explicit oath beneath his breath, he forced himself to look around the room. To look anywhere but at the bed.

It was a decidedly handsome room. Done in shades of deep green and brown, it was masculine and comfortable. He set his luggage down and walked over to the closet. It would still look empty with his few clothes hung in it. The bathroom was done in marble, and Matt decided that if one of the Roman emperors could be resurrected, he would feel right at home here. Matt wasn't at all surprised to discover that Charles had liked his creature comforts. The older man had worked hard to make something of his life, and Matt was glad that he'd enjoyed his wealth.

Walking out of the bathroom, Matt made his way quickly past the bed and studied the fireplace that served as a freestanding wall between the sleeping area and the sitting room. A fire, when the weather warranted it, could be viewed from either room. The hearth was brick and the mantel, with a traditional hunting scene hung over it, looked as if it had been taken from some European manor house. The sitting room beyond held a small sofa, a couple of large wing chairs, a desk and a television. It occurred to Matt that the apartments he'd lived in as a child would have fit into the master suite with plenty of room left over. Well, he'd finally made it to one of those big, fancy houses he'd dreamed of as a youth though he'd never, in his wildest imagination, considered that he might marry into it.

Deciding he'd wasted enough time on the decidedly unproductive act of reminiscing, he went to unpack his clothes. The problem was that when he finished, that damn lace thing was still lying across his bed.

He intended to toss it onto one of the chairs, but the pink froth seemed to cling to his fingers, and the scent reminded him of Charlotte. How could that be? he wondered momentarily, then remembered the kiss in the judge's chambers. The scent and taste of her was still with him. Uttering an oath, he strode toward the door. He knew there would be no sleep as long as this bit of seductive lace remained in the room.

Charlotte had removed her makeup and slipped into her favorite silk gown when she heard the tap on her door. Slipping into the matching robe, she brushed the hair back from her face and crossed to the door. When she opened it, Matt filled the doorway. Silently he held out her pink gown.

"It seems Mrs. Nguyen has had a busy day," Charlotte commented as she took the gown from Matt.

"Very busy."

It wasn't the words so much as the grim line his mouth had settled into that had her asking, "What else has she done?"

"Just more champagne and lots of candles."

"Oh, dear."

"I would never have guessed that she was such a romantic."

"She learned a lot of her English from old movies. Old romantic movies," Charlotte explained as she tossed her nightie onto a chair. "Well, I suppose we'd better give your room that lived-in look. Her feelings will be hurt if she thinks all her work has gone to waste."

Matt stepped aside just in time to avoid being run down by Charlotte. The silky gown she wore billowed out behind her like a vibrant blue sail as she glided toward his room. He wondered how she intended to give his room a lived-in look.

"Pop the cork on this," Charlotte instructed as she passed the champagne to Matt. "Then light the candles."

Matt was just removing the foil wrap from the bottle when he heard water running in the bathtub.

"I prefer a shower," he informed her when he found her bent over the Roman tub. Hot water was gushing out of the dolphin-shaped spout, and steam was rising in a heavy cloud. A *cold* shower, he decided when he saw the way the steam was giving her skin a sultry glow. That was how Charlotte's skin would look after making love.

"That's fine." Charlotte dragged two bath sheets off the towel rack. One she dropped beside the tub. The other she took into the bedroom and placed at the side of the bed. Turning back to him, she eyed the champagne bottle in his hands. "Don't you have that open yet?"

"I'll have it open by the time you turn off the bathwater."

Charlotte grabbed up the two glasses and fled to the bathroom. By the time Matt followed her in, she'd set the glasses at the edge of the tub and turned the water off—but not without getting splashed in the process. Matt could see the outline of her nipples through her robe, and his hand tightened around the bottle.

He held the uncorked champagne in the air. "What do you want to do with this?" Even to him, his voice sounded strange.

"Pour just a little in each glass. Now take a couple swallows from this one." When she saw he still held the cork in the other hand, she stood and lifted the glass to his lips.

"Is this really necessary?" Matt asked after the first sip. She held the glass up so he could take another drink.

"Absolutely. Mrs. Nguyen is a stickler for details." Charlotte took a sip from her glass. "A good year. It's a shame we have to waste any of it, but Mrs. Nguyen will be up here in the morning to clean up. If she even suspects that we haven't made use of her elaborate staging, she'll be like a bulldog with a bone. There will be no rest until she's gotten at the truth." Charlotte took another appreciative sip. "Remember that and we'll carry this charade off just fine. Slip up once," she warned him, "and like I said, she'll be after us like the dog after the proverbial bone."

Setting both glasses on the side of the tub, Charlotte snagged the bottle from him and headed for the sink. When Matt caught himself wondering how many dollars' worth of bubbly she was pouring down the bathroom sink, he realized that no matter how big the house or how much money he had, he'd never completely eliminate the part of him that had grown up poor.

When the bottle was half-empty, she set it beside the glasses. "There's enough for one more glass before you turn in."

Matt shook his head. "I need a clear head in the morning."

"If you'll light those candles, I'll get out of your way."

Matt turned and went back to the bedroom. He was making a mental note to put out all the candles before he went to sleep when Charlotte joined him. Picking up one of the tapers he'd already lit, she took it over to the hearth and began to light the fat candles Mrs. Nguyen had set on the brick. As he glanced around the room, Matt decided that he had to give credit to the little lady: if he was going to set the scene for a seduction, he couldn't imagine a better way of doing it. Despite what he'd told Charlotte about no long-term relationships, he'd staged his share of seductions. The problem was that the only woman he had any fantasy about seducing at the moment was his wife.

He was going to need a long, *cold* shower, he decided.

"Sleep well," Charlotte told him as she crossed the room. But her scent lingered after the door had closed behind her, and Matt uttered a short, succinct oath as he turned on the cold water.

Charlotte was still awake when the grandfather clock struck one. She wished the champagne bottle was in her room. Maybe a glass would calm her nerves and allow her to drift off to sleep. Instead she thumped her pillow and turned over again. This sort of restlessness was not like her. Usually she dropped off to sleep right away, slept six hours and woke up ready to conquer the world. Tomorrow she'd be lucky if she could conquer the mound of papers on her desk. She turned to her other side and decided her behavior was ridiculous. She should feel safer with Matt sleeping in the house, not jumpy over every little sound. But a rattle from somewhere out behind the house had her wondering if she'd remembered to lock up. Another noise convinced her that she hadn't checked the downstairs doors. Intelligent people did not leave doors unlocked for burglars, no matter who was sleeping just across the hallway. It would take only a few minutes to run downstairs and make sure things were locked up tight. She didn't bother with her robe, just slipped out the door and down the stairs.

Matt wasn't even close to drifting off to sleep when he thought he heard the sound of a door opening and closing. It sounded nearby, as if it might be Charlotte's, but he knew sound had a way of bouncing off walls that could fool you, especially in a house this size. He slipped out of bed, picked up a poker from the fireplace and made his way to the door. He thought about checking on Charlotte, but decided there was no reason to wake her for what was probably the normal settling of a house. Then he crept down the stairs, taking care to blend with the shadows.

It had been years since he'd stalked another human being. Then, he'd been in a steaming jungle with the smells of fecund earth around him. Now he was in the middle of civilization, but the old instincts were still good. One set of footsteps, he decided as he waited in the shadows at the foot of the stairs. One set of light, rapid footsteps and the sound of things rattling every so often. One person who was going quickly through drawers and cabinets, probably stuffing valuables into his pockets as he went along. Matt had listened as the thief made his way through the kitchen and into the back of the house. The intruder was in the living room now and should be making his way past the shadows at the foot of the stairs any second—the shadows where Matt stood shrouded in silence.

Matt set the poker against the wall and waited. He'd have a better chance of immobilizing the thief with only his hands. In a matter of seconds a figure rounded the corner. Matt already had his right arm around the person's throat and was twisting a slim left arm behind the back when his brain finally recognized the soft skin and sultry fragrance.

He let out a grunt when Charlotte's foot connected with his shin, then spun her around to face him. With his hands on her shoulders, he held her firmly in place and said her name. He knew the moment recognition replaced fear in her eyes, and he gentled his hold on her.

He was prepared for her anger, but he wasn't prepared for the soft squeal she let out or the way she stepped into his embrace. Her arms came around his waist, and Matt held her tightly to him until her body quit trembling.

Charlotte sensed the strength of his arms around her and felt safe again. She couldn't understand how the same arms that had terrified her moments before were the only place she wanted to be right now. She kept her head burrowed against his bare chest and her arms locked around his waist even when she felt his hand glide gently over her hair.

"Are you all right?" he asked softly.

She nodded and tried to nestle closer to him, but his hands skimmed up her back to rest on her shoulders and hold her away from him. His brown eyes studied her from beneath drawn brows.

"I didn't hurt you, did I?"

She shook her head.

"You're sure?"

She nodded.

One hand moved from her shoulder to her neck. His thumb covered the pulse that still beat wildly there.

"I could have snapped your neck." There was an edge of anger in his voice. "What the hell were you doing wandering around a dark house?"

"Checking the doors."

"Why?"

"I thought I heard a noise out back and I didn't remember locking up—"

"So you came downstairs in a darkened house in hopes of stumbling over a burglar?"

Charlotte shook off his hands. "I came downstairs to be sure I'd locked the house up. How was I supposed to know you were lurking in the shadows?"

"The best way to be sure no one is lurking in the shadows is to eliminate the shadows. Why didn't you turn on the lights?'' Matt demanded as he reached over and punched the switch.

The light from the chandelier was nearly blinding. Charlotte blinked several times, then crossed her arms in front of her. Without her robe, she knew that the silk nightgown did more than hint at what lay beneath. She could tell as Matt's heated gaze followed the contours of her breasts, her hips and her legs that her body must be plainly silhouetted through the sheer fabric.

"I'm used to having the house to myself," she said simply as she reached back to turn the lights off.

Matt said nothing, but she was reminded of how she'd felt when first meeting him, like a deer caught in the gaze of a hungry mountain lion. She wondered, as they stood there, if the deer ever had the urge to run headlong into the lion's embrace? She murmured his name, she thought she'd even taken a step toward him when he bent to retrieve the poker and headed up the stairs. The closing of his door was the only sound she heard.

Chapter Five

It took a long time for Charlotte to fall asleep, and when she woke the next morning it was to discover that she'd overslept by thirty minutes. She was just stepping into her sensible pumps when Mrs. Nguyen burst through the door of her bedroom.

"What are you doing in *here*?" the housekeeper demanded.

Charlotte blew a lock of hair out of her eyes as she reached for her earrings. "Getting dressed, of course."

"No 'of course' to it. You should be in the master bedroom now. I'm going to move all your clothes in there today."

There was nothing the housekeeper could have said that would have caught her attention faster, Charlotte decided as she took a moment to brush her hair back off her temple. She'd known she wasn't any good at subterfuge, but she hadn't thought that the first time she was running late she'd forget the role she was playing. She took a deep breath before turning to face the older woman.

"Actually, Matt and I have decided to keep our separate spaces," Charlotte said with what she hoped was just the right touch of worldly sophistication. "After all, this is a modern marriage. We both have professional commitments and busy schedules. There will be times when we need our privacy."

Mrs. Nguyen crossed her arms and stared at the rumpled bed Charlotte hadn't had time to make.

"On your wedding night?"

Charlotte crossed her arms and stared right back.

"That's not . . . healthy," the older woman finally decided. With her mouth set in a thin, disapproving line, she began to straighten the bed.

Charlotte wasn't sure if it was "healthy" or not, but she knew it wasn't restful. She hoped Matt had managed to get more sleep than she had. And she wondered how she was going to face him after last night's encounter. All the more reason to be on her way, she told herself.

"I just have time for a quick glass of juice. I've been letting the paperwork pile up lately."

"But breakfast—"

"Is the most important meal of the day," Charlotte finished for her, and was relieved to see her housekeeper's usual smile. "When Matt gets up—"

"Mr. Oliver is already eating his breakfast. Says he has an early court date."

"I knew that," Charlotte said when Mrs. Nguyen continued to study her. "It's just that 'early' is such a relative term."

So much for avoiding Matt this morning! She glanced at the bedside clock. Who would have thought that a lawyer would need to be on the road by six-thirty? Somehow she'd always thought they kept banker's hours.

When her housekeeper had nothing else to say, Charlotte turned back to the mirror and clipped her other earring in place. Glancing out of the corner of her eye, she waited until Mrs. Nguyen had turned her attention back to making the bed before she spoke.

"That was a great dinner last night."

Mrs. Nguyen smoothed out the blanket. "You two eat a lot for newlyweds. Bride and groom usually pick at their dinner."

Charlotte sidestepped that conversational land mine and went on the offensive. "Why'd you fix it, then?"

"I thought there would be enough leftovers for you to eat on my bingo night. Now I'll have to fix a whole meal." She fluffed a pillow before adding, "Newlyweds usually have *big* appetite for breakfast."

Charlotte shot her housekeeper a quelling look. "Don't expect my eating habits to change because I've married."

Mrs. Nguyen crossed her arms and stared back. "I'm not a very modern lady, so let me be sure I get this straight. Your room isn't changing, your dinner isn't changing, and your breakfast isn't changing. Anything else isn't changing?"

Charlotte threw her hands in the air. "What else do you expect to change?"

"I expect you to get up every morning with a smile on your face."

Matt sat at the kitchen table and looked from the teenage boy to the strange contraption that hovered beside him and back at the boy again. Matt had been so concerned about how to greet his bride this morning that he'd been mentally preparing himself since the early, restive hours before daylight. The fact that he was happy to be eating his pancakes in the presence of a teenage boy and his robot was an indication of just how nervous he'd been.

Tommy Nguyen didn't look like the kind of kid he'd expect to find puttering around in the garage. He was of an average height and build, without wire-rimmed glasses or a calculator hanging off his belt. He looked like the kind of kid who'd be right at home with a baseball bat or on a skateboard, yet here he sat with a robot not three feet from him. While there was no mistaking the gleam of intelligence in Tommy Nguyen's dark eyes, Matt still doubted that the device would ever be able to execute the intricate maneuvers the boy was describing. Actually he wasn't sure the strange amalgamation of household items and state-of-the-art robotics could be termed a *robot*. It looked like something devised by a demented prop man for a low budget sci-fi movie.

The wheels, Tommy had told him, were taken from a remote-controlled car; the antenna sticking up in the back looked like a tail. The body was made of a large metal cooler, the kind that could hold Kool-Aid for about sixty kids. The spout, which was still attached, looked like the remnant of an umbilical cord. Attached to the cylindrical body was a small keyboard not unlike the one on the electronic phone book and calendar Matt carried in his suit pocket.

The robot's neck was made of plastic pipe and the head was composed of two stainless-steel mixing bowls held together by a strip of foam with lights imbedded in it.

Only one amber light was glowing now, but when Matt had first seen it, the whole strip of lights had been on. For one insane moment Matt had wondered if he was having a strange encounter with an alien life-form. Once he'd gotten over the shock, he'd had to suppress the urge to laugh as the thing bumped along toward him.

A microphone on the bottom bowl looked like a mouth, and the two round speakers attached to the top bowl made the machine look like a giant, electronic ant. An antenna intended for a car phone stuck out of the head and waved jauntily with each movement.

The only sophisticated parts of the machine were the two robotic arms. Those, Tommy had told him proudly, Charlotte had purchased from a company that made industrial robots.

"Do you have a name for your invention?" Matt asked.

"VASSAR. Voice-Activated Security System and Robot," Tommy explained.

"That's some science project," Matt said admiringly. "When I was in school we tried to make a gasoline engine. As I remember, my neighbor almost blew up the apartment building. What is VASSAR's energy source?"

"Batteries. They're in the cooler."

"And what's in the head?"

"The brains."

Tommy swung the top bowl back on its hinges so that Matt could see the maze of wires and circuit boards. It was obvious VASSAR was much more sophisticated than he'd given Tommy credit for. Which meant that the young man before him must be pretty sharp.

No wonder Charlotte had been worried about convincing the Nguyens, both mother and son, that their marriage was the real thing. It was going to be tough to pull anything over on this kid. And the mother, Matt knew from previous visits to the house, was one very shrewd lady.

"How did you come up with the idea?"

"To be honest, this was my second choice. What I really wanted to do was build a miniature space shuttle, but Charlotte talked me out of it. That's when I hit on the idea of the robot—one that could help her out."

Matt could envision it lending a touch of comedy to Charlotte's life, but he didn't see how it could help out.

"How so?"

"Besides being hooked up to a security system, VASSAR will be able to lock and unlock the doors and windows. My mom says Charlotte is always forgetting to check the doors at night, and that isn't good for a woman all alone. Oh, I forgot..." he added in a small voice, "she's not alone now."

"I'm sure there will still be times when she'll be by herself. But how does it work?" Matt asked, and then listened as Tommy explained about microchips and electrical impulses and circuit boards and such.

When he finished, Matt sat back in his chair and looked at him in a new light. Tommy Nguyen was a genius, Matt decided. And a nice kid, as well. He was so busy mulling over everything Tommy had said that he didn't realize Charlotte was in the room until she spoke.

"I see you've been introduced to the mechanical member of the family."

"Charlotte," Tommy cried as he rose to stand beside her.

Matt stood, too, but was saved from deciding how to approach her this morning when the young man caught her in a friendly embrace and congratulated her on her marriage.

"Why didn't you tell us you were getting married? We would've come to the ceremony."

"Why didn't you tell us you won the state-wide science contest last year?"

He had the grace to look chagrined. "I thought you'd make a fuss."

"Same here," Charlotte said as she put her arm over his shoulders in a friendly embrace. "Now, what's new with VASSAR?"

"Well, I've made a couple modifications," Tommy began, and for the next few minutes he demonstrated his improvements.

The three of them were watching VASSAR run a slalom course through the pots and pans Tommy had scattered around the room when Mrs. Nguyen returned.

"What you really need," she informed her son, "is a watch that keeps accurate time. You're going to be late for school if you don't hurry."

Tommy stopped VASSAR and gingerly picked it up.

"I'm gonna start work on the door locks after school," he informed Charlotte.

"Good."

"You're going to be late and get detention," his mother interjected. Tommy just grinned and ambled out the door. "And you," Mrs. Nguyen said as she rounded on Charlotte, "are going to take time for breakfast. You make her eat," she commanded Matt. "Eat a good breakfast like you do."

"Juice and a roll," Charlotte said. "We've been having this argument for eight years," she informed Matt with a grin. "I let her win about two days out of seven. Today is not one of the two. Unless you have any pizza in there."

Mrs. Nguyen let out a long-suffering sigh from where she stood assessing the contents of the refrigerator.

"No pizza for breakfast. No lasagna either. I've got eggs, pancakes or broccoli."

"Broccoli," Charlotte decided. "And put a little cheese on it. Don't look so horrified," she told Matt. "You aren't one of those narrow-minded people who thinks you can only have breakfast food for breakfast, are you?"

"I prefer to think of myself as a traditionalist."

"Let me guess. Pancakes for breakfast, sandwiches for lunch, and roast beef for dinner."

Matt rose and took his suit coat off the back of the chair. "Guilty as charged."

She let out a small whoop of laughter. "Then you are definitely in for a few surprises."

"Dinner at six-thirty," Mrs. Nguyen called as he adjusted his coat collar.

"What are we having?"

"Don't tell him," Charlotte commanded. "We'll surprise you," she informed Matt.

Matt rolled his eyes toward the ceiling. "What have I let myself in for?" he asked no one in particular.

"*Modern* marriage," Mrs. Nguyen answered with a frown. "A man who agrees to a modern marriage deserves any kind food he gets."

He looked at Charlotte. "Have I missed something?"

"Nothing important," she assured him as she hooked her hand through his arm and walked him to the door. But she could feel Mrs. Nguyen's eyes boring into her back, feel her disapproval at the way this modern marriage was starting, and she knew she was going to be left alone with this tiny whirlwind of a woman who would keep at her until she got the truth—unless she could sidetrack her. And the way to do that was to give her something else to think about.

"I'll miss you," she told Matt to get his attention.

When he cast her a curious glance, Charlotte grabbed his tie and pulled him toward her. Her lips managed to cut off whatever he'd intended to say, and her hands in his hair kept him from pulling back. But in only an instant Charlotte felt his arms slide around her and his big body enfold her. And suddenly she forgot why she'd started this kiss. She forgot everything and concentrated on how good it felt to be in his arms, how wonderful his lips felt on hers, how well her body fit against his. When his big hand pulled her closer, she went willingly. And when, moments later, the kiss ended as abruptly as it had begun, she stood stone still and watched him drive away. It wasn't until she heard Mrs. Nguyen's voice that she came out of her trance.

"Nice to see they still have old-fashioned kisses in a modern marriage," the older woman said with a smug smile.

Casually Charlotte strolled to the juicer, took several oranges from a nearby basket and dropped them in. That had been too easy, she thought as Mrs. Nguyen sprinkled cheese over the steamed broccoli. She generally liked a challenge. But she would have felt even better about her ploy if she didn't suspect that her housekeeper wasn't the only one who'd be thinking about that kiss today.

Matt was sitting in his office with his elbows on the desk and his head in his hands when the phone rang. It seemed as if every time he tried to make sense of the past forty-eight hours of his life he ended up in this position. He picked up the phone.

"Matt Oliver."

"Alice Kelsey here. How's married life?"

"Different," Matt answered before he thought.

When Alice laughed, Matt wondered if every woman was born with the instinct to delight in driving a man crazy. Maybe even logical, conventional women like Alice drove their husbands mad. Maybe he shouldn't take the emotional roller coaster Charlotte had him on personally.

"Listen, I think I have some good news," Alice informed him while he was still juggling maybes around in his head. "Are you going to be in your office for a while?"

Matt stared at the work he hadn't begun to make a dent in. "Yeah. I'll be here."

"Good. I'll be down in about fifteen minutes."

The line went dead and Matt cradled the receiver. He'd get fifteen minutes of work done in the meantime, Matt told himself. Fifteen minutes' worth of good, solid work would be more than he'd done since he'd gotten out of court two hours ago.

He flung the pen down on the desk and surged to his feet. Who the hell was he kidding? He wouldn't get two minutes' work done until he managed to forget this morning's kiss and erase the memory of Charlotte in that silky blue thing last night. He had to get himself under control. Had to return to living the rational, civilized life he'd made for himself. He didn't need the kind of desire that tied him up in knots or the violence that lurked just under his skin these days.

He squeezed his eyes shut and tried to blot out the image of Charlotte's slim neck with his arm around it, but the image continued to haunt him. He could have hurt her last night. Could have left bruises on her soft skin or, worse yet, snapped her neck like a twig. With an oath he shoved his hands into his pockets and turned to study the traffic on Wilshire Boulevard.

Why couldn't he get himself under control when she was around? Because she never did the predictable, he decided. The predictable reaction to being assaulted in her own home was the fear he'd seen in her eyes when she first turned to face him. That, he was prepared for. The unpredictable was for her to throw herself into his arms and hold on to him as though her life depended on it. That had been his undoing. That had started him thinking about picking her up and carrying her to his bed. That was when he'd stalked off before he lost all his control.

But Alice had just said something about good news. Maybe she'd heard from Charlotte's relatives. Maybe they were relinquishing any claim on the Lambert estate. Maybe then he could return to the logical, rational, predictable life he'd created, rather than this roller coaster he'd gotten on with Charlotte. So why wasn't he delighted at the prospect?

A tap on the door followed by Alice's greeting effectively cut off his rambling thoughts.

"I received a call from the court clerk," she said quickly. "He'd put us on the docket for the end of June, but there may be a cancellation for Monday. Think we can be ready in five days?"

Matt nodded. "I think so. It's fairly cut-and-dried. The will states that Charlotte has to be married. She is married." He shrugged. "I don't think that's going to be too difficult to prove. It's mostly a matter of getting the paperwork ready."

"My thoughts exactly. The clerk won't be certain about the cancellation until Friday, but we can't wait until then to prepare."

"You have all my notes?"

Alice smiled. "They make interesting reading."

"It's an interesting family."

"Is Charlotte as . . . interesting as the rest?"

Matt laughed. "Do you mean is she as avaricious as her uncles or as dotty as her aunt?"

Alice settled onto the corner of his desk. "I don't know that I would have stated it quite that way, but yes."

"Charlotte doesn't have an avaricious bone in her body. Her mother died when she was just a child, so I'm only guessing when I say she must have been the sensible one in the Rutherford clan. God knows they needed one sensible sibling. Charles Lambert was a self-made man. He grew up in a middle-class family and had made his first million before he married Charlotte's mother.'' Maybe there was something about their backgrounds that had drawn the two men together, Matt mused. "Charlotte has a lot of her father's qualities—they're just hidden beneath the Rutherford flamboyance. I hope.''

"I hope so, too." Alice studied him a moment before saying, "You know, you're like the son I never had.''

Matt grinned. "Five girls weren't enough?''

"I always wanted a boy," she admitted. "That's how we had the last two girls. Anyway, that's why I'm going to break one of my cardinal rules and give some unasked-for advice: You marry the family, not just the person. Try to keep that in mind.''

"You mean I shouldn't pick Uncle Howie up by the throat every time he says something stupid?''

"Something like that.''

"That was just to get his attention." Matt's smile faded. "I like to think we have an understanding now.''

Alice stood. "Make sure you and Charlotte keep Monday clear. Let's hope we can get this estate settled and you two newlyweds can concentrate on each other." She was almost to the door when she turned back. "And don't forget the annual dinner.''

Matt groaned and checked his calendar. The black-tie affair hosted by the wives of the senior partners was less than two weeks away. "In all the excitement, I'd forgotten.''

"I thought you might have, so I RSVPed for you this morning. I also took the liberty of informing Mrs. Winslow of your marriage. She said that Charlotte was, of course, to be included in the festivities.''

Matt nodded. "I'll see if she's available.''

"No. *Make sure* she's available. You're going to be up for a junior partnership this year, Matt. It's vital that Charlotte make the right kind of impression.''

It was typical of Alice to worry about him. She'd been his mentor and his shepherd since he'd begun working for the firm. He supposed that just having read over his notes on Charlotte's family, Alice had reason to worry.

"She'll be great," he assured the older woman. "She's very charming.''

"She'd have to be, for you to fall in love with her. But promise me you'll explain how important this is to your career.''

"I promise. Now you promise that you won't worry about it.''

Alice gave him her innocent look. "Me? Worry? I won't have time if I'm going to get our case ready by Monday.''

Once Alice was gone, Matt was left to wonder how a logical man like himself had ever gotten into this predicament. He'd hoped that he would be nominated for a junior partnership this year. He had even considered that possibility when he'd first thought about proposing marriage to Charlotte. But he'd decided that a possible nomination wasn't as important as a definite miscarriage of justice if RP went to her relatives. Now he was wondering if he'd still be married when the annual dinner came around.

He supposed that a man who married and divorced in less than two weeks wouldn't represent the stable, sober type that Mr. Russell and Mr. Winslow usually added to the firm, but he wouldn't even consider asking Charlotte to carry on with their marriage until he had his partnership. The effect she'd had on him during the past twenty-four hours had him tied in knots; over several months she'd probably drive him mad. No, Russell and Winslow had never allowed a madman to join the firm. He had a better chance of becoming partner if he was divorced rather than crazy.

"You've verified these prices?" Charlotte asked John Everling as she glanced up from the folder he'd passed her moments before.

John sat relaxed and smiling in the chair across her desk.

"Just pulled those figures off the fax machine myself. I also have it on good authority that they're going to have a ten percent price increase the first of next month."

Charlotte nodded. "Then let's order now. Today. I want the material on hand at this price when we sign the Bixby contract."

"*If* we get the Bixby business," John cautioned.

"We'll get it. I've got Melinda Johnson handling that account. And even if we don't, we'll need these materials for another job."

"Then we get into the problems of storage and—"

John stopped in midsentence as the door to Charlotte's office opened and a woman's voice said, "Darling, what are you doing in this dreary place the day after your wedding? I thought you and that handsome husband of yours would be taking a few days for yourselves."

"Aunt Rhue," Charlotte said as she went around the desk to be enclosed in her aunt's arms and several yards of chiffon. She eased out of the embrace and stood back to examine her aunt, the better to take in the full effect of her outfit of vivid orange and fuchsia with a flowered shawl to match. Not many women of her aunt's age could carry off that outfit. She felt fortunate to be related to a woman who could.

"We went by the house and couldn't believe it when Mrs. Nguyen said you were at work today. So we rushed over here to talk to you, didn't we Carver?"

Charlotte glanced up when she heard Carver murmur his agreement.

"John," she said to the accountant, "you simply must make her take some time off. You need a honeymoon, darling. Some place far away from the ordinary. Hong Kong perhaps. Or maybe Vienna. Don't you agree, Carver?"

"Absolutely." Carver stepped forward and put his arm around Rhue. "I know I intend to whisk you away for a relaxing honeymoon. I want you all to myself for as long as you'll agree. Just you and me—'far from the madding crowd's ignoble strife.'"

"Oh, Carver, you're too good to me."

Charlotte fought to suppress a smile, but when she saw John's look of disbelief, she couldn't help herself.

"So when are you two going to tie the knot?" Charlotte asked.

"The moment your aunt will set the date," Carver answered without taking his eyes from Rhue. "I'd marry her today if she'd agree."

Rhue patted his face. "Just give me a little more time. I've made four mistakes. I want everything to be perfect this time."

"As long as you want, my love."

"So, um, what brings you two over here?" Charlotte finally asked when they continued to gaze into each other's eyes.

"Oh, darling, I've had the most wonderful idea. Since you slipped off and got married like you did, I daresay

Matt hasn't met all your friends and family. I'd like to rectify that with a reception in your honor.''

Charlotte's immediate response was guilt. It was terrible to have her aunt be so generous when she was living a lie.

"Matt is very low-key. I don't think he'd want a big party."

"We'll keep it small. Not more than two hundred. It just so happens that we were at the country club for dinner last night and I heard they have a room available next month. Something about a wedding cancellation. The bride ran off with the golf pro or some such thing."

"That's very generous, Aunt Rhue, but I really don't want you to go to so much trouble."

"No trouble, darling. I'll contact the caterer and see about an orchestra."

"No, really I don't think Matt would like it. He's very...shy, you know."

"You must be joking! He's always been so 'take charge' when I've dealt with him."

"It's big groups," Charlotte decided quickly. "He hates crowds."

"Well, we'll keep it small. Maybe a hundred."

"Too big."

"Fifty?"

"Oh, I don't think so. He gets so nervous in group situations. I want him to be at his best when he meets everyone."

Rhue looked crestfallen. "I have my heart set on it. Haven't I, Carver?"

Carver nodded.

"It's sweet of you," Charlotte tried to forestall the inevitable. "Really sweet, but why don't the two of you come to dinner instead. Just the four of us. Wouldn't that be nice?''

"What a wonderful idea!"

Charlotte wasn't used to her aunt capitulating so easily. "Really?"

"We'll have an intimate family dinner instead. The four of us...and Howie...and Walter...and their families. We'll have it at home."

Charlotte barely suppressed a moan. Poetic justice, she told herself. She'd lied to her family, and now she was going to be forced to endure her various cousins and their mates. Still, it was a small price to pay for saving RP. She only hoped Matt would agree after an evening with the Rutherford clan.

"It sounds wonderful," she lied. "Why don't you work out the details and get back to me about a date." If she was lucky, Rhue wouldn't be able to come up with a caterer on such short notice. And Rhue never cooked.

"Maybe we should have a theme party. I do so love those. Come along, Carver. We have so much to see about."

After walking her aunt to the lobby, Charlotte returned to find John grinning from ear to ear.

"What are you so happy about?"

"Not happy. Amused."

"About what?"

"That guy your aunt's dating. Is he for real?"

"Carver? He seems very sweet."

"Sweet? He's as phony as they come. Real men don't talk like that. 'Just you and me,'" John mimicked. "'Far from the madding crowd.' I say she'd better think long and hard before she marries that guy."

"And I say you'd better have someone get on that order right away."

"Sure thing, boss." John ambled toward the door. "But I say you shouldn't trust a guy who talks like some eighteenth-century poet."

Charlotte had thought the same thing on several occasions, but at the moment she was hardly in a position to suspect someone else's sincerity when she was lying to everyone she cared about.

Chapter Six

Matt turned up Los Feliz Boulevard and headed toward home. Instead of being exhausted from the week, he felt a certain elation and a very real sense of anticipation. And he couldn't help wondering what Charlotte had dreamed up for tonight's dinner. His wedding dinner of lasagna had been the only traditional meal he'd had this week. Wednesday night Mrs. Nguyen had served eggs Benedict with sushi; he'd found it an interesting combination. Thursday night the menu had consisted of a shrimp-and-crab salad with French fries—real, honest-to-God home-made French fries. Heaven only knows what strange combination Charlotte had dreamed up for tonight's dinner, but Matt was anxious to find out. Almost as anxious as he was to be home.

Home. Who would have thought that after three days he'd already feel as if he belonged in the household? Slowing down for the sharp curve, Matt checked for traffic before making the turn into the driveway. For a man who'd never experienced this sort of thing, the sense of belonging made for a very heady experience.

When both his parents had been alive, home had been nothing but a battleground. He remembered his father as a big, angry man who'd delighted in bullying his family. The only person he'd felt any real connection to had been his older sister, and she'd run away from home when he was ten. To this day he had no idea where she'd run to. After his father's death, he'd felt obligated to take care of his mother. He'd even dreamed of buying her a house where they'd become a real family, then his mother had died while he was in law school and denied him even that.

This made it all the sweeter to be accepted into Charlotte's "family." The nightly conversation, the good-natured banter, the feeling of belonging—it was like nothing he'd ever experienced. Matt parked his car beside Charlotte's and took a moment to study the house. From the outside it was imposing, but inside there was a homeyness that was as real as it was unexpected.

He hoped Mrs. Nguyen was in the kitchen, because then Charlotte would come running the minute he stepped inside. They'd exchange a hug and kiss for the housekeeper's benefit, then sit side by side in the living room until dinner was ready. They were getting pretty good at this marriage stuff, he thought. Then Mrs. Nguyen would leave them to have dinner alone.

That was his favorite time—the hour or so when he had Charlotte to himself. Admittedly the first night had been awkward. That was when he'd decided to clear the air. He'd tried to apologize for his actions the night before. He'd wanted to assure her that his streak of violence rarely surfaced. But she'd just smiled and shook her head and told him not to worry. She'd said she trusted him. She'd even thought him brave for going downstairs to confront a burglar. It would take some time, she said, but they'd get used to living in the same house. Later they'd said goodnight and gone to their own rooms. He'd discovered that was the toughest time—the hours he was by himself.

He was glad to be bringing home good news tonight. Alice had indeed gotten the Lambert estate on the docket for Monday morning. If they were lucky, RP would be Charlotte's by noon that day. That also meant there would be no reason to continue this charade. He'd pack up the few possessions he'd brought with him, and by Monday evening he'd be back in his own place in Santa Monica. He wouldn't be lonely, of course, because he was used to living alone, but there was no denying the pang of regret he felt.

If he hadn't been expecting Charlotte to greet him at the door, he wouldn't have been so disappointed, he told himself. That was the problem with getting dependent on people: it hurt when they let you down. Of course, it was impossible for her to hear him over the sounds of good-natured shouting coming from the family room. He detoured in that direction and arrived in time to see Charlotte take out Tommy's last four starfighters on the video game.

"Gotcha!" Charlotte chortled as the TV screen flashed her score in bright red letters and VASSAR's lights flickered off and on. Tommy touched one of VASSAR's buttons and the TV screen announced the beginning of another intergalactic war.

Matt couldn't help smiling over Charlotte's childlike enthusiasm. "I see you've been saving the galaxy while I was stuck in traffic."

"Oh, Matt, did you see that?" Charlotte jumped up from the sofa and raced toward him. In her jeans and oversize sweatshirt she looked as if she could be Tommy's contemporary. Throwing her arms around his neck, she gave him an exuberant kiss. "He's beat me at least a zillion times but now I've finally won."

"Pure luck," Tommy informed them both. "Want to try it again?"

Charlotte shook her head. "Let me enjoy the thrill of victory for a while."

"How about you?" Tommy asked Matt.

"It wouldn't even be a contest," Matt kept his arm around Charlotte while he talked to the boy. "I've never played one of those games before."

"Never?" Charlotte looked up at him with real concern in her eyes. "You've led a pretty boring life, haven't you, Counselor?"

"Not boring, just too busy for games."

"I'll teach you how," Tommy volunteered.

"You don't have time to teach him anything," Mrs. Nguyen said from the doorway. She was carrying her purse and sweater. "We've got to get going."

"Ah, Mom. I was going to finish hooking VASSAR up to some of the appliances tonight. I've got this great idea," Tommy told Charlotte. "I'm going to fix it so you can start the appliances by remote control. When you get up in the morning you just press a button on the remote control to start your coffee. It'll be ready when you get downstairs. Put the oranges in the juicer the night before, and with the press of a button you can squeeze them while you're coming downstairs. Won't that be great?"

"Will it be so great when you have push-buttoned your mother out of a job?" Mrs. Nguyen asked her son. "It's a good thing I'm taking you away from here."

"Where are we going, anyway?"

"I'm going to bingo. But first," she said when he started to protest, "we're going to go buy that new video game you've been wanting."

Tommy was already on his feet. "Really?"

"Got to hurry. Dinner is in the oven," she told Charlotte. "You two enjoy."

Once the Nguyens were gone, Matt followed Charlotte into the kitchen. He was almost disappointed to find they were having roast beef with mashed potatoes.

Charlotte sliced the roast and put it on the table. "Mrs. Nguyen told me she thinks you're really a meat-and-potatoes man. She vetoed my suggestion for dinner in favor of something more traditional."

What Mrs. Nguyen had really said was that a bridegroom needed more substantial food if he was to fulfill his husbandly obligations. Charlotte had replied that if beef was a necessity, there wouldn't be so many children in Hindu countries. Mrs. Nguyen had still insisted on a hearty meal.

"What had you suggested?"

"Don't think you can get it out of me so easily. If I tell you now it won't be a surprise when I talk her into fixing it. If you want catsup, get it out of the fridge."

Matt got his catsup like the good meat-and-potatoes man he was, and they settled down to a quiet dinner.

"Alice called today," Charlotte said after Matt finished off his first helping. "She said the Monday court date is definite."

Only her sense of fair play had kept Charlotte from asking Alice to cancel it. Just because she'd come to enjoy Matt's company was no reason to keep him here any longer than necessary. Oh, but she was going to miss him. How had their lives become so entangled in less than a week? It occurred to her that if her marriage had been this satisfying, she would have moved heaven and earth to save it.

"I have a feeling she called in a couple favors to get us on the docket so quickly. Is there any more gravy?"

Charlotte went back to the stove and refilled the gravy bowl. "She also mentioned some black-tie dinner that's coming up. Alice seems to think this event could be very important to your career." She set the gravy on the table. "Why didn't you tell me about it?"

"I try not to think about the one time each year I'm required to wear a penguin suit. Besides, I think Alice overestimates the importance of these social occasions. The partners are more likely to look at my professional experience than my manners when they make nominations for junior partnership."

"I got the distinct impression that it wasn't *your* manners she was worried about."

Matt smiled. "She's just had the pleasure of going through my file on your family. You can't really blame her for being a little cautious. But since we'll have the estate settled by that time, you won't have to worry about the party. I hadn't even planned to inform the senior partners that I'd married. That way I wouldn't have had to explain about the divorce."

Charlotte pushed the food around on her plate. "What will you tell them now?"

"That it didn't work out, I guess." Matt helped himself to more meat and carrots. "Considering the divorce statistics these days, they shouldn't be surprised. Hell, divorce makes up at least twenty percent of Russell and Winslow's business."

"Will they think any less of you for having married and divorced so quickly? And not just married, but married to one of the firm's clients."

Matt put his fork down and looked her in the eye. "Don't worry about it. I'm not."

"I can't help feeling responsible. After all, if it wasn't for me, you wouldn't be in this situation."

"I weighed all the facts before I proposed this solution. I can take care of myself."

"I know that. It's just that . . . well, I only thought . . ." Nervously she twisted the wedding band on her finger. It was the plain gold ring her father had given her mother when they'd first married, but now, instead of being a symbol of love, it was just another part of the charade. "If it would be any help, I'd be happy to go to the party with you. I'd even let them think that things were working out with us."

Matt stopped eating and stared at her. "You'd really do that for me?"

"After what you've done, it's the very least I can do. Besides, I have a little party . . . I mean problem of my own." She tried not to blush when he grinned.

"You do?"

"It's not a formal black-tie affair like yours. Just a little family get-together."

"Your family?"

Charlotte nodded.

"I'd rather put on a tux."

"It's Aunt Rhue's idea. She wants to give a reception to introduce you to the family. She really has her heart set on it. Anyway, I just thought that maybe we could agree to keep up the appearance of being married long enough to get through these two social occasions. What do you think?"

"Do you think that's fair to your aunt when we know that our marriage is only temporary?"

"I thought about that, but then I remembered that we're talking about a woman who's made four trips to the altar—and divorce court. And she *loves* to give parties. If I'm not careful, she may even insist on a party to celebrate our divorce. She had a doozy to celebrate the end of her last marriage."

"Does Carver know about her track record?"

Charlotte nodded. "He was at her divorce party, in fact. Don't try to change the subject. Do we have a deal on the parties?"

"Sure. As long as I don't have to wear a penguin suit to your family festivities."

"Thanks for helping with the dishes." Charlotte rinsed out the sink and hung the cloth to dry. "Tomorrow is Mrs. Nguyen's day off, so I didn't want to let them sit."

Matt watched her bend over and put the pot away on the bottom shelf. He'd never liked those oversize shirts on women, but he had to admit there was something tantalizing about the way it molded to Charlotte's figure when she moved, reminding him of what she looked like underneath all that bulky material. He wondered why he'd never realized just how sexy jeans and a baggy sweatshirt could be. Maybe because he'd never seen them on Charlotte before.

Charlotte smiled at him. "Do you have work to do tonight?"

"Yeah, I do actually. I need to take care of some paperwork that I'd scheduled for Monday morning."

"Me, too." Charlotte retrieved the dishcloth and wiped off the already spotless stove top.

Matt leaned one hip against the counter. "Just another exciting Friday night?"

Charlotte smiled. "Not exactly life in the fast lane, is it? What do you usually do on Fridays?"

"Pick up a pizza and watch a little TV."

"Somehow I'd pictured you doing something more exciting."

"Singles bars aren't my scene," Matt informed her.

"Mine, either."

He shifted his weight and leaned down on one elbow. "What do you usually do?"

"Friday is Mrs. Nguyen's bingo night, so sometimes I meet friends for dinner. If I'm home, Tommy usually comes over and we play video games or watch a movie. We used to spend the time working on his inventions, but lately his projects are too complicated for me."

"I can understand that." He hung the dish towel and looked at the clock. "I guess I'd better get busy."

"Yeah, me, too." She watched Matt start for the door. She didn't want to go to her own room tonight. If things went as expected on Monday, their marriage would be over. She wanted to enjoy the time they had left together. "Or I could teach you how to wage intergalactic mayhem."

"What?"

"The video game. You said you'd never played before, so I figure I can probably beat you. I wouldn't mind shooting a few more starfighters out of the sky before I get to work—all in the interest of intergalactic peace, of course. What do you say?"

"I've never played before."

"All the better." She grabbed his hand and tugged him toward the family room. Smiling up at him, she asked, "I don't suppose you'd like to make a little wager on who's going to save the universe?"

* * *

"One more game?" Charlotte asked from where she sat Indian-style on the floor.

Matt moaned and leaned his head against the back of the sofa. "Show a little mercy. I've crashed and burned over three hundred times tonight."

"You're showing some improvement."

"Uh-huh, I winged one of your planes and flew into two others during this last game. You call that progress?"

"I call the fact that you have now been introduced to one of the great inventions of the twentieth century a real step forward."

"Somehow I don't think this is going to go down in the history books with electricity and the telephone."

Charlotte paused in the act of putting away the game controls. "You know what your problem is? You don't take time to enjoy yourself. What do you do just for the sheer pleasure of it?"

Matt shrugged. "I go to the gym about three times a week and work out."

"So you count and sweat for fun?"

"It gives me time to sort things out."

"See, that's just what I mean. What do you do to make yourself *forget* about things?"

Matt thought for a minute. "Engage in intergalactic mayhem?"

"Exactly. Now you see why it's one of modern technology's greatest creations."

"You could be right. I didn't think about the Gilbert estate even once."

"And I bet when you go back to work, you'll be able to look at it from a fresh perspective."

Matt raked a hand through his hair. "Not a chance on this one, I'm afraid."

"That's a defeatist attitude if I ever heard one."

"Nope. This is one case I can't lose—even though I wish I could. There are times when the letter of the law has nothing to do with justice."

"And that bothers you, doesn't it?" She leaned back against the sofa and looked up at him. "Want to talk about it?"

"Not much to tell, really. Ron Gilbert made his money in oil. Started out as a roughneck and got lucky. He was married to the same woman for over thirty years. They raised five kids. About three years ago his wife died and ol' Ron was lonely. So lonely that he fell for the first cute young thing in tight pants. Unfortunately, all she had in her eyes was dollar signs. When Ron's health began to fail, he became increasingly dependent on her. Toward the end, she told him she didn't want him to worry about anything. She said that if he left everything to her, she'd be sure his kids and grandkids were taken care of."

"And he believed her?"

Matt nodded. "It's a helluva thing to see a man who's been so sharp most of his life make one dumb mistake that'll affect his family like that."

"Where do you fit in?"

"Technically, I'm representing the estate. In actuality, I'm the man who's going to make sure the second wife gets everything that should have gone to Ron's children and grandchildren." He ran his hands over his face in a gesture of utter weariness. "It wouldn't be so bad if it was an isolated case, but in estate law we see it all the time."

"Maybe you'll get used to it."

"I sure as hell hope not."

Charlotte placed her hand over his. "I'm glad."

"Thanks for listening." Matt turned his hand over and laced his fingers with hers. "You're right. It helps to get a little emotional distance. It also helps to talk about it."

"Any time."

With his other hand, Matt reached down and brushed a lock of hair from her temple. "I may take you up on that. You're a great listener."

"And somehow that surprises you?"

"Yeah," Matt said with a grin. "I've always thought of you as moving at the speed of light. I didn't realize anyone with that kind of energy could sit still this long."

"And I never realized that a man who seemed so in control could keep so much emotion hidden."

"It's nice to be able to surprise you."

Charlotte smiled. "I like surprises."

"Good," he said as he leaned down toward her. "Because I think I have another one for you."

But she wasn't really surprised by the feel of his lips on hers. She remembered how they felt from before. She even remembered how he tasted. What did surprise her was his hesitance. She would have sworn that he was a man of decisiveness, yet he almost drew back. It wasn't until she lifted her free hand to his cheek that his kiss became insistent. Demanding.

Unable to get enough of him, unable to give enough, she came up on her knees. He plunged his hands into her hair as he deepened the kiss. That took her breath away and made her head swim. Her arms went around him. To steady herself, she thought. Then she found she was pulling at him, trying to draw him closer. She wasn't sure she would have been able to let go if the phone hadn't rung.

Shrill and insistent, it pierced the cocoon of emotion they'd created. Even then it was hard to pull back. Hard to brush away the haze of desire. She was sitting on her heels, trying to understand what had happened when she heard Matt answer the phone.

"Rhue," he said. "Nice to hear from you."

Charlotte wondered if her aunt noticed the husky timbre of his voice. Wondered if she could feel the vibrations of desire over the phone lines.

"No, we're not doing anything special. She's right here," Charlotte heard him say. Then he was extending the phone to her.

Her hand was still trembling when she accepted the receiver.

"Hi," she said, and watched Matt get up from the sofa. His expression was unreadable as he turned and left the room, but Charlotte felt suddenly small and alone.

"Darling," Aunt Rhue began without preamble, "I have the most wonderful idea. What do you think about doves?"

Charlotte pulled herself back to the conversation. "I think they make a mess out by the gazebo."

Rhue laughed. "No, I mean for the reception. I thought we'd release white doves into the sky."

"It's your patio."

"Hmm. I see what you mean. What about heart-shaped balloons?"

"The EPA has asked people not to do that anymore. It pollutes the environment."

"Oh, dear. I did so want to do something romantic. Would you two consider reaffirming your vows? After all, we did miss it the first time."

"Well..." She wasn't sure how Matt would feel about that, but it made her very uncomfortable.

"Never mind. I'd forgotten how shy Matt is."

"Shy?"

"You told me about that earlier this week. I can't imagine how I forgot. Well, don't worry. I'll think of something."

"I know I can depend on you."

"Quite right. I've tentatively set the date for next Friday."

"One week from tonight?"

"That's right. Sevenish. How's that?"

"Fine."

"Now you get back to that handsome husband of yours. I've got work to do. Maybe heart-shaped pâté... I'll work it out. Night, darling."

"Good night, Aunt Rhue," she responded, though she was sure her aunt was already concentrating on other things.

She cradled the receiver, then sat on the sofa—in the very spot Matt had sat—and wondered how things had gotten out of hand so quickly? One minute she and Matt had been decimating starfighters and the next they'd been necking like a couple of teenagers. Where had all that raw emotion come from? And where was it headed?

She closed her eyes and leaned back against the sofa. She had enough sense to know exactly where it had been headed before her aunt called. She owed Aunt Rhue, she decided. Maybe even enough to eat heart-shaped pâté.

Pulling her bare feet onto the sofa, Charlotte wrapped her arms around her legs and rested her chin on her knees. She was still having trouble thinking straight, but she wasn't naive enough to believe that the sort of emotion she'd just experienced would go away. She hadn't felt that tug of desire in a long time. She wasn't sure she'd ever felt anything quite that intense.

And she had enough experience with men to know that Matt had wanted her, too.

She wished fleetingly that the passion was genuine. That it could lead to something beautiful and solid that would last a lifetime. That would be ironic, wouldn't it? To marry because of her father's will and then fall in love. That was exactly the kind of absurdity her father had loved.

Of course, that wasn't what was happening. Matt had married her because the injustice of her father's will stirred his conscience, precisely as the injustice done to Ron Gilbert's family tormented him. So the question remained: what should she do about this unwanted passion? There was only one answer, as far as she was concerned—face it head-on. Resolutely she stood and pushed up the trailing sleeves of her sweatshirt.

Because she was evidently weak where Matt was concerned, they were going to have to reach an agreement. She started for the stairs only to be brought up short by a horrible thought: what was she going to say? It seemed a little presumptuous to knock on his door and inform him that she wasn't interested in going to bed with him. There was always the chance that he hadn't been nearly as overwhelmed by that kiss as she had been. By the same token, it seemed dangerous to wait until the topic came up in conversation. Considering what had happened earlier, she wasn't sure she'd remember what she wanted to say if he kissed her again.

Perhaps this was one time in her life where subtlety might be effective. He'd said he would be working tonight, so she'd take up a pot of coffee. Then she'd find a way to segue into the fact that she wasn't interested in a physical relationship with him. Surely he'd see the logic in that.

Why was nothing ever easy? Charlotte wondered as she crossed her arms and stared at the coffeepot. She'd plugged it in five minutes ago and nothing had happened yet. Probably had something to do with that thingamajig on the end of the cord. It looked like a little black box, and it was probably part of Tommy's plan to "push-button" her world. She removed the plug and looked at it. Yep, there was definitely a thingamajig on the end of the cord. She pushed it back into the outlet, but nothing happened.

If this was, indeed, Tommy's doing, then the black box must have something to do with VASSAR. She stalked back into the family room and glared at the robot. Tommy had turned it off before leaving, but maybe if she turned it on... She hit the On button, waited for the row of lights to come on, then headed back to the kitchen.

Sure enough, the coffee maker was on—and there was smoke coming out of the black thingamajig. Grabbing a pot holder, she hit at the first few sparks, hoping to smother them. When that didn't work, she yanked on the cord. The plug didn't budge, but she noticed that the pot holder had begun to smolder. This time she gave the cord a powerful tug and succeeded in pulling the plug out of the wall—and in knocking the coffee maker onto the floor. With the now-flaming pot holder still in her hand, Charlotte ran for the sink. Tossing the burning material into the basin, she turned on the cold water. Once the small blaze was extinguished, she plunged her burned hand under the cold water.

Chapter Seven

"What the hell is going on down here?" Matt demanded.

"I was making coffee."

He eyed the mess on the floor. "I see. What are you doing now?"

"Running cold water over my burn."

He was across the room in three long strides. "How bad is it?"

"Not bad."

Grasping her wrist, he turned her hand so that he could see the burn. It wasn't bad, as burns went, but it made his stomach churn.

"You'll live," he told her. "Where's your first aid kit?"

"In the laundry room. Wait," she called when he started in that direction. "I want a leaf from the aloe vera plant."

"We'll worry about your plants later."

"It's for my burn. It's an old folk remedy, but it works better than anything that comes in a tube."

He hesitated. "Where is it?"

"There are several in the solarium. They look like a succulent with big, fleshy, triangular-shaped leaves. Just break the tip off one—but be careful not to let the liquid drip on the carpet."

"The hell with the carpet," Matt muttered as he went through the dining room and into the solarium. The plants were easy enough to recognize, and he was back at her side in a matter of minutes.

"It stinks," he commented as he watched the thick greenish liquid ooze onto her skin. "Does it really work?"

"You bet. I just need to let it sit on there for a while."

"You might as well sit down then."

Holding the dish towel under her hand, he guided her to the breakfast table.

As she sat watching, he set the coffee maker back on the counter and used paper towel to blot up the liquid.

"You ought to let Mrs. Nguyen make the coffee next time."

He heard her sigh. "I'm perfectly capable of making coffee. It was the black thingamajig that caused the trouble."

"Uh-huh."

"The one on the end of the plug."

Matt inspected both the cord and the little black box. "What is it?"

"Darned if I know, but it must be connected to VASSAR somehow. Oh, my gosh! I left VASSAR running."

Matt pushed her back in the chair as he strode past her toward the family room. VASSAR was idling beside the fireplace. The only indication that it was working was one dim amber light.

"The robot's fine."

"Will you turn it off?" Charlotte called back.

Matt was happy to switch it off. The thing showed all the earmarks of becoming a menace.

"Want to tell me how the robot managed this?" he asked once he'd finished cleaning up. He sat at the table and listened to her story.

"The kid needs to go back to the drawing board with that thing," was all he said when she finished, but he made a mental note to talk to Tommy. Electrical fires could get out of hand quickly. He hated to think of anything going wrong when Charlotte was here alone.

"You ready to rinse that green stuff off?" he asked after a moment. "I'm going to get some real medicine to put on your hand."

He brought the first aid kit to the kitchen table and began to lay out whatever he thought would be useful. As he applied the antiseptic salve, Matt was happy to see that the burn hadn't formed a blister. Without comment, he took out a roll of gauze and began to wind it around her hand.

"Don't you think that's a bit much for such a little burn?"

He ignored her remark. "Next time you want coffee," he advised as he tied the bandage in place, "consider instant."

"It wasn't for me. You said you were going to work late, so I was making you a pot."

He thought of the mess he'd just cleaned up and couldn't help smiling. "Don't do me any more favors, okay?"

He was putting the supplies away when she placed her hand on his. The white of the bandage was stark against his skin.

"It isn't your job to go around cleaning up everyone else's messes, you know."

He glanced over at the kitchen floor. "I think I did okay."

"Matt."

The way she said it, all soft and gentle, made his insides melt. He didn't think any other woman had ever said his name quite that way.

"I mean that you can't go around trying to make everything right. The world isn't always fair."

"You don't have to tell me that," he responded, thinking of the way he'd grown up.

She shook her head and smiled at him. "I'm not saying this right. What I mean is that you can't take responsibility for the mess other people have gotten their lives into. I appreciate what you've done for me, but you can't marry every woman who needs a husband and you can't make all the gold diggers in the world give back the money they shouldn't have."

"I know that."

"No, you know it here," she said, touching her fingers to his forehead. "But I don't think you know it in your heart, where it really counts."

Grabbing her wrist, he pulled her hand from his brow. It burned where she'd touched him, and it was the kind of burn that couldn't be treated with medicines.

"What makes you such an expert?"

"I don't have to be an expert. It's there in your eyes. It's in the things you do. You try so hard to make everything right, but you're only human."

He thought of how he'd reacted to her earlier. "I think I proved that before your aunt called."

"I think we both did."

"I suppose you want me to apologize."

"Not necessarily. Do you want me to apologize?"

"For what?"

"For kissing you back."

"Dammit," he muttered, and began shoving supplies back into the first aid kit. "I'm the one who initiated the kiss. I'm the one who'll apologize." He slammed the metal box so hard it made her wince. "I'm sorry. It won't happen again."

"Oh? How are you going to guarantee that? Do you think you can control my emotions, too? Or didn't you notice that I was just as involved as you were?"

"I won't let things get out of hand again," he insisted.

"See, there you go again trying to take on everyone else's responsibilities. What if I want it to happen again?"

He went perfectly still. "Is that what you want?"

"No," Charlotte said with a gentle shake of her head. "I don't believe in casual sex, but I can see how that sort of thing was almost inevitable given our present circumstances. We're actually married and living under the same roof. Even though we're not...not intimate, the situation creates a deceptive amount of familiarity. If we both recognize that fact, we'll be less likely to get caught up in the moment again."

"That seems reasonable," Matt conceded. But he couldn't help wondering why, if she was making so damn much sense, he still wanted her so badly that he needed to stuff his hands into his pockets to keep from reaching for her.

"I admit our reaction was perfectly normal under the circumstances, but I know we're both mature enough to see that it doesn't happen again. I'm sure you feel the same way."

"Are you planning to talk this into the ground?" he asked when she paused to take a breath. "Or do you want to agree to stay out of each other's way during the next couple of days?''

He was being wonderfully sensible about the whole episode, she decided. She should have known he would be. So why did she feel betrayed? Why did she find herself staring at his hands and remembering how they'd felt against her face, her scalp? Why did she want to feel them on her again?

Charlotte stood. "I have plenty of work to do over the weekend."

"So do I."

"By Monday this will all be behind us."

"Right."

Charlotte smiled at him. "Good night." She resisted the ridiculous urge to touch him. Instead she watched him walk out of the room, then scooped up the first aid kit and returned it to the cupboard.

Monday morning dawned dreary and overcast. A typical June morning, Matt decided when he glanced out his bedroom window. He adjusted his tie and began packing his papers into his briefcase.

It had been a particularly productive weekend. Of course, that was exactly what he'd expected when he kept himself locked up in his room all weekend. He'd ventured out only long enough to find food when he was hungry and to talk to Tommy. Finding Tommy had been easy since the boy had been fiddling with the door locks all weekend. Sleeping had been tougher; he'd spent Saturday night watching various movie monsters destroy Tokyo, and even that hadn't put him to sleep.

Snatching up his suit coat, he started downstairs. All he had to do was get through this morning, then he'd be home free. By noon RP would be Charlotte's, and by tonight he'd be back in his own bed. He always slept well in his own bed.

As soon as he stepped into the breakfast room, he decided it wasn't going to be an easy morning.

"I have plenty to do without doing extra work," he heard Mrs. Nguyen say.

"What extra work are you talking about?" Charlotte asked.

"Got to fix two different breakfasts every morning. Got to clean two different bedrooms each day. Got to make two different beds."

"Hire some extra help you if you need to," Charlotte snapped. She was sorry the minute she'd said it. She'd spent a restless night—make that *three* restless nights—and she wasn't handling Mrs. Nguyen very well this morning. She knew the older woman's grumbling only masked her concern. However, Charlotte couldn't confide in anyone, not even Mrs. Nguyen.

"I just want juice and toast this morning," Charlotte said, hoping to defuse the situation. "Please."

"Humph. You should be wanting a *big* breakfast," Mrs. Nguyen informed her as she stomped over to the toaster. "You *should* be waking up with a smile on your face."

Charlotte was shaking her head when she saw Matt standing in the doorway. He looked wonderful, she decided. She hadn't seen him since he'd doctored her hand, though she'd heard him rattling around in the house. She supposed this would be the last morning she'd sit across from him at the breakfast table. She was surprised to realize how much she was going to miss him.

"Good morning," she said, trying not to let her voice reveal how she felt.

He came over to give her a perfunctory kiss. Only his lips touched her cheek, but Charlotte couldn't resist resting her hand on his arm. She wanted to rest her head on his shoulder.

"How's your hand?" he asked after staring at it for several seconds.

Charlotte removed her hand with its two Band-Aids from his arm. "Almost as good as new. I told you that aloe vera is good stuff."

"I hope you want a *big* breakfast," Mrs. Nguyen said from across the room.

Matt smiled. "You bet. I'm starving."

Charlotte watched the smile spread across Mrs. Nguyen's face.

By the time Charlotte had made her fresh juice, Mrs. Nguyen had slapped her toast on a plate and plunked it on the table. Matt poured himself some coffee and sat across from her.

"We need to be at the courthouse by nine," Matt told her.

"I'm ready to go."

"I talked to Alice last night. She said everything looks good."

Charlotte ignored the way Mrs. Nguyen's head swiveled around at that bit of information. "Good."

Charlotte toyed with her toast as Matt ate his breakfast. She tried to pretend the silence didn't bother her, but she was extremely grateful when Tommy came in the kitchen door with VASSAR.

"I've got the door locks hooked up," Tommy announced without preamble. "See," he said as he closed the door, "I installed these little boxes on all the doors and doorjambs. Now all you have to do is press a button and the doors will lock or unlock."

Charlotte couldn't help responding to his enthusiasm. "How does it work?"

"A lot like the remote control on the garage doors. You just press a button and the two boxes form an electronic lock. It's virtually burglarproof, too."

To demonstrate, Tommy pressed a couple buttons then tried to open the door. It wouldn't budge.

"That's wonderful!" Charlotte told him.

"What happens if the doors aren't closed?" Matt asked.

Leave it to Matt, Charlotte thought, to look for the flaws.

"VASSAR can't close the doors, but it buzzes. Then it's up to you to come close it."

Charlotte nodded. That sounded reasonable.

"Will we be able to use our keys to get in?"

Another reasonable question from Matt, Charlotte decided. She wondered if he ever accepted anything at face value.

Tommy shook his head. "Right now you'd have to carry the remote control with you, but I'm working on electronic keys. Then you could secure the house when you're gone, too."

"Speaking of being gone..." Matt tossed his napkin onto the table. "I think it's time for us to leave."

Tommy pressed one of the buttons.

Carrying his briefcase and jacket, Matt crossed to the door and turned the knob. The knob turned but the door didn't open.

"You want to unlock the door?" he said to Tommy.

Tommy pressed some more buttons, and Matt tried the door again. Nothing happened. Matt gave the boy a withering look. Tommy went to the door and tried it. When he couldn't open it either, he tried pressing more buttons and in different combinations.

"Look what you've done now," Mrs. Nguyen wailed.

"I'm sure it will be okay," Charlotte told everyone.

Matt checked his watch and began to pace as Tommy worked frantically, first with the remote control and then with the keyboard on VASSAR.

Charlotte sat back in her chair and decided this was great fun. It's too bad no one else has the sense of humor to see it, she thought. As Tommy continued to work with VASSAR, Matt stalked toward the front of the house. Charlotte heard him rattle the front door and the doors in the solarium. He returned looking grimmer than when he'd left.

"Now what?" he asked with a scowl. "We need to be in court in thirty minutes."

"I'm working on it," Tommy assured him. "But I can't figure out what's wrong."

Charlotte stood and smiled. "I guess we'll just have to crawl out a window."

"A window?" Matt asked as though she'd just suggested they find a black hole in space to crawl through.

"Yeah, you know those things in the wall made out of glass. The one in the dining room is probably best."

He sent her a fulminating glance. "Cute."

"You have a better suggestion?"

"We could unscrew one of those black boxes."

Tommy coughed. "The tools are in the garage. And VASSAR locked the garage doors, too."

"My car?" Charlotte asked.

Tommy gave her a sheepish grin. "In the garage."

"I'll drive," Matt told her. "Then I'll drop you at work."

Charlotte didn't see what else they could do.

"Let me out first," Matt said once they'd reached the dining room.

"Be careful of the azaleas," Charlotte warned as he eased over the windowsill.

She'd just decided this wasn't going to be too difficult when she heard the sound of tearing cloth. Matt fingered the rip in the shoulder of his shirt and muttered an oath.

"At least it wasn't your pants," Charlotte said when he caught her smiling. "Want me to get you another shirt from your room?"

Matt sighed. "We don't have time. Besides, my jacket will cover it. Hand it to me. Now the rest of the stuff," he said, once his jacket was on. "Okay, now you. And watch that catch on the window.... Well, come on," he urged when she didn't move.

But Charlotte just stood there. No matter how she figured it, getting out the window in a skirt and high heels presented several problems. She took off her pumps and handed them out first. Matt stuck one in each pocket.

"What's the problem?" he finally asked. "This was your idea."

"I'm trying to figure out a way to do this without my skirt ending up over my head, if you must know."

She watched the muscle in Matt's jaw clench several times. Finally he said, "You just sit on the window ledge, and I'll lift you out."

Charlotte nodded and stuck one slender leg through the window. Her skirt was hiked up above midthigh, and Matt felt his body tense. When she straddled the windowsill and lifted the other leg to bring it through, he closed his eyes and concentrated on reviewing the elements of a contract from his days in law school—in the order of ascent. First, identify the parties. Second, have a meeting of the minds. Next a statement of... He didn't open his eyes until he heard Charlotte's voice.

"Well," she said.

The morning breeze molded the silky material to her legs, and Matt wasn't sure if he was relieved or disappointed to find that she'd pulled her skirt down as far as she could. Placing his hands at her waist, he lifted her away from the window and set her on the ground in front of him. There wasn't much space between the house and the azaleas, and he found Charlotte too close for his peace of mind. After avoiding her all weekend, he found the softness of her body even more tempting.

Her legs were long and slender and practically molded to his. Her feminine curves fit perfectly against the planes and angles of his body, and her breasts rose and fell with each breath she took. He'd done nothing good enough in his life to deserve this moment of pleasure and nothing bad enough to deserve the torture of knowing this was all wrong. He stepped back and thrust her shoes at her before he did something foolish.

"It's a good thing I hadn't fixed the locks on the windows, huh?" Tommy asked from inside the house.

Speechless, Matt turned toward the boy. He would have grabbed the kid by the collar and hauled him out the window if Charlotte hadn't been in his arms.

"I think you'd better perfect the doors first," was all she said.

But the laughter in her eyes when she looked up at Matt told him that she wasn't the least bit angry at Tommy. Actually, he decided, she found the situation wildly amusing. There was no denying the fact that Charlotte was gorgeous and so desirable that she had him tied up in knots. Too bad she also had a few screws loose.

The sound of Matt's steps seemed to echo in the hallway of the courthouse, and Charlotte was forced to trot along at a very undignified pace to keep up with him. Even though dignity was not high on her list of priorities, she was delighted to finally turn the corner and see her family and Alice Kelsey only a few yards away. Putting her arm through Matt's, she dug in her heels and tried to slow him to a dignified pace. Alice Kelsey broke away from the group and came to meet them.

"There you are." Alice glanced pointedly at her watch. "I was beginning to wonder if something had happened."

"We couldn't get out of the house," Matt said.

"You should have planned to leave earlier."

"You don't understand." Matt gave her a direct look. "The doors were all locked and we actually couldn't get out."

Alice's laugh was disbelieving. "You make it sound like the house from hell."

Matt glanced meaningfully at Charlotte. "We had to crawl out the window," he informed his colleague without taking his eyes from Charlotte. "We were lucky the freeways were clear."

"Darlings," Charlotte heard from behind Alice. She turned just in time to see a flash of emerald green before being enveloped in one of Aunt Rhue's enthusiastic hugs. "I told your uncles you'd be here."

Charlotte glanced past Carver, who hovered at Rhue's side, to where Howie and Walter stood with two of their attorneys.

"Morning," Uncle Howie called cheerfully, as Walter nodded. "I see you and the gigolo made it on time."

Charlotte tightened her grip on Matt's arm as Carver, the quiet, colorless little man at Rhue's side, said quite clearly, "That's uncalled-for."

Rhue patted her fiancé's arm. "No one pays much attention to Howard when he's in this kind of mood. Try to ignore him."

"But, Sweetie," Carver said to Rhue, "the world is so cruel to lovers. It seems unfair that these two young people who have just embarked on a life together should be subjected to such insults. I hate to say it, but your brother has no romance in his soul.''

Howie laughed. ''Romance and a dollar will get you a cup of coffee.''

''Pay no attention,'' Rhue commanded.

Carver sighed. ''I'll try. For your sake. But I still can't fathom how a warm and loving person like you can have such a cold, uncaring clod of a brother.''

Charlotte couldn't help smiling over the little man's flowery language, though she noticed that the effect on her aunt was quite different. Rhue's expression took on the glow of a simpleminded teenager, and Charlotte couldn't help remembering John Everling's warning. She hoped, for her aunt's sake, that John was wrong.

''We can go in now,'' Alice said, once the doors were opened.

''Thank God,'' was all Matt said. But Charlotte had the distinct impression that he could hardly wait to rid himself of his wife and her eccentric relatives.

Chapter Eight

When Matt stepped back into the hallway an hour and a half later, he was convinced that the rest of the world had gone mad—and that he wasn't far behind. How in the world was he going to endure six months married to the woman at his side? Six months of Charlotte's smiles and laughter. Six months of being so tied in knots that he couldn't sleep without dreaming of her. Six months of her relatives. Six months in the house from hell. There was a good chance he wouldn't make it.

"That was certainly . . . unexpected," Alice murmured. "Their attorneys are more resourceful than we gave them credit for."

Matt nodded. They had anticipated that the attorneys for the Rutherford clan would make a token contest of Charlotte's marriage. What they hadn't expected was her relatives to allege that their niece had fallen into the hands of a madman who'd married her only for her money. It had been particularly damning when Charlotte's own attorney had been forced to tell about Matt manhandling Howie during the first meeting.

"Unexpected," Matt agreed. "And effective."

"But not really a problem," Alice finished. "They've only postponed the inevitable. The judge stated for the record that if you and Charlotte are still married six months from now, he will order an immediate disbursement of the estate. But who would have thought that Charlotte's crazy relatives could persuade anyone that they want Charles Lambert's wishes carried out? Sorry," she said to Charlotte with a friendly pat on the arm. "The 'crazy' part just slipped out."

Charlotte smiled at the older woman. "They've been called worse."

"Charlotte, honey, wait up," Howie said as he hurried over to her.

Matt stuck his hands in his pockets so that he wouldn't give in to the urge to rub that smug expression off the man's face.

"No hard feelings, I hope," he said as he removed a cigar from his pocket. "We only want what your father wanted, you know." Pausing to light the cigar, he blew a few puffs of smoke in Matt's direction. "You know how Charles felt. He wanted you to settle down with some nice young man and have children of your own." *Puff. Puff.* "Yes, sir. Your father wanted you to have children to carry on the bloodline."

"The conception of children is not mentioned in the will and has no bearing on this case," Alice pointed out.

Howard Rutherford stuck the cigar back into his mouth and chewed on it. Matt smiled.

"But, Sweetie," Matt heard Carver say in the silence that followed, "how could you be a party to this? You're not like that brother of yours. You believe in love. Don't you?''

"How can you even ask?" Rhue's voice sounded weepy.

Matt turned to look at the couple and had to grit his teeth. That's just what they needed, a tearful scene in the hallway.

"Then why did you agree to this six-month waiting period?"

"Howie only wants what's best for Charlotte."

"But, Rhue, how can it be right to put love on a time-table? I loved you just as much the moment we met as I love you now. Are you so heartless that you would doubt your niece's love?"

"Oh, Carver," Rhue whispered as the tears began to fall. "You're right, of course. Can you ever forgive me?"

That brought Howie to life. "Stuff a sock in it," he told the man who embraced his tearful sister. "Remember, Rhue, you promised we'd stick together on this. You can't go back on your word now."

Rhue produced a lacy handkerchief from her pocket and sniffed prettily. "That's true."

"Even if you know it's wrong?" Carver tightened his embrace.

Howie waved his cigar in the air. "A bargain's a bargain."

"How can you say that? Can't you see how upset she is?"

Howie rocked back on his heels and puffed thoughtfully on his cigar. "As far as I can see, you're the one who upset her. She was happy enough before you put in your two cents' worth. What's it to you, anyway?"

"Anything that affects my sweet Rhue affects me."

Rhue went from sniffling to sobbing, and several people turned in their direction. Matt couldn't help heaving a sigh.

"Your Sweetie is going to be even more upset if that niece of ours falls victim to some bluebeard. How do you think she'll feel then?"

Rhue's sobbing increased in volume and enthusiasm, and Matt shook his head. Bluebeard? During the past ninety minutes he'd somehow gone from gigolo to serial killer. The Rutherford clan obviously went for the drama of the moment. And they were just as obviously used to drawing a crowd; everyone within earshot was giving the scene their undivided attention.

Carver gave his weeping fiancée several pats on the shoulder as he glared at Howie. "Don't be an ass. If he had planned to murder Charlotte, he can't do it now. There'd be no advantage to it until after the six-month waiting period."

That did it, Matt decided. He and Charlotte were leaving before he did something incredibly stupid. The only thing keeping him from physical violence right now was the fact that he couldn't decide which man to go after first. But before he could reach for Charlotte, she was stepping between the two men.

"Stop it, both of you," she admonished. "You're upsetting Aunty Rhue. Are you all right?" she asked the woman who peeped out from between her hands.

"I only want what's best for you," Rhue said between sniffles.

Charlotte smiled at her. "I know that."

"I want you to be happy."

"I am," Charlotte told her aunt, and realized it was the truth.

When the judge had granted her relatives a six-month extension, she'd had to stuff her hands into the pockets of her silk skirt to keep from clapping. She'd been so delighted that she'd wanted to shout. Six months of having Matt around. Six months of sharing breakfast and dinner with him. Six months to explore the possibility that fate—and her father's will—had thrown her together with a man she could learn to respect and love. The last thought had shocked her right down to her toes. But she'd told her aunt the truth: she was happy.

"Now dry your tears," Charlotte instructed. "And don't worry about me."

Rhue dabbed at the corners of her eyes then extracted herself from Carver's embrace. Pulling her niece into her arms, she whispered, "Do you think you'll be safe living in the same house with . . . *him?*"

Traffic on the Harbor Freeway was incredibly heavy for the middle of the day. Matt cut into the fast lane and accelerated past a car belching exhaust into the already hazy L.A. basin. He slanted Charlotte a look.

"Did you get your aunt settled down?"

Charlotte smiled sweetly at him. "Carver and I convinced her that there was absolutely no reason for you to put a pillow over my face during the night. At least not for another six months. She'll sleep fine until then."

"Thanks a lot."

"It seemed the most expedient solution at the moment."

Matt cut around a truck doing forty-five in the fast lane. "You know, that little guy can be real annoying."

"Carver?"

"Yeah. If he'd just dropped the subject we could have avoided the whole scene, but somehow he couldn't let go of it."

"He seems to bring out the worst in everyone," Charlotte agreed. "I still haven't figured out what she sees in him."

"Your family feels the same way about you and me."

"Listen, I'm sorry about what they said...you know, about being a gigolo and a...a bluebeard. I never dreamed you'd have to put up with *that* kind of talk."

Charlotte glanced into the car next to them. It was a small economy car occupied by a young couple in the first blush of love. The young man drove with only one hand on the wheel; his right one was entwined with his girlfriend's. Charlotte couldn't help comparing that closeness to the way she and Matt sat.

"If you want to back out of our agreement, I'll understand," she told him. "Six months is a lot longer than we'd expected."

"Twenty million dollars is a lot of money."

Charlotte shrugged. "It's only money. I can always make more. But once this half year is gone, you can't get it back."

"It's more than that now. They've attacked my integrity."

"You think so?"

"Sure. If I walk away now, everyone will think I married you for your money but abandoned the plan once I was found out. My reputation will suffer and probably my career. No, thank you."

"But I'd explain...."

He slanted her a cutting look. He was angry, she realized, although he was doing a good job of hiding it.

She looked away and concentrated on keeping the tears out of her voice. "I shouldn't have asked you to marry me in the first place." *Tell me I'm wrong,* she prayed silently. *Tell me you want to stay. Please.*

"I believe the marriage was my idea."

"Yeah, but I turned you down at first. I shouldn't have let Uncle Howie scare me into changing my mind. I shouldn't have gone through with it."

You're babbling, she admonished herself. And you're wishy-washy. That wasn't like her. She was usually decisive. That didn't mean she never changed her mind. She did that often enough, but she was always sure of her decision at the moment she made it. Now she was saying one thing and thinking another—and not sure which one she believed. You're definitely losing it, she told herself. The sad part was, she wasn't sure "it" was worth looking for at the moment.

"Are you through?" Matt asked when Charlotte was finally quiet.

"Yes. No. I guess so." She threw her hands in the air. "Oh, I don't know."

"You're through," Matt informed her. "Now it's my turn. First of all, this marriage business was my idea. I still think it's a good one. Secondly, if I wanted out, I'd damn well tell you so. Thirdly, if I'd even considered backing out—which I hadn't—that little maneuver your relatives pulled this morning made it nearly impossible. Bluebeard," he muttered with an exasperated shake of his head. "I don't like being thought of as the kind of man who would marry for money, let alone being accused of planning to kill for it. I'm committed to this marriage for however long it takes. Is that clear enough for you?"

Charlotte looked at him from the corner of her eye. "You sure?"

"Hell, yes, I'm sure. Unless you want to back out."

"Take the next exit," Charlotte told him.

He steered across four lanes of heavy traffic, all the while waiting for her answer. The silence was driving him crazy, but he'd be damned if he'd let her know that. They were passing in front of the Walt Disney Company corporate headquarters when he lost patience.

"Well?" he demanded, then was as silent as Snow White's seven dwarfs who held up the templelike facade of the building.

"I'd like to follow through with the original plan," Charlotte finally said.

Matt tried not to let out a sigh of relief. "Good." He didn't say anything else until he was stopped in front of RP. "I'll pick you up after work. Probably around six-thirty."

"That's fine." Charlotte opened the door. "You don't have to rush. I have enough paperwork to catch up on to keep me busy till midnight. I'll just have to take home what I don't finish here." She got out and slammed the door. Leaning down to look through the open window she said, "Thanks. I appreciate everything."

"No problem," Matt told her, then watched her walk into work humming the same song Snow White's little friends had sung—and looking just as happy.

Right, Matt told himself as he pulled away from the curb. No problem. Half a year wasn't so long. He'd probably survive the next six months without cramming his fist down Howie's throat...or tossing VASSAR into the nearest trash can...or dragging Charlotte into the bedroom and making passionate love to her. He might even survive the next six months without going completely crazy. But he wasn't willing to put any money on it.

* * *

Despite his good intentions, it was almost eight by the time Matt stopped in front of RP again. He'd been to Charlotte's office a couple times since her father's death. It was in an older section of town where the buildings had been thrown up during the fifties with no thought to aesthetics. Rutherford Packaging had its headquarters in a one-story L-shaped building. Charlotte's office was in the back next to the factory and warehouse. Closer to the action, was the way she'd put it the first time he'd been here.

As he crossed the empty parking lot, he noticed that the reception area was dark. He couldn't even see the light from her office. The main gate was locked, preventing him from going around to tap on her window. He'd just have to beat on the door until she heard him. His hand had already formed a fist when he saw the neat little rectangle that had been cut from the glass door. The piece of glass lay next to his feet, and the door was open by a scant half inch. It didn't take long for Matt to realize that someone had broken into RP—and that Charlotte was in there alone. He knew that the smart thing to do was find the nearest phone and call the police, but doing the smart thing could leave Charlotte alone in the building with a thief.

Pushing the door open just wide enough to accommodate his size, Matt glided silently into the darkened room. It took a moment for his eyes to adjust to the darkness, but his sense of hearing was fully functioning. There was music. Not that elevator stuff, but something with a fast tempo and lots of bass. It figured that Charlotte would like rock and roll. When he listened carefully enough, he could make out footsteps around the corner. Slow, stealthy footsteps. They weren't Charlotte's; he was sure of that. Charlotte had never moved so slowly in her life.

Flattening himself against the wall directly opposite the door, he inched his way toward the right angle of the hallway. He listened, but it was hard to hear over the beating of his own heart. He didn't remember having that problem in 'Nam, but then he'd been young and foolish with nothing to lose. Now he had the kind of life he'd dreamed about, and he'd earned it by using his intellect rather than giving in to violence. But intellect wouldn't help Charlotte right now, and she was the only thing he really feared losing. He waited for his heart to slow down, then he edged closer to the corner. He was sure he heard a noise, perhaps the movement of a foot on the tile floor and the sound of someone breathing. The music was turned off.

"Who's there?" he heard Charlotte call out. He was relieved to hear her voice even though there was a thread of fear in it. "Matt, is that you?"

Matt tried to recall everything he'd ever read about burglars. They favored easy targets, buildings that were empty and had no alarm system. Someplace they could get in and out of without having to worry about running into people. Matt's personal opinion was that burglars were cowards. They liked to sneak around at night stealing things they'd be afraid to take during the day. Matt hoped the fact that someone was in the building would be enough to send this particular burglar running out the way he'd come in—running past where Matt stood now. Matt tensed, ready to spring when the intruder passed him, but there were no footsteps. No neck for Matt to slide his arm around. No convenient target for Matt's anger.

Bending slowly forward, Matt peered around the corner—and what he saw made his heart stop beating. The burglar was standing in the shadows opposite Charlotte's office. It was too dark for Matt to make out his features, but he had the impression that the man was watching Charlotte. Watching and waiting.

Matt heard movement in Charlotte's office. The scraping of a chair. The opening and closing of drawers. Did Charlotte keep a gun? he wondered.

"I know someone's out there," he heard her say. This time he was certain he heard the fear. "I'm calling the police."

Matt thought that would galvanize the thief into action, but the man didn't move—except to raise his arm. It took Matt several seconds to realize that there was a gun in the man's hand, for it seemed almost a part of him. An extension of the dark figure hidden in the shadows like the angel of death.

"Charlotte," he yelled. The weapon swung in his direction. "Get down! He has a gun!" Then everything happened so fast he could barely separate one event from the other.

Two gun shots rang out just as he ducked back behind the wall. He heard Charlotte scream—he thought it was his name she called—as two more shots were fired. There was the sound of footsteps retreating toward the other end of the hallway and the crack of the doors being kicked open.

Matt came around the corner in time to see the burglar make his escape out the back door, but he paid little attention to the fleeing figure. His attention was centered on the light spilling from Charlotte's office, and in his mind was the question of where the last two shots had been aimed. Nothing in his life—not his angry youth, or his time in the steamy jungles of Vietnam—had prepared him for the fear he felt now.

"Charlotte!"

He could think of no one else. His brain could conjure up no other word. Before he could call her again, she came running out of the office and directly into his arms. She cried his name while he held her tight against him. Nothing in his life had ever felt as good. Nothing in his life had ever mattered more.

"Are you all right?" he asked, then held her at arm's length to see for himself.

When she nodded he hauled her back against him. In the distance he heard a motor start and the screech of tires as someone took off at high speed. Matt relaxed, certain that they were rid of their burglar.

"It's okay," he crooned. "He's gone now. You're safe."

Charlotte thought nothing had ever felt as good or as strong at Matt's arms. When she'd heard his voice, her first instinct had been to run toward him. Then he'd said to duck and she'd heard the gunshots. She never wanted to relive those moments again. Never wanted to feel the heart-stopping fear that had had her rooted to the floor. Never wanted to endure the minutes until she'd heard his voice again.

"You weren't hurt, were you?" she demanded as she pushed against his chest. Cupping his face in her hands, she said, "Let me look at you." Once she was satisfied he was unhurt, she threw her arms around his neck and gave in to the tears.

"Shh," Matt said gently. "There's nothing to cry about."

She tightened her grip on him. "I thought he'd shot you," she said against his shirt. "I was so scared."

"I was, too." She felt his kisses on her hair, his hand caressing her back. "I've never been so terrified. If anything had happened to you . . ."

She lifted her head from his shoulder and looked up at him. His dark eyes were filled with emotions. Anger and determination and . . . desire.

"Matt."

Had any woman ever touched his soul with a single word? he wondered. Had any woman ever drawn such emotions from him? There was a storm building inside him. A storm of fear and rage caught in dark, swirling passions that he'd fought and controlled before. But there, amid the dark shadows, swirled another emotion. Desire, he named it. And the desire was a pulsing, keening wind he could not deny. He wanted the woman in his arms as he had wanted no one else in his life. If he didn't kiss her, he thought he would go mad. And if he did kiss her? That way lay another kind of madness, he was sure, yet he was powerless to resist her.

His lips took hers with an urgency that surprised him. He told himself that he would have been satisfied with one brief, desperate kiss if she hadn't melted against him. He would have pulled back if her hands hadn't found their way into his hair. Then he was lost.

Charlotte thought she'd been kissed before, but nothing in her life had prepared her for this. She thought she'd experienced desire before, but she'd never been possessed by such need. There was nothing controlled in the way his lips slanted over hers. No holding back. No restraint. She met his demands with her own. Her fingers twined in his hair. Her body arched against his. Her passion flared to match his. When his hands gripped her upper arm to push her away, she tried to hold him to her. When he dragged his lips from hers, she murmured a protest.

"Charlotte," Matt whispered. His breathing was harsh and ragged. "We've got to stop." When she reached blindly for him, he cursed vividly. "Do you hear me?" He gave her a brief, hard shake to emphasize his question.

When she dropped her hands from around his neck, he saw a potent mixture of passion and confusion in her eyes.

Because he wanted to drag her back into his arms, he thrust her into one of the chairs.

"I'm going to call the police," he told her. When he reached for the phone, he noticed that his hands were still shaking.

It was an odd time to realize she was falling in love, Charlotte decided as she looked at the uniformed policeman sitting opposite her. Fighting the urge to throw herself back into Matt's arms, she curled one leg beneath her and kept her seat. Matt had thrust her into the chair little more than an hour ago, and she'd felt abandoned ever since. Glancing up at Matt, where he was perched on the edge of her desk, she wondered where the heat and passion had gone, for now he looked cold enough to kill and not regret it.

When had she started losing her heart to him? she wondered. When had he become both her strength and her weakness? And where would it end? She shook her head, refusing to contemplate the answers.

"I think that's about all the information I need," the officer told them as he looked up from his notes. "From what you've told us, I'd guess it was a small-time thief out to grab whatever he could lay his hands on."

"With a gun?" Matt asked.

The officer shrugged. "A handgun doesn't mean much anymore, Mr. Oliver. We're taking them off kids of ten or twelve. The point is that he didn't shoot anyone and, as far as Mrs. Oliver can tell, he didn't take anything."

"No." Matt rose to his full height. "The point is that she could have been killed."

"I understand what you're saying, Mr. Oliver." The officer rose, too. The creaking of his leather belt and holster were loud in the silence of the room. "But you've got to understand the reality of the situation. We've had two drive-by shootings, an armed robbery and a rape reported over the last twenty-four hours. The fact that someone fired a couple rounds into the wall comes in way down the line."

"Not with me."

The officer sighed. "I understand that. But if you really want to do something about it, don't let your wife work here late alone. Take her home."

"I intend to," Matt assured him.

Turning to Charlotte, the officer said, "We'll be in touch if anything turns up. Sorry there isn't much more I can do."

Charlotte only smiled and nodded as Matt escorted the officer to the door. She wasn't sure what had her more stunned—the fact that she'd almost been shot or the fact that she was falling in love with her husband. She certainly hadn't intended for her emotions to get involved when she'd married Matt, but she realized now that her intentions had very little to do with reality. So here she sat, free-falling into love with a man whose emotions could go from hot to cold in the space of a heartbeat. How he could control his emotions like that was a mystery to her.

Although there'd been no mystery about that kiss. Or about his desire. He'd wanted her, of that she was sure. But she was equally certain that he didn't want to want her. With a sigh, she rose and went around her desk to begin stuffing papers into her briefcase. She couldn't make any sense of this tonight, but tomorrow...

"Zeb Tibbens just arrived," Matt said from the doorway and made her jump.

Charlotte placed her hand over her heart and willed it to quit racing. "Don't sneak up on me." Because her voice sounded shaky, she forced a smile to her lips. "Think you can hum or whistle for a couple of days so I'll always know where you are?"

He was across the room in three swift strides. "Get your stuff together. I'm taking you home. Now."

His anger confused her, but at least it was better than the coldness he'd shown her earlier.

"Just let me talk to Zeb. I want him to board up that door until we can get the glass replaced."

"He's already on it. Come on. I'm taking you home."

Home. That would be nice, but what she wanted more than anything was to feel Matt's arms warm and strong around her. What had happened to the passion they'd shared earlier? What had happened to the man she was falling in love with?

Chapter Nine

Matt scanned the front page of the Friday *L.A. Times* and tried to ignore the fact that Charlotte was sitting across the breakfast table from him. When Mrs. Nguyen placed his breakfast on the table, he set the paper aside and pretended to concentrate on buttering his toast.

Charlotte was reading the sports page as she did everything else—with complete concentration. With her flawless complexion and her dark hair shimmering in the morning sunlight, she was incredibly beautiful, he decided objectively, despite the faint shadows beneath her eyes. The long hours she'd spent at her desk over the past four days were beginning to show. He'd say something to her if he hadn't been working himself just as hard.

But no matter how many hours he spent in his office or how many times he visited the gym, he still couldn't sleep at night without reliving Monday in his dreams. It seemed that no matter how tired he was when he fell into bed, he always woke in a cold sweat with the sound of gunshots ringing in his ears—and the sound of Charlotte calling his name. Maybe the same memories were haunting her, he thought. Maybe she too was trying to work herself to exhaustion so she could fall into a dreamless sleep. He hoped she was having better luck than he was.

As he picked up the second piece of toast and began to slather butter on it, he admitted that it wasn't only the memory of violence that kept him awake. Sometimes he remembered how Charlotte had kissed him, and then he'd be up pacing the floor for hours. It would be easier to sleep if she wasn't in her bed just across the hall. Hell, it would be easier to sleep if he'd never met her.

But he had.

And he wanted her.

She was a beautiful woman and he wanted her almost as much as he wanted his next breath. But he couldn't have her. He couldn't seduce her into a short-term relationship and then leave her in six months' time. He knew instinctively that she wasn't the kind of woman who could come out of an affair unhurt—and he was beginning to suspect that, should their relationship become any more involved, he wouldn't be able to walk away unscathed, either. It was a helluva position to be in—married to a gorgeous, desirable woman that he wanted desperately, yet condemned to his lonely bed. If he wasn't a man who had his emotions under control, he could easily be driven crazy.

"You're going to drown that toast," Charlotte said without taking her eyes off the newspaper. "And I don't even want to think about the amount of cholesterol involved."

She had the satisfaction of looking up in time to see him scrape some of the butter off. She was certainly glad to have some triumph—no matter how small—after the past four days. The aggravating man was driving her mad! Considering his cool treatment of her, she would have thought she'd only imagined the passion if she didn't see the fire in his eyes every once in a while. It had been there only a few minutes ago—the glow of a fire smoldering deep down in his soul—and as usual, it had ignited something within her. She'd make him look at her that way again today, just see if she didn't. And she'd find a way to fan those embers into flames.

"Tonight is Aunt Rhue's party," she reminded him.

"I'm not likely to forget a thing like that."

Oh, yes, she liked that look, too. The one that said he'd like to strangle her for even being in the same room with him. She liked anything other than that cold, controlled gaze he gave her most of the time.

"It starts at seven, so we should leave here by six-thirty. Will you be home in time?"

"I told you I'd go. If I'm going, I'll damn well be on time."

She smiled, delighted to rile him so easily. He wasn't unaffected by her, no matter how he tried to be. When he tossed his napkin onto the table, she took a quick swallow of her orange juice and rose.

"Gotta run," she said.

He was already halfway out of his chair, and there was no way he could sit back down without being incredibly rude; he was going to have to walk out to the car with her. Her day seemed to be going rather well.

Charlotte didn't mind that the short walk was silent. It only mattered that he was forced to deal with her rather than ignore her. The kiss he gave her for Mrs. Nguyen's benefit was only a quick peck on the cheek, but she was gratified to see that look in his eyes again. The way he slammed his car door was icing on the cake.

"Morning, Tommy," she said. The young man was already fiddling with VASSAR in the garage workshop. "How are things going?"

"Great. You haven't had any more trouble with the door locks, have you?"

Charlotte shook her head as Matt gunned his engine. Oh, yeah, she had him steaming.

"I've already put the locks on the windows. They're having parent conferences all day at school, so I have the day off. I thought I'd hook everything up."

"Okay." She heard Matt's car stall and couldn't suppress a smile.

"My teacher's real impressed with VASSAR so far."

Matt's car stalled again, and she looked back at him. "Good," she told Tommy.

"He thinks we have a good chance of taking at least the county science prize. Maybe the state."

Dragging her gaze away from the black Jaguar, she zeroed in on Tommy. "Another feather in *his* cap. But let me give you a bit of advice. This time when he wants to take you out to dinner to celebrate, pick some place fancier than a burger stand."

"But I like Barney's Burgers." When the Jaguar stalled again, he added, "Sounds like Matt has car trouble. I'd better see what I can do."

"Good idea." Charlotte tossed her briefcase into the back of her Corvette before following Tommy across the driveway.

The young man already had the hood up and was listening to the engine by the time she joined him. After a moment, the engine sputtered and died.

Matt got out of the car and slammed the door. "Well?"

"I think it's the fuel pump."

"Can you do anything so I can get by for the day? I'll take it to the garage over the weekend."

Tommy shook his head. "I can replace the fuel pump for you, but that'll take a while. If you drive it, it's only going to get worse."

"Damn." Matt pounded the top of his car. "What lousy timing. I'm supposed to be in court at ten."

"I can't promise I'll be done by then."

"If you drop me at RP, you can use my car," Charlotte said.

Matt was forced to look at her then. Forced to look at the way the breeze blew her short hair back from her face and molded the navy-and-white dress to her body. He didn't understand how any dress that was supposed to look like an old-fashioned navy uniform could be so damn sexy. He didn't understand how she could stand there looking so beautiful he almost forgot what she'd said.

"Yeah, that might work," he murmured, to give the impression he'd been thinking it over. Actually he couldn't see that he had any other choice, and the sooner he dropped her at work, the sooner he'd be able to concentrate again. "I'd have to leave work a little early to pick you up, but I think I can swing that. Here." He threw his keys to Tommy then reached into the car to get his briefcase. "I'll pay you what I would have paid the garage. Deal?"

Tommy tossed the keys into the air and caught them. "Deal."

Stalking over to Charlotte's red sports car, Matt put his briefcase in the back and eased his body into the passenger seat. He'd just found his seat belt when Charlotte gunned the motor and accelerated down the driveway. Slowing just enough to check the traffic, she cornered sharply onto the street and made another turn at the intersection. The neighbor who was out watering his roses shook his fist and yelled as they sped past.

"Don't worry about Mr. Morris," Charlotte said casually. "I've been making that turn since I was sixteen. And he's been yelling the same thing since then."

Matt snapped his seat belt into place and checked the fit before looking out the rear window at the neighbor who was still standing beside his wrought iron fence shaking his fist. Behind him, an Olympic-sized swimming pool gleamed in the morning sun.

"Important case this morning?" Charlotte asked once they were breezing along the freeway.

The traffic was moving quickly, and Matt hoped they would make exceptional time. He needed to get Charlotte out of the car while he was still in control. He wondered what she would do if he turned to her and said she was so gorgeous she had his tongue tied in knots. Probably laugh. He reminded himself that trust was more important than a few moments of shared passion. A few moments? Who was he kidding? He'd never be satisfied with just that.

"It's the preliminary hearing for the Gilbert estate."

"The one where the second wife aced out the man's kids?"

Matt nodded as Charlotte downshifted. A traffic jam brought them to a complete stop, and she reached over to place her hand on his arm.

"I told you before that you can't go around cleaning up everyone else's messes. You can only do the best that you can do—and let life take care of itself."

Matt raised his gaze from her hand to her eyes—and he was lost. Four days of working late and leaving early were rendered meaningless in that instant. He wondered how long they would have sat there if the driver behind them hadn't leaned on his horn.

Charlotte shifted into second as they rounded the high-way patrol cars, and she kept her eyes on the road until they pulled up in front of RP. Leaving her keys dangling in the ignition, she stepped out of the car.

Matt came around to the driver's side and tried to resist the urge to touch her. Dragging his gaze away from hers, he looked at the entrance. "I see you got the door fixed."

Charlotte shrugged as if to say she'd almost forgotten about it. "Zeb had it fixed the next day."

"Good."

"And he's walked me to my car every evening since the break-in. He'll be happy to know you're picking me up today."

"I'll be here by five."

"Don't you dare be late," Charlotte told him with a smile. "Zeb will read you the riot act if you leave me here after everyone else is gone."

Lifting herself on tiptoe, Charlotte planted a kiss on his cheek, then turned and dashed into work. She'd had the satisfaction of seeing his eyes go dark with passion, however, and she was smiling when she stepped into the building. It wasn't until she was in her office that she realized she'd left her briefcase in the car.

When Matt returned to Charlotte's car shortly after noon, he was actually humming. It had been a good morning. Much better than he'd expected.

The attorney representing Ron Gilbert's children had asked for a delay in order to investigate some new information that had just become available. Matt might have thought they were simply engaging in a fishing expedition except he knew the private investigator who had been sitting with the family. Bob Stone ran one of the best investigative services in the state, and the fact that he was present meant something was up. Matt's hunch had been confirmed when his client turned a sickly shade of green all the way to the roots of her dyed blond hair.

He wished he had someone to share this with, he thought as he unlocked the car door. The sun had warmed the car's interior, and Charlotte's scent enveloped him as he slid into the driver's seat.

The car was an extension of Charlotte—her scent, her zest for life, her endearing habit of dropping things where she took them off. On the console was a pair of red earrings and one white one; God only knows where the mate to that might be. Behind the passenger seat was a gray sweater and a pink scarf, and behind him was her briefcase. He wondered how she ever got dressed in the morning when half of her clothes were left in the car or strewn around the house.

But he remembered her bringing the briefcase out to the car this morning. She might need it. No, she undoubtedly needed it. RP was a few miles out of his way, but he decided to take the briefcase to her. He could share his good news at the same time.

Matt leaned against the counter and waited while the receptionist dialed Charlotte's office on the phone. The reception area was done in soothing grays and blues with vivid splashes of burgundy and fuchsia in the abstract paintings. He didn't usually like that sort of art; he liked to know what he was looking at. But otherwise the room was pleasant. It was hard to believe he'd confronted a burglar here only four days ago. Hard to believe he'd been shot at here, amid such civilized surroundings.

"I'm sorry," the receptionist said after hanging up the phone. The woman was somewhere in her early twenties, with pale blue eyes and dimples in her cheeks. The smile

she flashed him didn't interest Matt in the least. "Ms. La—
I mean, Mrs. Oliver isn't in her office just now. Was she
expecting you, Mr....?"

"Mr. Oliver," Matt said. "And no, she wasn't expecting me. I thought I'd surprise my wife."

"Mr. Oliver? Charlotte's Mr. Oliver? I mean, Charlotte's husband? Oh..." The flustered woman took a deep
breath and smiled. "Charlotte didn't tell me you were so
good-looking." She rolled her eyes toward the ceiling and
blushed prettily. "Tell me I didn't say that," she moaned.

"Problem, Gracie?" a man asked.

"Mr. Everling, this is Charlotte's husband."

Matt turned to confront a long, lanky fellow with an
easy grin and thick glasses. The gray sprinkled in his brown
hair couldn't dim his boyish enthusiasm.

"John Everling," the man said as he extended his hand.

"Matt Oliver."

"Looking for Charlotte?" John asked.

Matt nodded.

"She isn't in her office," the receptionist said.

"She's probably back in the warehouse then. Why don't
I walk you back there, Matt? Don't worry about paging
her, Grace. I'll take care of Mr. Oliver."

John led the way to the back of the building. "I hear you
two had a little excitement on Monday. Come to check up
on her?"

"No, actually I'm bringing her briefcase. She left it in
the car this morning."

"That sounds like Charlotte," John said with a laugh.
"Never can hang on to things."

Matt nodded and wondered why it bothered him that
John Everling knew Charlotte so well.

"My car's being fixed, so I'm driving hers. We were in
such a hurry this morning that she forgot it."

John nodded. "I noticed her car wasn't on the lot. Is Tommy working on yours?"

"Yeah."

"Better watch those speed limits when he's finished."

"He's worked on yours?" Matt was annoyed at the spurt of jealousy. Jealousy wasn't a reasonable emotion—especially given the circumstances of his marriage.

"A couple times. He's great, but he likes to really cut loose with the power."

"What does your wife have to say about it?"

"My wife?"

"You have one, don't you?"

John smiled. "A wife, two kids, a dog and a cat. Charlotte and I are friends and co-workers. And my wife wasn't real happy when the family station wagon took off like a bat out of hell."

Matt felt himself relax. "I can understand that."

Matt followed John into the lunch area, where he was introduced to several of the employees. Everyone told Matt how lucky he was to have married Charlotte. Employee morale was obviously high at RP, as was employee loyalty.

"Mrs. Oliver was headed for the loading dock," Zeb Tibbens informed John. Matt recognized the man from Monday night.

"Charlotte told me you've been walking her to her car." Matt offered his hand to the man. "Thanks for taking care of her."

The man smiled, his dark skin wrinkling around his eyes. His handshake was brief and strong. "She didn't like it much at first. Said I was making a fuss. But I was firm with her. Told her I'd want someone to do it for my daughter."

"I appreciate it," Matt said, then followed John out through the warehouse.

Matt had never been in this part of the plant before and was surprised at the amount of activity. All four of the loading docks were busy, and boxes were piled high all around. Considering the bustle of activity, it was easy to understand why Charlotte loved it.

"She's down at dock four," John shouted as he pointed to the other end of the building.

Matt followed his gesture and saw her talking to one of the employees. With her short hair and her sailor dress, she looked like a kid from where he stood, but there was an air of authority about her that had the burly man at her side nodding.

Matt gave in to the ridiculous urge to shout her name and was pleased when she saw him and smiled. She was waving at him when the stack of boxes behind her began to shake. He shouted her name again when he realized that the whole thing was tumbling forward onto her, then he was sprinting toward her, trying to block out the image of Charlotte buried beneath the avalanche of wooden pallets and cardboard boxes. He was still shouting her name when he reached the first carton.

The heavy boxes hadn't all settled, and the rumble and crash still echoed in the cavernous warehouse. He'd thrust aside two of the heavy boxes and was struggling with a third by the time John Everling arrived. The damn things were surprisingly heavy, and the accountant, though he tried to help, simply didn't have the muscle for it. But it was only a matter of seconds before other hands were pushing at the boxes and other voices were shouting Charlotte's name. Matt was struggling with another heavy carton when Zeb Tibbens's dark hands grabbed hold of the other side. Between the two of them, they managed to heft the thing aside.

Matt heaved another box out of the way and found Charlotte's navy-and-white pump. The heel was broken off and the shoe mashed flat. No matter how he tried to fight it, his mind kept conjuring up images of what the heavy boxes could have done to Charlotte's soft body and delicate bones.

"Charlotte," he yelled again. "For God's sake, answer me! Charlotte!"

"Take it easy, boy," Zeb told him. "We're gonna find her."

Matt nodded, but called her name again.

Her voice, when he first heard it, was so faint that it frightened him more than not hearing her. Someone yelled that the paramedics had been called, but all he could think of was getting to her as quickly as possible. With Zeb's help, he made a path through the debris.

Matt spotted her first. She was curled up between two of the boxes. On top of those was another huge carton. Matt felt the color drain out of him when he realized what could have happened had it fallen directly onto her.

"Charlotte. Are you okay?"

When she looked up at him, her face was unnaturally pale against her dark hair. "I'm glad you're here," she told him. "Are you okay?"

"How badly are you hurt?"

"I crawled in between these two boxes and rode it out. Help me out of here, so I can evacuate the place before it starts again."

Matt decided she'd probably been hit on the head; that was why she wasn't making any sense. Gently he asked, "Before what starts again?"

She gave him an exasperated look as she struggled to pull her dress from under the box. "The earthquake. We're bound to have some big aftershocks."

"There was no earthquake," Matt said as he pressed her back down. "And I don't want you to move until the paramedics get here."

"No earthquake?"

Matt shook his head.

"I wondered why nothing was falling at that end of the building." But instead of lying still, she gave another futile tug on her skirt. "And I don't need any paramedics."

Matt pulled her skirt free. "You're in no position to give orders."

Instead of pointing out that she was still the boss at RP, she lay still while he and Zeb pushed the carton off the top and moved aside one of the two boxes she'd squeezed between.

Somehow, she felt safer as soon as Matt was kneeling beside her. She wondered how that could be, while he brushed the hair back from her forehead and cupped her face in his big hands. She closed her eyes and nestled her cheek into the warmth of his palm. The shock was starting to wear off now and she could feel some bumps and bruises, but she knew she'd be fine—as long as Matt was with her. That was ridiculous, of course, but she was willing to give in to the emotion for just a minute or two.

Opening her eyes, she smiled up into Matt's worried gaze.

"Help me up," she whispered. "I've lain around long enough."

"Not until the paramedics get here."

She noted the stubborn set of his jaw. "Fine. I'll get up on my own," she told him.

Grabbing hold of the nearest box, she managed to drag herself to her feet—and she felt fine, she told herself. Just a little light-headed. She leaned against the carton and closed her eyes until the dizziness faded. The first thing she saw when she opened her eyes was Matt standing next to her with his arms crossed and an I-told-you-so expression on his face. Straightening to her full height, she took a step away from her support—and promptly fell into Matt's arms when her ankle gave way.

"Don't say it," she told him as she clung to his shoulders.

"I wouldn't dream of it."

"Good."

"Talking to you doesn't do any good."

She glared up at him. "And what do you mean by that?"

He didn't bother to answer, just swung her up into his arms and started walking. Charlotte decided to ignore the grins of her employees.

"What do you think you're doing?" she demanded.

"Taking you home."

Charlotte crossed her arms and informed him, "I'm not going anywhere until I find out what happened."

When Matt stopped walking, she was sure he'd come to his senses and would put her down. Instead, he shouted for Zeb.

"Find out what happened," he told the older man, "and come into Charlotte's office. We'll be waiting in there."

If she'd had her feet under her, Charlotte would have stood her ground and gotten Zeb's explanation right away. As it was, all she could do was look over Matt's shoulder as Zeb directed men to start the cleanup.

Matt had barely settled her in one of the chairs when the paramedics arrived. Charlotte admitted to some bumps and bruises but maintained she was fine. The paramedics told her she had a sprained ankle and needed rest. Matt informed everyone that he'd see that she got to bed right away. Charlotte was still fuming over his high-handed attitude when Zeb entered the office.

"What did you find out?" Charlotte asked as soon as the three of them were alone.

"Someone rammed into that section with a forklift," he said. "Whoever it was abandoned the machine with the ignition still on." He shook his head. "Don't know who could have been that stupid."

"We'll have to fill out an accident report. Get John to help you." She sighed. "The insurance guys will be all over us."

"Is everyone accounted for?" Matt asked Zeb.

Zeb nodded.

"Damn."

"What do you mean 'damn'?" Charlotte demanded. "You wish someone else was hurt?"

"No, I do not. I was just hoping that whoever was driving the forklift had gotten scared enough to run. Then we'd know who did it."

"Thought of that already," Zeb said. "That's why I checked. But everyone who reported to work is still here."

"Thanks," Matt said to Zeb. "And thanks for your help out there. I'm grateful to you again."

"Sure thing."

As Zeb exited the room, Charlotte could see John Everling and several other employees standing in the hallway, but before they could even get into the room, Matt had scooped Charlotte into his arms and was striding toward the door.

"Charlotte will be at home if anyone needs her," he informed the knot of people in the doorway. "And if anyone calls, it'd better be important. A life-or-death emergency."

"I am not going to see the doctor," Charlotte informed Mrs. Nguyen. She was certain her declaration would have been more impressive had she been standing on her own two feet rather than languishing like some Victorian maiden in Matt's arms. Nevertheless she meant what she'd said.

"I think what she really needs is rest," Matt said reasonably. "The paramedics checked her over, the only thing they found was a twisted ankle. We need to elevate that foot and keep some ice on it."

"Right," the housekeeper said as she scurried over to the refrigerator.

Charlotte heard the rattle of ice cubes as Matt whisked her through the kitchen and up the stairs.

"I'd appreciate it if you'd let me make my own decisions."

Matt nudged open the door to her bedroom. "Normally I would, but you and Mrs. N. looked like you were going to go into one of your lengthy face-offs." He laid her gently on the bed. "And you were getting too damn heavy for me to stand there while you glare at each other."

"How sweet of you to mention it." She looked up in time to see his grin. "Besides, I didn't ask you to carry me around like a sack of flour."

"You're welcome. Pass me one of those pillows so I can elevate your foot."

She threw it as hard as she could, but he was too fast for her. He ducked, then picked it up off the floor as Mrs. Nguyen bustled in with an ice pack.

"There," Matt said when he was satisfied that her foot was positioned correctly. "Keep your foot elevated tonight, and if the swelling hasn't gone down tomorrow, we'll go to the doctor."

"I don't need a doctor! And I can't keep it elevated all night. We're going to Aunt Rhue's tonight. Remember?"

"You're not going anywhere tonight," Matt informed her. When Mrs. Nguyen nodded her head in agreement, Charlotte scowled at the woman.

"I may not be able to dance tonight, but I am definitely going to the party."

"You are not leaving this house tonight."

This time Mrs. Nguyen's nod was more vigorous.

"Don't you have something else to do?" she asked her housekeeper. Once the woman was gone, she turned to Matt and asked, "Do you think you can stop me?"

"I'm going to do better than that," Matt told her in a deceptively calm voice. "I'm going to call Rhue and tell her to cancel her party—heart-shaped pâté and all."

As Matt stalked out the door, Charlotte wondered what had ever made her think she was falling in love with such an overbearing man.

Two hours later Matt again used his shoulder to push open the door to Charlotte's bedroom. This time he carried a tray with tea and sandwiches that Mrs. Nguyen had prepared for Charlotte.

Charlotte looked up from the magazine she was reading. "Is that a peace offering?"

"Mrs. N.'s idea," Matt told her. He didn't mention that he'd volunteered to carry it up. "How's the ankle?"

"Good as new. Look," she said as she threw back the covers. "It's the same size as the other."

"Pretty close," Matt agreed.

"Exactly the same size. Are you going to hold that tray all day or is there something on it to eat? I didn't get lunch and I'm starved."

Matt set the tray on the bed beside her and then settled on the chaise in front of the window.

"Is your life always so eventful?" he asked.

Charlotte finished her sandwich as she thought about it. "My life isn't the least bit eventful. At least it wasn't until I married you."

"That's what Rhue told me."

"Uh-oh. What else did she say?"

"That if anything happened to you, she'd hunt me to the ends of the earth."

"She means well. Besides, I'm healthy as a horse."

Matt didn't bother to remind her that even a horse could be killed by a bullet or by hundreds of pounds of boxes. "She got me to thinking, though. If anything should happen to you—or to me—our marriage would certainly muddy the issue of who inherits the deceased's property."

Charlotte leaned back against the pillows. "I'd never thought of that."

"Neither had I," Matt told her. And he was annoyed with himself; he was usually such a stickler for details. "I have a will. You should have one."

"Let's not go into that again."

"Since you don't, I've taken the liberty of drawing up a postmarital contract." He drew the folded pages out of his jacket pocket. "I want you to look over it. Basically it states that my will remains in effect and that your property should be divided among your relatives." He rose and tossed it onto her lap.

"It seems fine," Charlotte said when she finished. "And it might even keep Uncle Howie from mentioning his bluebeard theory again."

Matt smiled. "I wouldn't count on that. But it might make your aunt rest a little easier. She's really very sweet."

"When did you decide that?"

"We had a long talk when I called her. I think I convinced her that I can be trusted with her favorite niece's welfare."

"Thank you." He could be sweet, though he'd probably bristle at that description. "But how did she take the cancellation of the party?"

Matt pulled a pen from his pocket. "I've already signed the agreement. You sign on this line."

"Don't we need witnesses or something?"

"Not for this one, it's only temporary. We'll go into the office next week and sign a more official document." He handed her the pen and watched as she signed both copies.

"There. Now tell me exactly what my aunt said when you told her there wouldn't be a party tonight."

Matt smiled. "That isn't exactly what I told her."

"What did you say?"

"That you'd twisted your ankle and I didn't think you should be on your feet tonight."

"And?"

"She agreed with me."

"She did?"

Matt nodded. "She even said that she didn't think the night air would be good for you. I can't see any connection between a twisted ankle and the night air, but I decided not to pursue the point." Truth was, Rhue had already had him so confused that he wasn't sure he could have pursued it.

Charlotte crossed her arms and smiled at him. It was almost as if she knew what was coming. "Then what happened?"

Before Matt could decide how to frame his answer, there was the sound of several vehicles turning into the driveway and the slamming of doors. Matt crossed to the window and looked out. Rhue was standing in the middle of the driveway, issuing directions like a drill sergeant. She was wearing some sort of long, flowing gown of iridescent pink.

Matt looked over at Charlotte and gave a helpless shrug. "Rhue said she'd bring the party to you."

Chapter Ten

He could see that Charlotte was trying not to laugh. "Bring the party here, huh?"

"You don't look surprised."

"Nothing surprises me about Aunty Rhue. How did Mrs. Nguyen take the news?"

Matt shrugged. "Okay, I guess. She just said that when she came to work Monday morning she wanted the house in the same condition she left it." At least that's what she'd told him in English. What she'd said in her native tongue during the first fifteen minutes remained a mystery—and he wanted to keep it that way.

Charlotte got out of bed and limped over to the window to stand beside Matt. Entire armies had marched off to war with less food, she decided as she watched the caterer and his four assistants make numerous trips to the kitchen.

"What instructions did Aunt Rhue give?"

"She said not to worry about a thing. That everything would be ready 'sevenish.' "

"That means seven-thirty at the earliest. My advice is to hide out until then."

Matt swallowed. "She was so sweet about the whole thing that I'd planned to go down early and help out."

Charlotte shook her head. "You'll be sorry. Stay in your room and lock the door. Pay no attention to shouting, screaming, or the sounds of breaking dishes."

"Oh, God."

"If you can stall until seven forty-five, you'll miss all the fuss and probably have the time of your life."

Wondering if anyone would notice if he didn't show up at all, Matt started across the room. On the chair by the door was a dress in shades of red with glittering sequins and layers of ruffles. He turned back in time to see Charlotte smother a grin.

"You knew all along that I wouldn't be able to cancel out, didn't you?"

"I've never seen anyone stop Aunt Rhue."

He looked at the dress then back at Charlotte. "You could have told me that."

"Some things have to be learned the hard way."

He sighed as he looked at the dress once more. On the floor beside it lay a pair of high-heeled black sandals. Hell, they were hardly more than four inches of heel, a sole and a couple black velvet straps. They were sexy little numbers that conjured up visions of black net stockings and lots of leg.

"Show a little intelligence and wear some sensible shoes. I don't think your ankle can take those," was the last thing he said before he closed the door.

* * *

When Charlotte hobbled down the stairs at seven-thirty, the noise from the kitchen had settled to a low hum and the first guest had yet to arrive. As soon as she was on a flat surface, she was able to walk a bit more gracefully and so she concentrated on gliding into the kitchen, where she found Aunt Rhue making a final check of the food.

"Darling," her aunt cried as soon as she spotted Charlotte. "Let me look at our blushing bride." She gave her niece a hug and then walked all the way around her. "You're quite right not to wear white. And you look wonderful. No one will ever guess you were almost smashed to a pulp earlier today. Should you be walking on that ankle?"

"It's fine now." Charlotte stuck her foot out and wiggled it around. "I'll sit down if it starts to hurt."

"Unusual shoes," Rhue commented. "Thomas," she said as VASSAR and its inventor came into the kitchen, "Do try to keep that mechanical beast out of the way."

Tommy grinned. "You should see the food," he told Charlotte. "Everything is in the shape of hearts and bells and stuff. And the cake has real flowers on it!"

"I think the balloons are here," Rhue announced when another truck pulled up to the kitchen entrance. She glanced over the shoulder of one of the caterer's assistants on her way to the door. "How are those butter patties coming along? Thomas, be a darling and show the balloon man to the dining room."

"Do you think that many balloons are absolutely necessary?" Charlotte asked when the delivery man made his fourth trip through the kitchen.

"You can't have too many balloons. They add such a festive touch." Leaning closer, she whispered to Charlotte, "But I am worried about the fellow making the butter patties. One of the caterer's regular workers had an accident at the last minute, and Carver hired that fellow to fill in." She glanced over her shoulder to look at the burly man who was scraping butter out of the mold and slapping it onto a crystal dish. Rhue shook her head. "I'm afraid Carver doesn't have much experience hiring kitchen help." In a louder voice she said, "Here's the bridegroom," and rushed over to greet Matt.

Matt glanced over Rhue's shoulder as he was enveloped in a generous hug. Things appeared to be going well, at least to his inexperienced eye. The only problem he could see was the fellow working at the kitchen counter who looked like a prizefighter and was flinging butter all over the counter.

"Oh, dear," Charlotte's aunt murmured as she stood back. "My good man," she called out to him. "That isn't the way to use a butter mold."

"No one told me I'd have to make butter hearts," he complained. Glancing at the plate, Matt decided none of the yellow globs looked particularly heart shaped. "What's wrong with the regular butter?"

"See," Rhue whispered to Charlotte. "He hasn't the faintest idea what to do." To the man she said, "Why don't we ask Henri if he has another little job for you. Henri!" As Matt watched, she sailed off in search of the caterer with the reluctant assistant in her wake.

"She's really something," Matt said once Rhue was out of earshot.

"Yes, she is."

Matt looked around the room, but his eyes came back to Charlotte. "Has anyone else arrived?"

"Since it's family, they all understand that when Aunt Rhue says 'sevenish' she won't be ready before seven-thirty. So they'll be here around eight."

Matt nodded and wondered what he could do other than stand there and stare at Charlotte. "You look great," he finally said.

Great? She looked absolutely gorgeous. The dress, which was made up of several different red-and-white-patterned materials, had looked like nothing more than sequins and ruffles as it lay on the chair, but it took on a whole new style when it was on Charlotte.

The neckline was big and scooped and hung off one gorgeous, tanned shoulder that had a sort of iridescent glow. Did her skin shimmer like that all of the time, Matt wondered, or had she put some kind of sparkly stuff on it?

As far as he could tell, the only thing that held the neckline of the dress together was a string tied in a loose bow. Matt couldn't help speculating on what would happen if someone pulled on the string—and his fingers itched to get ahold of it. In the shadowy area below the bow, he could just glimpse the swell of her breasts and the same sheen that made her shoulders so damn sexy.

The dress was gathered at the waist and then flared out into a full skirt with rows of ruffles at the bottom. It was full enough and long enough that he couldn't see if she'd taken his advice on the shoes.

"You look pretty good yourself," Charlotte told him.

"Thanks." Matt coughed and wondered what he could do other than speculate on how tightly she'd tied that damned bow. "How's your ankle?"

"Much better. And I took your advice," she told him as she hiked up her skirt enough for him to see her feet.

Matt laughed when he saw the pink high-top tennis shoes.

"Sensible enough for you?" Charlotte asked.

"Absolutely."

"Good." She studied her foot for a moment. "Although I do think something in red and white would have been better. What do you think?"

He thought she was showing off a bit more of her leg than was necessary. "The pink looks good." When she continued to study her foot, he added, "But red might have been better," and was relieved when she nodded and dropped her skirt.

He was glad she'd taken his advice, but he couldn't help wondering how many women could pull off red silk, sequins and high-top sneakers. He couldn't think of another woman who'd even have the nerve to try.

"The doorbell," Charlotte called out.

"I'll get it, darling," Rhue said as she sailed back through the kitchen. "It may be your house, but I'm the hostess."

"Think you're ready for this?" Charlotte asked as she looped her hand through Matt's arm and led him into the dining room.

Matt's confidence almost failed him when he got a good look at the rest of the house. There were helium balloons dripping with colorful ribbons, an ice sculpture of two lovebirds in the middle of the dining room table, and hors d'oeuvres molded into the shapes of wedding bells or hearts. As he was trying to take all of it in, he heard a laugh that reminded him of the wicked witch in *The Wizard of Oz*.

"Good God. What's that?"

Charlotte smiled sweetly up at him. "My cousin Nedra. Uncle Walter's daughter. We've never figured out how anyone as quiet as Uncle Walter managed to spawn a child with a voice that could cut through steel."

* * *

"Rhue has really outdone herself this time," Carver said.

Charlotte, who was surveying the room, hadn't heard him walk up beside her, but that wasn't really surprising considering the noise level.

Still studying the fascinating assortment of people she called family, she said, "Yes, she has." Satisfied that her relatives were as interesting—and eccentric—as ever, she turned to face Carver, only to discover that the little man was sporting a black eye and an arm in a sling. "Good heavens, what happened to you?"

"Fell down the stairs the day before yesterday. It's not quite as bad as it looks. I wouldn't have this on," he said, looking down at the bandaged arm, "except that sweet Rhue insisted I go to the doctor. You know how determined she can be."

Charlotte nodded.

"Rhue tells me you had an accident today."

"At work. I don't mind admitting that it was scary—though I seem to have come out better than you did. Only a twisted ankle." She lifted her skirt to reveal her sneakers. "This is my concession to sensibility."

"You know I'm still upset about the judge's decision on Monday. So unfair."

"Life isn't always fair," Charlotte reminded him with a smile.

"Rhue feels awful about it. I almost had her convinced to petition the court for a change—then Howie talked to her. I think she'd change her mind if you asked her."

Charlotte shrugged. "Aunty's only doing what she thinks is right."

"No, she's doing what Howie and Walter think is right. It seems to me that a marriage should be as valid the moment it's performed as it is thirty years later."

Oh dear, she thought, he's going to start on that again. "Speaking of marriages, have you gotten Aunt Rhue to set a date yet?"

He sighed and shook his head. "Just because she made a mistake before—"

"Four mistakes."

"Yes... well, just because she made some previous errors in judgment is no reason to put off our marriage. I hope that seeing you two lovebirds together will make her realize that. You two are happy, aren't you?"

"Ecstatic."

"What?" Carver shouted. "I can't hear you over the music."

"Ecstatic," Charlotte shouted back.

When Carver shook his head to indicate that he still couldn't hear her, Charlotte realized that the volume of the music had risen dramatically over the past few minutes. She motioned to him that she was going to see about it.

As she hobbled toward the central control for the music system, she noticed Matt talking with several of her cousins—all female, of course. She also noticed that he was taking everyone, from Nedra in brocade and feathers to Cousin Alexandra, who was wearing camouflage pants and boots, in stride. Mentally she gave him credit for aplomb and tolerance, two of the most important traits when dealing with the Rutherford clan. A sense of humor still ranked number one.

Limping slightly, she continued toward the kitchen cabinet that housed the controls for the built-in music system. She was surprised to find Carver in the room, talking to the burly caterer's assistant. He must have moved quickly to get there before her.

"And furthermore—" Carver was saying as she entered.

But before he could say anything else, the big man turned on his heel and left. Obviously embarrassed by the situation, Carver plucked an orange from the basket, tossed it into the air and followed him out. Aunt Rhue was right; Carver didn't have any experience with kitchen help.

Kneeling in front of the controls, Charlotte tried to adjust the sound level. Unfortunately, turning the volume down didn't help. Neither did turning the system off. The music was still blaring when Tommy came through the door with his science project at his heels.

Charlotte sighed. "I should have known this had something to do with VASSAR."

"I don't understand, Charlotte. It worked just fine this morning. Honest." He began punching buttons on VASSAR's control panel. "I thought I'd made it self-controlled so that the music would get louder when the conversation did and then softer when it was quiet. Great idea, huh?"

"Uh-huh," she agreed as the noise level from the other room escalated. The volume of the music did the same.

When Nedra's laugh cut through the clamor like a knife through butter, VASSAR's lights flashed off and on. Matt and Aunt Rhue were charging through the door when Tommy finally hit the magic button. Barbra Streisand was cut off in the middle of "Evergreen," and the chatter died immediately afterward. Charlotte counted to twenty-three before the hum of conversation resumed. She was at twenty-seven when Matt spoke.

"No more music," he said with quiet authority. "Don't even hum."

Charlotte was glad to see that Tommy remained wisely silent.

"What in the world happened?" Rhue demanded as she fanned herself with her hand. There was a sheen of perspiration on her upper lip.

"VASSAR's controls went haywire," Tommy began.

Rhue looked totally confused. "What has my alma mater got to do with the level of the music?"

"Not your college," Charlotte began. "Tommy's robot. And it's a long story."

"One we won't go into now," Matt informed her.

Rhue looked from one to the other. "Don't bother me with details, just tell me if this robot will turn down the heat, as well."

Matt and Charlotte looked at each other—then at Tommy.

"I'll work on it," the teenager promised.

"Meanwhile we'll get some fresh air in the house." Matt looked at Charlotte. "You open the French doors in the solarium. I'll take the dining room."

Charlotte nodded once. "Right."

Less than a minute later they were back in the kitchen.

"The damn windows—" Matt began.

"Are locked," Charlotte finished.

"I'm working on it," Tommy told them.

"Oh, dear," Aunt Rhue murmured. Picking up a small tray from the counter, she began to fan herself.

Afraid the older woman might faint, Matt grabbed her by the elbow and half led, half carried her to a chair. Taking the tray from Rhue, he handed it to Charlotte.

"Fan," he commanded. Going back to Tommy, he said in a barely controlled whisper, "Get those windows unlocked before everyone is overcome with the heat." He winced when the sound of Nedra's laugh ricocheted through the house. VASSAR flickered once more then twisted from side to side like a helicopter trying to take flight. "And make sure those damn doors are kept *un-*locked. I can't imagine anything worse than being trapped overnight with these . . . characters."

By ten-thirty what was left of the melted ice sculpture had been tossed onto the lawn, most of the balloons had popped in the heat, and Cousin Nedra was almost dry after falling into the pool when Matt suggested that everyone step out into the cool night air. Now, Charlotte was happy to note, the house had been cooled down by the cross breeze from the open windows and even the doors Matt had insisted upon propping open.

When Aunt Rhue tapped a spoon against her crystal champagne goblet, everyone became quiet. Despite all the complications, she seemed determined to make this a festive occasion.

"This evening wouldn't be complete without our best wishes for the happy couple."

There was a smattering of applause and shouts of Hear! Hear! VASSAR began to emit a low-pitched hum.

"First of all, we want to extend our wishes for a long and fruitful marriage to Mr. and Mrs. Matthew Oliver."

Everyone clapped as Rhue herded the two of them into the center of the room. VASSAR's lights went from yellow to orange and the hum became shrill.

"And of course we want to welcome Matthew into our family," Rhue continued as though she weren't forced to scream over the high-pitched sound.

There was more applause while Charlotte and Matt smiled. VASSAR's hum became ear piercing. Almost as quickly as it had begun to screech, the robot fell silent though the lights went to a bright, winking red.

Rhue held her glass aloft. "To these two wonderful young people. May their dreams never tarnish and their love never die."

It was so quiet as everyone sipped their champagne that the sound of barking dogs—lots of dogs—could be heard in the distance.

"I'd like to add to that," Howie began as VASSAR started to vibrate. In the background the howling grew louder as the robot's lights glowed brighter. "To Charlotte, my sister Gwen's little baby girl. And to Matt Oliver, the man she married. He'd better take good care of her—or else."

Everyone was drinking to that when the first dog came though the front door.

"What the—" Matt began.

"Close the doors," Tommy cried as two more dogs ran inside and began to circle VASSAR. A third dog went straight for the pâté as Tommy went to work on the robot's control panel. "VASSAR's calling the dogs."

"I'm going to take a can opener to that machine," Matt vowed as he slammed the front door on a particularly mangy-looking mutt. Glancing out the window, he discovered that a whole pack of dogs had formed on the front lawn. Several had begun to howl ferociously. The damn robot had turned into a giant dog whistle.

It was well past midnight by the time the last guest had left and the caterers had cleaned up. Disgruntled neighbors had rescued their precious family pets, and the humane society had rounded up the last of the strays long before that. Now Charlotte and Matt sat side by side on the living room sofa. Charlotte had taken off her sneakers and put her feet up on the coffee table. Matt had loosened his tie and unfastened the top button of his shirt.

Charlotte held her fluted champagne glass up to the light and watched the bubbles. "I think the party was quite a success."

Matt was certain he hadn't heard her correctly. "A success?"

"Uh-huh. The kind of party that people will be talking about for years to come."

"That's how you judge a party?"

"Aunt Rhue does. Besides, she took that adorable little puppy home."

"Mutt," Matt amended.

Charlotte smiled at him. "She's going to name him Oliver, after us. Isn't that sweet?"

Matt shook his head and rolled his eyes toward the ceiling. "Sweet," he agreed, and wondered how Charlotte could sit there looking so desirable after everything that had happened. The funny part was that while he was exhausted from the evening, she seemed to have come alive during all the excitement.

"You were brilliant," Charlotte told him after another sip of champagne.

"I was?"

She nodded. "Especially when you led everyone to the backyard."

"I was only trying for unflappable." He took a sip of his champagne and basked in the knowledge that Charlotte thought he was brilliant. Sitting here, talking over the evening with Charlotte was the perfect way to end the day. It was the way he'd always thought a family would be. "Although I think it would have been less chaotic if Nedra had refrained from jumping into the pool."

"I thought we were lucky everyone didn't join her."

As she turned to smile at him, her diamond earrings caught and refracted the light, and the diamond pendant at her throat sparkled as brightly. But it was the twinkle in her green eyes that held his attention. He'd never thought of laughter as being seductive, but he found himself wanting to take her in his arms and turn the laughter to desire. To see the sparkle of delight turn into smoldering flames of passion. He wanted to feel all her energy and excitement centered on him.

"Does your skin always glow like that?" he found himself asking. He watched her smile falter and her eyes turn dark, and he was gratified to know that she felt the pull, too.

"Shimmer?" she asked in a small voice.

"Like it has diamond dust on it."

Her laugh was nervous. "That's only bath powder."

Matt said nothing, but ran his thumb along her collarbone. His fingers skimmed the pulse in her throat and he felt it race beneath his touch. When he pulled his hand away, he saw that some of the shimmering powder had clung to his fingertips—and that Charlotte's pulse still raced where he'd touched her. It was unsettling to realize that his own blood pounded as fiercely after that fleeting contact.

Charlotte yawned daintily behind her hand. "Aunt Rhue told me you were wonderful."

"That's not what she told me. She said I was making great strides in overcoming my shyness." When Charlotte smiled, he asked, "You don't have any idea what she might mean, do you?"

"I wouldn't lose any sleep over it."

"If I lose sleep," Matt murmured, "it won't be over anything your aunt said. I might, however, lose sleep over this little bow on your dress." So saying, he fingered the tassels on the end of the string. "I've been wondering all night if this little string is all that holds your dress together. And I've been wondering what would happen if I pulled on it."

Charlotte stopped breathing. She looked down as his strong fingers closed around the string and began to tug on it. Slowly, inexorably, the bow became smaller. She could still stop him, she realized, but she didn't. She wanted him, and—God help her—she loved him. She savored the thrill, anticipating the feel of his hands upon her skin, waiting for the moment his kisses drove her beyond thought and rationality.

But there was another part of her, the part that knew that by loving him she gave him the power to hurt her. Was she willing to risk her heart because of the passion that smoldered in his eyes? She smiled. It was too late to save herself; she was already in love. Besides, caution had never been one of her strong points.

Matt held his breath when the bow finally came undone. The neckline of her dress, which already hung provocatively off her left shoulder, opened wider. The material glided slowly downward, revealing more of her shoulder and the shadowy area between her breasts but not far enough to reveal the nipples that he could see beaded beneath the clinging silk.

His hand was shaking when he cupped her breast; he could feel the heat from her skin through the material. His breathing was unsteady as he bent down to kiss her; he was surprised to discover that the taste of her was intoxicating. The way she leaned into him, the moan of surrender as her arms came around him aroused and inflamed as nothing else could.

Whatever remnant of control he'd held on to shredded beneath the onslaught on his senses. Her taste, when he swept his tongue inside, was wild as summer honey. Her skin, where he slipped his hand beneath her bodice, was warm and soft. The sound of his name on her lips was sweeter than music, and the fragrance of her skin more potent than wine. When he summoned enough control to drag his lips free, the sight of her mouth, swollen from his kisses and her eyes dazed with passion, pulled at him more forcefully than gravity.

His lips returned to plunder hers. His hand swept away the material and kneaded her soft breast. His last rational thought was to wonder why he had fought this so long.

Charlotte had known there was a wildness beneath all that restraint. She'd known the emotions he kept so tightly controlled would be fierce. But she hadn't been prepared for her own response. There was the wildness in her that answered his, and there was passion. She had expected those. But she hadn't expected to feel peace at the core of the storm. She hadn't expected to feel as if she'd been waiting for this moment all her life. With a sigh, she melted against him. With love, she returned his passion.

"Charlotte," she heard Tommy call. "Are you downstairs?"

Charlotte pushed against Matt's chest. When he relinquished her lips, she wanted to weep; and when she rested her cheek against his shoulder, she felt the pounding of his heart. His colorful expletive made her smile.

She pulled the neckline of her dress together and fumbled with the string until Matt swept her shaking fingers aside and tied the bow.

"I'm in the living room," she called out once Matt's hand had dropped away. She couldn't resist the urge to place a quick kiss on his cheek as Tommy entered the room.

The fact that the young man was the picture of dejection almost made his interruption forgivable.

"I came to apologize. I'm sorry about the mess I made of the party."

"I thought you added a little excitement," Charlotte said to cover the heavy silence. Tommy didn't seem to notice.

"I still haven't figured out what went wrong. It might have been all the sharp noises, like people clapping."

"And Cousin Nedra's laugh," Matt put in.

Tommy smiled at that. "I've disconnected most of VASSAR's peripherals, but it's still hooked up to the security system. You'll need these remote controls to turn the alarm on and off tonight." He handed each of them devices that were smaller versions of VASSAR's keyboard, and he showed them which buttons activated the alarm system. "I'll run some more tests on VASSAR tomorrow," he promised before saying goodnight.

When they were alone again, Matt sat staring at the remote control in his hand and wondering what to do now. He should be grateful Tommy intruded when he did. He should be grateful the young man saved him from further complicating an already complex situation. Matt shifted to accommodate the bulge in the front of his pants and wondered why, if his mind was so damn grateful, his body was still aching with need.

Charlotte looked at the remote control she held and wondered how it could feel less real than the emotions still vibrating within her. How was it possible to want a man so much that reality faded to oblivion? What would have happened if Tommy hadn't come back? She couldn't help smiling; she knew exactly what would have happened. Would she have regretted it in the morning? She didn't think so, but one look at Matt told her he would have. She would try to be grateful for Tommy's intrusion, she decided. When they made love, she wanted no regrets.

"I'm sorry—" Matt began.

"Don't apologize. You have nothing to apologize for."

He'd known she would say that. "Yes, I do. I generally keep my promises."

"What promises?"

"I told you before the wedding that this would be a marriage in name only. I had every intention of keeping my word. I told you the other night that I wouldn't let things get out of hand again. I meant that, too. The problem is—" Wanting to phrase the next part very carefully, he stopped to gather his thoughts.

Charlotte smiled. "Yes?"

"The problem is that you're a very beautiful woman—"

"Thank you."

"And living under the same roof with you is making it difficult to remember my promise." Not to mention difficult to sleep or keep his train of thought. But he wasn't about to admit to that.

"Let me see if I have this straight." Charlotte was still smiling. "Because you think I'm beautiful, it's hard for you to remember that you promised to keep this strictly business?"

Matt nodded.

"It has nothing to do with my brain or my personality? Is that right?"

Because just the opposite was true, Matt was ruthless. "Don't read any more into this than there is," he warned. "What I feel for you is simply the desire a man has for a beautiful woman. Nothing more and nothing less."

But Matt was more honest with himself. He knew that a woman's body, no matter how beautiful, had never kept him tied up in knots like this. To himself he even admitted that no other woman had ever had him up at night pacing the floor.

She gave his words some consideration. "Perhaps I could help."

"How's that?"

"I could run around in an old bathrobe with curlers in my hair and a pound of cold cream on my face."

Matt laughed but realized that it wouldn't solve his problem, because he'd still remember how she looked beneath it—and because it wasn't just her body that intrigued him.

He was equally entranced by the brilliant CEO with a wicked sense of humor and by the long-suffering niece who not only tolerated her eccentric family but actually loved them and by the employer who gave as much loyalty as she asked for and by the starfighter pilot who shot down intergalactic invaders with childlike abandon. In fact there were so many facets to the woman he had married that he couldn't begin to explore them all if they were married fifty years.

But that was the problem. Their marriage was only temporary, and he was showing signs of forming some very permanent attachments to the lady. A smart man would walk away while he still could. Matt had always prided himself on his intelligence—so why was he sitting here getting lost in her eyes?

"I don't think the cold cream and rollers are going to help," Matt finally said.

"What will?" she asked, and smiled when he frowned at her.

"Damned if I know," Matt asked as the grandfather clock struck two. "But I don't think sitting here talking about it is going to do either of us any good. Maybe a good night's sleep will help us think more clearly." But he doubted it.

Rising, he took Charlotte's glass and set it on the table, then reached down to take her hand and pull her up to stand beside him. He kept the touch casual and his smile friendly, but he couldn't stop his pulse from accelerating. When he noticed she was favoring her bad ankle, he swept her up into his arms—and silently cursed himself for being a masochist.

"Thank heaven, it's Saturday," Charlotte said as she snuggled sleepily against his shoulder. "I have all weekend to get the house straightened up before Mrs. Nguyen sees it."

Matt forced himself to concentrate on what she was saying instead of how easy it would be to carry her to his bed.

"I'll help after lunch, but I'm planning to go to my place early in the morning. I didn't bring enough clothes for six months."

"Wake me up when you get back. I'm planning to sleep until noon."

"Here we are," Matt said when they stood outside Charlotte's door. "Think you can make it from here?"

Charlotte yawned and stretched in a way that made his body clench. "Sure. Oh, and Matt . . . thanks for being so patient tonight. I know my family can be a little overwhelming, but they're lovable in their own way."

Lovable as a nest of rattlers, Matt thought, but he said, "I found them to be . . . interesting. I especially liked your cousin in the army fatigues and boots. I think I talked her into shaving her head."

"You didn't?"

"Do you doubt my ability to sway a jury—let alone one woman?"

Charlotte laughed at that. It was a sleepy, intimate sound that had his stomach tightening. "No, I have great faith in your lawyerly skills. Pleasant dreams," she told him just before she stepped into her room.

Right. Pleasant dreams. And they'd probably all be of her.

Stuffing his favorite sweats into the cardboard box, Matt surveyed his condo. It was spotless; he'd continued paying the lady who cleaned for him even though he wasn't living there. It was neat; there was a place for everything, and everything was perfectly in place. And, he realized as he looked around, it was about as lifeless as the artificial plant on his kitchen table.

Damn. That wasn't what he'd expected to find. He'd thought it would restore his emotional equilibrium to be back in his carefully organized world again; instead he felt as though he'd walked into the Arctic Circle. The place was exactly as he'd left it, but he didn't feel at home here. That wasn't logical, of course. So what had happened to cause this change? He set the box next to the others stacked by the door and turned to look out over the Pacific Ocean.

Charlotte had happened.

He no longer sought solitude. He no longer wanted his life calm and predictable. He no longer enjoyed the kind of orderliness that should be relegated to a museum. He wanted laughter and warmth and excitement and chaos.

He wanted Charlotte.

Could such a profound change be summed up so simply? He smiled; there was nothing simple about Charlotte. She was the most complex and enchanting creature he'd ever encountered. And there was nothing simple about the emotions she evoked. Or about the way he desired her.

The only simple part was the fact that he'd never have her. He'd given his word that their marriage was in name only, and he'd promised not to let things get out of control again. He was a man of his word, but that didn't ease the pain that came with wanting, especially since he knew he could have her. Hell, he would have seduced her into his bed last night if Tommy hadn't come back. And he would have hated himself this morning.

It didn't matter that they were legally married. It didn't even matter that she'd wanted him. She deserved a gentleman, not a man who'd camouflaged his violence with silk suits and a law degree. But even that couldn't keep him from dreaming—and the dreams were a big part of his problem. The only chance he had of keeping his promise was to spend long hours at work and make sure that when he went to bed at night he was too tired to dream.

The last items he wanted to take with him were his weights and rowing machine. He'd decided early this morning that these pieces of equipment might be the key to his peace of mind. If he worked out every night so that he fell into bed exhausted, maybe he'd quit dreaming of how she'd felt in his arms. And maybe he could wake up in the morning without wanting her. And maybe he'd be able to forget those awful moments when he'd thought she was dead.

He closed his eyes against those memories only to discover that such strong emotions couldn't be banished. He remembered how helpless he'd felt when the boxes toppled forward. As awful as the reality had been, in his dreams it was worse—for then his feet were mired in quicksand so that he couldn't get to her. Or sometimes he was trapped in a maze of boxes where he could hear her calling his name, but no matter where he turned, no matter how he searched, he couldn't find her.

Even worse than that were the dreams where he saw the gun pointed at Charlotte. He'd relived that moment a thousand times. Sometimes he was mute and was forced to run down a long hallway to reach the man with the gun. And no matter how fast he ran, the hallway went on forever, and he woke to the sound of gunshots and the knowledge that Charlotte was dead. And sometimes, in the strange way dreams have of changing reality, he could see Charlotte in her office at the same time he saw the man with the gun take aim at her. And, though he shouted, she didn't hear him. So he shouted louder and louder but never loud enough to divert the intruder from his purpose. And never loud enough to block out the sounds of the gun or the sight of Charlotte lying dead on the floor.

Matt opened his eyes. Hazy sunlight poured in through the windows. The sound of the waves mingled with the cries of sea gulls circling offshore. But in his mind's eye he was seeing it again, the man with the gun taking careful aim into Charlotte's office.

My God, why hadn't he realized it before? That hadn't been a burglar trying to sneak off into the night. That had been a man waiting and watching for the perfect moment and the perfect target. That had been a man whose sole purpose was murder. And Charlotte had been his intended victim.

Chapter Eleven

For the first half of the drive home, Matt tried to think of a subtle way to broach the subject of murder, but he could think of no easy way to inform Charlotte that someone was trying to kill her. By the time he turned onto Los Feliz Boulevard, he wasn't so much worried about how to tell her as much as he was about finding her safe at home. It was logical to assume that if there had already been two attempts on her life, there would be more. Logic was making his life a living hell.

Tommy called a greeting from the garage where he was working on VASSAR, but Matt didn't bother to do more than wave as he headed straight for the house.

"Charlotte," he shouted as threw open the kitchen door. When there was no answer, he dashed into the foyer. "Charlotte, where are you?"

He was halfway up the stairs when she came out of her bedroom, still fumbling with the belt on her bathrobe.

"Okay, okay, I'm up," she mumbled.

She was on her feet, he decided, but not really awake. He was surprised she'd been serious about sleeping until noon.

"I think I should warn you that I'm not a morning person on the weekend. At least not right away," she added around a yawn.

He felt his heart settle down to a natural rhythm. "We need to talk."

"Let me take a shower and—"

"No." He caught her arm. "We need to talk right away."

She yawned again then ran her fingers through her short hair. The bleary-eyed look she gave him made him fear she'd go back to sleep standing on the stairs.

"Sure this can't wait?" she asked, then sighed when he shook his head. "Let me splash some water on my face. You put the coffee on."

He was pacing the floor when she came downstairs. Though he was relieved that she showed her usual animation, he couldn't help noticing how young and vulnerable she looked with her damp hair combed back out of her face and no makeup. There were freckles on the bridge of her nose that he'd never noticed before.

He poured two cups of coffee and waited until she'd settled at the table before beginning.

"If this is about last night—" Charlotte began.

"No, it's not. Actually, it's about the break-in at RP."

She looked up sharply. "Has something else happened?"

"No." He took a sip of coffee. "But I've been remembering certain things about the one last week."

She didn't bother to stifle a yawn. "Couldn't we have reminisced later in the day?"

"Listen, I'm being serious here."

She held up her hand. "I've already contacted the alarm company. We're upgrading security, and I've talked several other businesses in the area into going in on a private patrol. It's nice of you to worry, but I really think we have the problem covered."

"I don't think it was a burglary," Matt said as he shook his head. This was harder than he'd thought.

"That's because you scared him away before he could take anything."

Matt decided another approach might help. "Let's be logical about this. Of all the businesses in that immediate area, why would a thief pick RP? There's a camera company down the street and a warehouse for a video store next door. So why break into a place that makes boxes? It doesn't make sense."

"Of course it does. We have computers and typewriters and a TV in the lunch room. There are plenty of things to steal."

Matt couldn't help smiling. "I'm not saying that you don't have anything of value. I'm just saying that a thief could make a better haul at one of the neighboring facilities. Isn't that true?"

Charlotte scowled at him. "I suppose so."

"And if the thief had been planning to steal these things, he would have needed to get them to his car as quickly as possible. Right?"

"I guess."

"But this guy's car was parked at least half a block away, if that was him we heard speed away."

The nod she gave him was grudging at best.

"And why, when he discovered there was someone on the premises, didn't he hightail it out of there? Why did he pull a gun when he could have left without ever being discovered?''

Charlotte sipped thoughtfully on her coffee. ''Because he felt trapped between you and me?''

''No. He didn't even know I was there until I yelled. And I didn't yell until he took aim at you with the gun.''

''So what are you getting at?''

''I don't think he ever intended to steal anything,'' Matt said quietly. ''I think he was there to kill you.''

''Me?''

Matt nodded.

''Me?'' she asked again. ''That's crazy.''

''You didn't see him standing out in the hall, Charlotte. I did. He was watching you. And when he raised his gun, he took careful aim. There was nothing rushed or panicky about it.''

''That's ridiculous!''

''No more ridiculous than the idea that a thief would kill with no provocation.''

She stood up, almost oversetting the chair. ''I thought you were supposed to be logical.'' She turned and emptied her coffee into the sink, then stood there staring at the cup in her hand. ''I've never heard anything so preposterous.''

''Then there's the 'accident' with the forklift.'' He rose and walked over to her. He longed to put his arms around her, but the set of her shoulders told him she wouldn't welcome his touch. He couldn't blame her after last night. ''You never could find anyone who admitted to driving it. And none of your employees were missing.''

She turned to face him. ''So you're suggesting that the same man came back four days later and tried to kill me by burying me under a ton of cardboard?''

''Yes.'' Matt nodded. ''I am.''

Charlotte brushed back the hair that had fallen over her forehead. "I'm going to fix some juice. Do you want any?"

"No, dammit, I don't."

He poured more coffee and watched her drop oranges from the basket into the juicer while he tried to hold on to his temper. It was a lot to take in, he knew. In fact, it was so overwhelming that he still had trouble with it himself. But he was right. He knew he was. Not only was it the logical conclusion, but he felt it deep down in his gut. Now all he had to do was convince Charlotte.

"Who would want to kill me?" Charlotte asked.

"I can think of three people."

"Three?" Her finger hesitated over the button that would set the juicer into operation.

"Howie, Walter, and Rhue."

Charlotte's finger came down in a jerky movement that started the appliance even as it slid off into the air. She was whirling to face him as the machine began crushing the fruit. Before she could say anything else, the juicer emitted a low, whining sound. Matt saw the sparks bounce off the tiles. He'd started across the room before Charlotte could scream. Launching himself toward her, he managed to catch her around the waist and drag her away from the fire. Twisting his body, he landed with Charlotte on top of him then rolled so that he was between her and the flames.

"Where's your fire extinguisher?"

Charlotte pointed across the room. "Under the sink."

Matt had it out of the cabinet and turned on the flames before they could get a hold on the wooden cabinets. He doused the whole area with the fire retardant then pulled the plug out of the wall for good measure.

"Now do you believe me?" Matt demanded.

"It was an accident!"

"I don't think so."

"VASSAR. That's what caused it."

"No." Matt took her by the shoulders and held her fast. "Tommy has VASSAR out in the garage. Besides, he told us last night he'd disconnected most of the peripherals."

Matt turned back to survey the blackened cabinets and the melted appliance. It had happened so quickly and had been so intense that he didn't believe it was an accident. The thought of what could have happened made him angry enough to kill.

"I've never seen anyone but you use the juicer. And if you'd been leaning on the counter like you usually do, you would have gone up in flames with it."

Charlotte's eyes appeared bigger and rounder in her white face. "No," she whispered.

Matt shook her. "Yes. Someone wants you dead."

"They don't," she cried.

"And they aren't going to stop until they've killed you."

"Not my family." She closed her eyes, and Matt could see that she was battling tears, as well as the truth. "They wouldn't." When she opened her eyes, the first teardrop rolled down her cheek. "They couldn't. We love each other."

"Someone loves money more."

She opened her mouth as though to speak, but shook her head. The breath she took in was long and tremulous. Matt enfolded her gently in his embrace and held her while she cried and for several minutes after. When she pushed away from him, he saw that she was composed despite the tracks her tears had left.

"I can see how you might come to that conclusion. It's the logical one. But there's more to life than logic. There's love and trust and loyalty. I love my family and they love me—and I know in my heart that they'd never hurt me. All the logic in the world won't change my mind." She used the back of her hands to wipe away the vestiges of her tears. "Don't make me choose between you and my family. Please."

"I'm not asking you to choose—"

She cupped her hand around his cheek. "You are. You just don't know it."

"All I want is to keep you safe."

"How about happy?"

"Happy?"

Charlotte nodded. "Do you want to keep me happy, too?"

"Sure I do."

"Then you won't ever mention this again. Is that clear?"

Matt nodded. It was clear all right—clear that she was so blinded by her own love and trust that she couldn't see her relatives for what they were. He should have expected that. If he'd used one iota of that logic he was always talking about, he would have expected it.

He watched her walk out of the kitchen with her back and shoulders held stiff. She might not want him to discuss it, but he was damn well going to do something about it, because he was the only person who stood between Charlotte and a murderer—and because he was the one who had set the chain of events into motion.

Charlotte hadn't had any "accidents" before their marriage. It was only afterward that someone had become desperate enough to resort to homicide. That made it his responsibility. He flexed his fingers as he thought of getting ahold of the bastard's throat and choking the life out of him.

Matt took a deep breath. If there was any time in his life when he needed to be logical and objective, it was now. This minute. Charlotte's life depended on it. He'd give in to anger when he discovered the murderer—and he'd make the bastard wish he'd never harmed a hair on Charlotte's head.

"Been working on VASSAR very long?" Matt asked as casually as he could while he roamed around Tommy's garage workshop a little while later. A mad scientist or a terrorist would have a field day in here.

"Since early this morning."

"Have you figured out what went wrong?"

Tommy shook his head but kept working. "I've checked the wiring and the circuit boards. Now I need to check the programming. That's going to take some time."

"VASSAR hasn't been hooked up this morning?"

"Not since you left. I came downstairs just as you pulled out of the driveway."

"So there's no way VASSAR could be responsible for the juicer catching on fire?"

Tommy's head snapped up. "No way. I told you, I've been working on the unit since early this morning."

"Take it easy. I believe you. But the fact of the matter is that Charlotte's juicer just went up in flames. And I don't think it was any accident."

"What's that supposed to mean?"

"Can you keep a secret?"

"If I think it should be kept."

Matt nodded. He liked the young man's honesty—and his intelligence. Matt knew Charlotte well enough to know that one person couldn't keep an eye on her. He needed an ally, and there wasn't anyone else available.

"I think someone is trying to kill Charlotte." He expected Tommy to be shocked, but the teenager didn't blink an eyelash. "You don't seem to be very surprised."

Tommy laid down his tools. "I had my suspicions after the two accidents at work, but Mom said I'd been watching too much TV. But if the juicer just burned up like you said . . ."

He'd made a good choice, Matt decided. The kid wasn't just bright; he was levelheaded, too. "You have any idea who might want her dead?"

Tommy crossed his arms. "At first I thought it was you."

"Me?"

"That's why I was trying to get VASSAR into operation. I thought Charlotte might need protection. From you."

"Have you been talking to Howie, or is this your idea?"

"Mine."

"And you didn't say anything to anyone?"

"Just my mom. She thought I was crazy."

"Why didn't you go to Charlotte with your suspicions?"

"I'm not a kid, you know. I have enough sense to realize that it would be tough to convince a woman that her new husband is trying to murder her. Even when the woman is just like your sister." Tommy glanced back to where VASSAR lay on the workbench. "I was doing my best to make a machine that could help keep her safe—only it kept going wrong. And I was afraid that if I told her about my suspicions she wouldn't want me around anymore. I didn't want that."

"What makes you think I'm not the one who wants her dead? Maybe I'm trying to throw suspicion off myself."

"I told you I'm no kid. I've seen the way you look at Charlotte." Matt saw color stain the boy's cheeks. "You don't look like you want to kill her."

Not only bright and levelheaded but perceptive, too. The kid might be his only choice for an ally, but he was also the best one.

"What about her aunt and uncles?"

"No way. I mean, I can see that they'd be the logical choices, but I don't think they'd hurt her. You should have seen how they took care of her after her father's death. I think you can forget about them."

"You're wrong. We can't forget about anyone."

"Okay. So what are we going to do?"

"Damned if I know."

"We could call the cops."

Matt shook his head. "She got mad when I suggested that her family might want to kill her."

She'd been more than mad, she'd been torn. If he made her choose between her family and him, she was going to give him his walking papers. Then she'd be a wide-open target.

"However..." Matt looked around. "Is there a phone I can use where she can't hear me?"

"In our place," the boy said as he gestured at the second floor. "Mom's out for the day," he added when Matt hesitated.

"Great. I'm going to make a phone call. If she comes out, you give a blast on the car horn. Okay?"

"Yeah, but—"

"Just do it. I'll explain later."

Bob Stone wasn't in his office when Matt called, so Matt stayed on the line while the private investigator's secretary paged her boss. When Bob finally came to the phone,

Matt wasted no time filling him in on the details. In the end, Bob said he'd get right onto it and that Matt should stick to his wife like glue, a suggestion Matt was only too happy to agree with. He gave Bob carte blanche to do whatever was necessary and hung up hurriedly when he heard the prearranged signal from downstairs.

By the time Matt reached the garage, Charlotte was already there—and Tommy was standing between her and the Corvette. Not subtle but quite effective, Matt decided.

"Hey, Matt," the boy said with such obvious relief that Matt had to smile. "I was just telling Charlotte that it's too nice a day to go to work. Don't you agree?"

"Absolutely. Besides, I thought we were going to clean up the house so that Mrs. N. doesn't see the mess."

Charlotte shrugged. "The mess will still be here when I get back."

"That's true," Matt agreed. "But Tommy and I were just coming in to volunteer our help."

"You two?"

"We could make it three if you want VASSAR."

Charlotte laughed. "I thought you said clean up...."

"Aw, Charlotte. I'm sorry about ruining your party."

"Yeah, and the kid wants to make it up to you by helping."

The look Tommy gave him for that lie was almost comical. It was an indication of how seriously Tommy took his assignment that he didn't try to get out of it.

"Then Matt promised to treat us to pizza," Tommy finished. The look he flashed Matt this time was triumphant.

"I don't know," Charlotte said. "House cleaning and pizza are hard to turn down, but I have some work I need to catch up on."

"And the video arcade," Tommy added.

"The arcade? Really?"

Tommy nodded. "Right, Matt?"

"Right," Matt agreed, though he had the distinct impression that Tommy had just manipulated him. And very nicely, too.

"Well, why didn't you say the arcade to begin with? Just let me go inside and get my quarters."

"Wait a minute, you two." Matt tried to look stern. "I thought we were going to clean up the house first."

"The mess will still be here when we get back," Tommy reasoned.

"Yeah," Charlotte agreed. "But we need to get to the arcade before it gets too crowded."

Matt couldn't help laughing. "Okay. But we're going to clean up when we get home. After all, I'm the one Mrs. N. threatened if things weren't back to normal on Monday."

As Charlotte snuggled down in her lonely bed that night she wondered if she would ever get to sleep. It had been a wonderful day. No, better than that. It had been perfect. The three of them had played video games and eaten pizza and played more video games and eaten ice cream. Then they'd come home and cleaned up the house. Even that had been fun, since the three of them had worked together. After Mrs. Nguyen called Tommy home, Charlotte and Matt had gone out for a leisurely dinner.

It was sweet of him to apologize for that ridiculous accusation he'd made this morning. Not in words, of course. She knew enough about men to know they had trouble saying the words. But he'd been saying he was sorry all day long.

No wonder she loved him, Charlotte mused as she snuggled deeper under the covers. She would tell him so except that men had trouble with those three little words, too. If she told him now, it would only make him more determined to abide by those promises he thought he'd made.

But she knew he cared for her. Why else would he have let his imagination run wild enough to believe someone was trying to kill her? Especially since he wasn't a man who gave in to his imagination very often. But there would come a time—and it wasn't far away—when he'd discover the truth for himself. And she'd be waiting.

Her last thought, as she drifted off to sleep, was that Matt would hate being described as sweet.

Matt was still awake when the lights finally went out under Charlotte's door. Thank God, she'd finally gone off to sleep. He activated the security system as Tommy had taught him and waited another hour before he went in to check on her.

She was sound asleep and, judging by her smile, enjoying pleasant dreams. That figured, he thought, and he tried to dredge up some anger. Someone was trying to kill her, and he was up playing bodyguard while she slept the sleep of the innocent. She hadn't even locked her door. The Pollyanna attitude was likely to get her killed. Still, the emotion he felt wasn't anger. It was desire.

He wondered what she would do if he slipped into bed with her and caressed her awake. Would she turn to him with that soft, dreamy smile on her face? Would she moan with pleasure as his hands familiarized themselves with her sweet curves and valleys? When she opened her eyes, would she give herself to him with wild abandon? Her long looks and speculative glances made him believe she would. Then, when it was finished, would she feel used? Would she hate him? She should, and only that thought kept him from turning back the covers and slipping between her thighs.

Matt was up and dressed before he heard the shower in Charlotte's bathroom. He'd decided to ask her to go for a drive. Maybe to the mountains or the beach. Maybe Palm Springs. Anywhere, as long as he was with her and no one knew where they'd gone. They'd pick up sandwiches at the deli and have a picnic.

But before he could do more than think about it, Charlotte was downstairs and on the tennis court.

With an explicit oath, Matt changed out of his jeans and into sweats. Fortunately, he'd left his rowing machine and weights in the garage beside the tennis court, so he had a perfectly logical reason to be there. And at the same time he might be able to work off some of his sexual frustration.

Charlotte was gathering up the tennis balls in her bucket when she saw Matt go into the garage. She hadn't played tennis since her marriage, and her serve, which had always been the weakest part of her game, needed some serious work. She'd planned to get in an hour or so of practice, then go to RP and catch up on the work she should have done yesterday.

When she saw Matt go into the garage, she waved, but she refused to behave like some love-struck teenager. She would not follow him around. Glancing up toward the sky, she let the warm breeze play over her skin, then used her wristband to wipe the sweat from her brow. She wasn't going into the garage to see Matt, she told herself. She was going in to get a towel out of the cupboard where Mrs. Nguyen kept them.

It took a minute for her eyes to adjust to the interior light. Just a few minutes for her to focus on Matt as he worked out with the barbells. She'd always known that the kind of body he had under those conservative suits didn't happen by pushing paper. She'd never guessed that there was so much muscle beneath the material, though. No, this was one time when her imagination hadn't gone far enough.

"Oh, hi," he said casually. He was trying to give the impression that he hadn't known she was standing there, but she wasn't buying it for one second. She knew he was aware of her—just as she was aware of him. "Mrs. N. said I could keep my equipment here. I hope it's okay."

"Sure." Charlotte smiled and tried to keep her eyes focused on Matt's face. It was a losing battle.

She pointed toward the cupboards. "I just came in for a towel." Matt nodded but kept pumping those barbells. She wondered if he had any idea what number he was on now? The imp in her hoped he'd lost count. "You ever play any tennis?" she asked, just to ensure that he would lose his place.

"Some." He switched the barbell to the other hand.

"Want to play?"

"Against you?"

She nodded. "Why?"

"Just seems unfair, that's all."

"I'll go easy on you," she promised.

Matt's laughter caught them both by surprise. "You're on."

Unable to take her eyes off the ripple of muscle, Charlotte reached back and opened the cupboard. Matt looked from her to the cupboard and back.

"Charlotte, do you trust me?"

She was taken aback by the question as well as his suddenly serious expression. "Of course."

"Then don't move. Not one inch."

"What?"

"Don't even turn your head." He began to move around to the side, circling so that he could come up behind her.

If this was some kind of strange test of her loyalty, she was determined not to blow it. Maybe he was still hurt that she hadn't believed his theory that someone was trying to murder her.

She followed him with her eyes. "You want to tell me what this is about?"

"If you promise not to move."

Charlotte barely kept from nodding her head. "Scout's honor."

"There's about four feet of snake coiled up on top of the towels."

She tried to control the shiver that went through her. "A snake?"

"Yeah." His voice was pitched low. "And judging by the way it's jerking its head around and put up its tail, the damn thing isn't very happy."

"Oh." She tried to visualize four feet of snake and suddenly had trouble keeping her breathing regular.

"I'm going to slam the door on it—and hope that the whole snake is inside when I do." He was standing directly behind her now. He was also behind the open door, so she knew he couldn't see exactly what the snake was doing.

"Do you want me to turn around and see where the snake is? I won't make any fast moves."

Chapter Twelve

"No!" Matt controlled the panic and said, "No," more calmly the second time.

God, no, he didn't want her to move. He'd tell her to hold her breath if he thought she would do it. He could just make out the coils of the snake through the space where the door opened on its hinges, and he was still telling himself that the snake couldn't possibly be what he thought it was.

But the small, flattened head and dark body slashed through with light cross bands was like the many-banded krait he'd encountered in 'Nam. This snake was a little larger than he remembered, and what he could see of the underbelly was snow-white rather than showing any dark mottling, but he wasn't taking any chances. The krait was poisonous.

He took a calming breath. "As soon as I slam this door, I want you to run like hell. But not one second before." He knew that any movement would serve as a target for the excited snake. "Say yes if you understand."

"Yes."

He heard the quaver in her voice. It was time to act. He inhaled deeply then let out his breath as he lunged for the open door. Hitting the wood with both hands, he slammed it hard. But he wasn't quick enough since almost a foot of furious snake stuck out from the door. He was going to have to push hard enough to cut the snake in two—before it got him.

"Run," he shouted, never taking his eyes off the undulating head of the snake.

The krait lunged at him but was a scant inch too short to sink its fangs into his arm. Rearing back, the snake jerked from side to side and tried to pull the rest of its body through the opening. Matt was ready to give the door a quick—and he hoped deadly—thrust when Charlotte appeared in his line of vision.

Holding an empty trash can in front of her, she placed the cylinder over the snake's head. Confronted by the clanging metal container, the krait quickly thrust its head back inside the cupboard and pulled the rest of its body inside. Matt slammed the door and leaned against it.

He could feel the snake bumping around behind the cupboard door, but that meant it was still inside—and he was out here. That's the way he wanted it.

"I hate snakes," he muttered as he leaned against the door. "Hand me a broom, will you? I want to wedge this door shut."

Charlotte handed him a mop instead. "Well, now what do we do?"

Matt took his time wedging the cupboard shut. He wanted to make sure the snake would stay put while he fought the urge to strangle Charlotte.

"What the hell kind of stunt was that?" he asked once the handle was secure. "Do you have any idea what kind of snake that is?"

"Big," Charlotte responded quickly. "With beady little eyes."

"And poisonous."

He was almost satisfied with the way she went white.

"How do you know?"

Matt rubbed a hand over his face. The adrenaline was starting to fade. "I encountered a few of them while I was in 'Nam. They scared me more than the Vietcong." He walked over to the phone.

"How did a snake get here from Vietnam?"

"A good question. I'd like the number of the humane society," he said into the phone. "No, I damn well am not able to look up the number in my directory."

Charlotte looked up from the tuna she was mixing as Matt came in the door.

"Did they take it away?" she asked. Even now her stomach turned when she thought about how close she'd come to reaching for a towel.

"They called the zoo." Matt opened the refrigerator and grabbed a beer. "It turns out our friend is an escapee from there. According to these guys," he said with a jerk of his head in the direction of the garage, "some kids broke into the reptile section early this morning. They opened some of the cages and several snakes got lose. The only one they haven't recovered is an Indian krait."

"Not Vietnamese?"

"Many-banded," Matt corrected before he took a long drink from the bottle. "They're related. Only this one is usually lethal."

"Oh." The shaking of her hands indicated that she realized how close she'd come to being bitten. "So they think the snake made its way up here and hid in the garage?"

"Don't be an idiot." Matt slammed his beer down onto the counter. "Do you really think that snake crossed a freeway and several busy streets, slithered all the way up into the foothills, and then picked your garage out of all the others on this street? And how do you suppose he opened the damn cupboard so he could crawl in?"

"Don't make fun of me," Charlotte whispered. "This isn't a joke—and I don't know anything about snakes."

"You don't have to know much about snakes to realize this one had some help."

Matt watched her swallow several times as she fought tears. God, she'd been so brave when confronted by a snake, but now, forced to admit that someone in her family wanted her dead, she couldn't even talk.

Because he wanted to haul her into his arms and hold her tight against him, he forced himself to be gentle. He pushed back a lock of hair that had fallen over her forehead and cupped her cheek in his palm.

"It's time to face facts," he said quietly. "Someone is trying to kill you. And that someone is most likely a member of your family." He placed a finger over her lips when she would have protested. "Whoever it is tried to shoot you, then bury you under a ton of boxes. When that didn't work, he triggered an electrical fire—and now he's used a poisonous snake."

Charlotte turned her head. "No," she said once she'd shaken free of Matt's hand. "I don't believe you."

"God only knows what else might be booby-trapped around here," Matt continued. "Tommy and I have been trying to keep an eye on you, but this is too much for us. And that's only part of the problem. Whoever the murderer is, he's not a professional. But the odds are in his favor, and pretty soon he's going to be successful. The only thing is that he might get Mrs. Nguyen or Tommy first.''

"Or you?"

Matt shrugged. "Our murderer doesn't seem to care how many people get hurt. The question is, do you believe someone is after you?"

"I don't know." She looked as if she wanted to cry. "I suppose it's possible."

Matt put his arms around her and held on tight. "That's a step in the right direction. There's someone you need to talk to. Will you do it?"

"The police?"

Matt shook his head. If he took this to the police, they'd probably laugh him out of the station. "A private investigator. I called him from the garage and asked him to bring over whatever information he's gathered."

"What kind of information could he possibly get this quickly?"

"He'd better have something. I hired him yesterday."

As Charlotte stared at the array of printouts on the coffee table, Matt sat back on the living room sofa and studied the private investigator. Somewhere in his late fifties, Bob Stone was tall and thin with a carefully trimmed beard and mustache. He looked more like an English professor at some Ivy League university than an ex-cop turned private investigator.

"So most of the information you have so far has come from the computer?" Matt asked.

"We've had the case less than twenty-four hours," the private investigator said in his defense. Absently scratching his beard, he smiled at Charlotte. "If Matt hadn't said it was a matter of life and death, we wouldn't even have moved on it yet.''

''I didn't exaggerate.''

The other man's smile faded. ''No, you didn't. Which makes it all the more important that we put our heads together and come to some sort of conclusions.''

''You're the private investigator.'' Matt removed his glasses and stared at the other man. ''What do you think?''

''What I'd hoped to do with this information is eliminate some suspects. You know, discover someone has several million sitting in the bank and has no motive for murder.'' He glanced at Charlotte. ''Unfortunately, both your uncles, Howard and Walter Rutherford, are in debt up to their eyeballs. They stand to lose houses and other personal assets unless they can make some large payments—and make them fast. Your aunt—'' he picked up a paper and read from it '' '—Rhue Rutherford Amis Wilson Schoenborn Smith,' isn't in such dire straits because her parents left her a trust fund rather than money outright.''

Charlotte nodded. ''They were rather Victorian and hoped to protect their daughters from fortune hunters that way.''

''Although . . .'' Bob shuffled through the papers until he found the one he was looking for. ''She does have a habit of overdrawing at the bank. Whenever that happens, someone always covers for her.''

''That was supposed to be confidential,'' Charlotte complained.

Matt shot her a questioning look.

''I can't very well let my sweet little aunt go to jail, can I? She's never understood the relationship between the amount of money in the bank and how much she can spend."

"How often do you bail her out?"

Charlotte crossed her arms and stared at Matt. He didn't seem to understand that you weren't supposed to discuss family secrets in front of strangers.

Bob studied the paper in his hand. "At least once a month. Sometimes more."

"Wonderful." Charlotte rolled her eyes toward the ceiling. "Pretty soon you'll be discussing her sexual habits."

"I don't know about those," Bob assured her, "yet. But she does make a habit of picking the wrong husband. This guy she's engaged to now...Carver Cunningham...is probably the worst. He's a professional gambler—and not very good at it, judging by the information I've compiled."

"I think you've made a mistake," Charlotte said.

"He certainly doesn't seem like a gambler." Matt put his glasses back on and studied Bob's printout. "I think I'd find another profession if I was this bad at something."

"Actually, he owns a little import-export business," Charlotte explained.

Bob shook his head. "Not according to his tax records. It's been my experience that people are more honest with the IRS than with their hairdresser or bartender. The point is, your uncles and aunt all have a financial motive for wanting you dead."

Matt tossed the paper back onto the table. "Now what?"

"I've got to talk to Aunt Rhue," Charlotte said, but both men ignored her.

"Grunt work. We check alibis and opportunity. See if we can find a record of any cash withdrawals that might have been used to hire a hit man. All the basics. It takes time, Matt. Meanwhile, either you keep your wife out of trouble or we put men on her."

"I'm a lot more worried about Aunt Rhue than this murder conspiracy you've dreamed up. And I'd appreciate it if you two didn't talk about me as if I wasn't here."

"What do you suggest?" Matt asked the other man.

"That you two hide out until we discover who's behind this."

Matt nodded. "Sounds reasonable."

Charlotte looked from one man to the other. "Excuse me, gentlemen, but it's my life. Don't you think you should consult me?"

"Do you have any suggestions as to where?" Matt asked.

"I have a cabin at Mammoth Lake you can use. The fishing's good, too," Bob replied.

Charlotte sighed. "I don't like to fish."

"There's also a little place down in Cabo San Lucas where I've sent people under similar circumstances. Great fishing down there, too. Do you speak any Spanish?" he asked Matt.

"Enough to get by."

"I happen to be fluent in French and German," Charlotte said to no one in particular. "But I have no intention of hiding out in France or Germany."

"Actually, you don't have to go far. You could stay at any hotel in L.A. as long as you register under a false name, don't tell anyone where you are, don't go out, and don't make any phone calls that can be traced."

Matt shook his head. "Charlotte wouldn't last four hours under those conditions."

"I wouldn't last two hours like that—unless I was comatose, of course," she put in.

"Then it's either Mammoth or Cabo," Matt murmured.

"I'm not going anywhere," Charlotte told them. "Except to talk to Aunt Rhue."

Matt's gaze locked on hers. "We'll settle things with Rhue once we've tracked down whoever wants to murder you. Got that?"

"Mammoth," Bob decided. "That way there are no plane tickets to trace."

Placing two fingers in her mouth, Charlotte gave a shrill whistle she usually reserved for three-point plays at Lakers games. "I am not going anywhere," she said slowly and distinctly once she had their attention. "This is my home and I won't let anyone drive me out of it or make me afraid to live in it." She looked from one man to the other. "However, I will promise not to talk to Aunt Rhue right now."

"That's reasonable," Bob commented.

"Only because I see no reason to upset her until I've seen some corroborative evidence," Charlotte hastened to explain. "Now, if you'll excuse me, I'm going to take a shower. You may plot and plan as long as you want, but if you expect to move me out of my house, you'll have to do it with me kicking and screaming. Is that plain?"

She didn't wait for an answer, but glided out the door and up the stairs.

Charlotte woke up on Monday morning suffering from the same headache she'd gone to bed with. She'd expected all the tears she'd shed during the night to wash away the pain, but she'd been wrong about that, just like she'd been wrong about the reason Matt had spent so much time with her. She wasn't sure which was worse—the fear that one of her relatives wanted to kill her, or the knowledge that Matt had only spent time with her out of a warped sense of responsibility.

If she wasn't convinced that running away was the worst form of cowardice, she would drive to the airport and take the next departing plane. The only thing that kept her from doing that was the knowledge that one's problems had a habit of hopping into the suitcase and going along for the ride. No matter where she went, she'd still wonder if someone she loved could actually want her dead. And no matter where she traveled, she'd still love Matt. And he wouldn't love her.

Stepping into a hot shower, she decided that if this went on much longer, she'd be declared insane and negate the whole problem. One minute she was convinced that Matt was right, that someone was trying to kill her; the next minute she decided that was the craziest idea she'd ever heard. When, she wondered, had her life gone from simple to overwhelming?

"You're not going to work with me," she told Matt a half hour later when she found him standing in the kitchen doorway.

"No?"

"No," she informed him. "I will have you forcibly removed if necessary."

Matt decided he'd finally crossed the fine line into insanity when a threat like that could make him smile. It was the first sign of life he'd seen in Charlotte since Bob Stone had left the day before, and he was willing to slay dragons or fight entire armies, let alone brave the California penal system, if it could restore Charlotte's usual enthusiasm for life.

"I'm going to drive you to work and pick you up. Be ready to come home at four," Matt informed her.

"I don't get off until five."

"You do today."

"Mind telling me why?"

"For one thing, you're the boss."

She slanted him as exasperated look. "The boss should set a good example."

"Also tonight is the Russell and Winslow black-tie dinner."

She was instantly contrite. "Oh, Matt, I'd forgotten."

"You're not planning to go back on our agreement, I hope. I suffered through your family party, the least you can do is make an appearance tonight."

"I never go back on my word. But honestly, that's all the more reason I should drive myself. You'll have to leave work by three to pick me up, and I need to stop by the dry cleaners to pick up my dress."

"No problem."

"Be reasonable, will you? It will be much more efficient if I drive myself."

"I'm being extremely reasonable. You're the one refusing to understand the situation. If I don't drive you to work, you're not stepping foot outside this house."

Charlotte crossed her arms and stared at him. "Is that so?"

Matt did the same. "Yes, it is."

"I can live with that," Charlotte decided after a minute. "Let's go."

Matt continued to stand in her way. "As soon as you give me the keys."

"I'm perfectly capable of driving."

"I'm sure you are, but my nerves are already frayed enough without being subjected to one of your kamikaze rides through L.A." He held out his hand. "Give me the keys."

She slapped them into his palm. Infuriating man! But it wasn't worth standing here and arguing. In silence they walked to the car, and in silence he started the engine. He'd eased the car into drive and started down the long driveway before she spoke.

"You realize, of course, that I'm still not convinced someone is trying to kill me."

Matt slapped on the brakes hard enough to make her jaw snap. The look he gave her was incredulous.

"You think that snake just dropped by for a visit?"

"It could have been sheer coincidence."

"And your juicer, no doubt, was defective?"

"Don't be ridiculous. It's too old to be defective. It was just worn-out."

"And those boxes just happened to fall on you?"

"Industrial accidents happen every day of the year."

"And someone picked you out at random to use for target practice?"

"Have you read the statistics on violence recently?"

"You're certifiable," he decided, and stepped on the gas with more pressure than usual.

When Matt failed to slow down and check the traffic before pulling out onto the street, Charlotte decided he was truly angry. But she understood anger, so even the curse he muttered under his breath didn't alarm her. It wasn't until he ran the stop sign that she suspected something was wrong.

"What are you doing?" she screamed when he narrowly missed a car and took out two trash cans.

"No brakes," he shouted.

She watched as he fought for control of the car on the winding foothill road before finally aiming it toward the neighbor's yard. With his right hand he pushed her face down onto her knees just before the car bumped and swerved over the lawn. She still had her head down when she heard the tremendous splash and felt the car come to a sudden, floating stop.

Charlotte opened her eyes and looked at Matt when he shouted her name. There was blood on his temple and his tie was askew, but otherwise he looked calm.

"My God, we're in Mr. Morris's pool," Charlotte murmured. "He'll kill me."

"He's going to have to stand in line."

That was when she noticed that her feet were wet. She reached for the door but Matt stopped her.

"Not yet." He kept a hold on her hand with one of his and reached over to unfasten her seat belt.

"We're sinking."

It was the only time he'd ever heard true terror in her voice.

"We're in the deep end." Ten feet, it said on the side of the pool. "So we have to wait until the car settles to the bottom. Are you listening?" he demanded with a shake of her arm.

"Yes."

"If we open one of the doors now, water is going to pour in and the car will tilt over on its side."

Through the shattered windshield, he could see that the water was already over the hood. Soon it would come pouring in where the power windows were partially rolled down. He had to talk fast.

"Don't even touch the handle until I tell you to. We have to wait for the water pressure to equalize enough that we can open the door. When I give the word, push as hard as you can. Once you're clear of the car, you'll float to the top."

Water was starting to rush in through the windows. He unfastened his own seat belt and waited until the water was chest-high before shouting, "Now." He took a deep breath and made sure Charlotte's door was open before he pushed on his.

He broke the surface of the water looking for Charlotte, but she wasn't there. He called her name before looking down to see her suspended in the door of the car. Dragging another breath into his lungs, he dove across the car toward her thrashing figure.

She was struggling, and it wasn't until he was beside her that he realized her skirt was caught in the door. Hooking his foot under the edge of the car to keep from floating to the surface, he grabbed the heavy water-soaked material in both hands and yanked. As soon as the material gave way, Charlotte shot upward. He followed her up, surfacing just behind her. Grabbing her around the waist, he kicked toward the side of the pool where a crowd had gathered and handed her up to waiting hands.

Charlotte was coughing by the time he dragged himself out of the pool and collapsed on the warm concrete beside her. He'd never heard a more beautiful sound.

"You've got to quit doing this to me," Matt told Charlotte as they lay there looking at each other.

Charlotte coughed again. "Doing what?"

"Scaring me half to death."

"You were scared?" she asked with a laugh that started her coughing again. "I wasn't. I knew you'd come get me."

Matt pushed himself up on his elbow and looked down at her. Her dark hair was plastered to her face and her makeup was running. Even the cleaners wouldn't be able to save her dress. He decided she'd never looked more gorgeous. He would have told her so if she hadn't started coughing again.

From across the lawn, Matt heard Mr. Morris cursing and shouting. He could tell right away that the man wasn't going to be a good sport about this.

"It wasn't an accident, was it?" Charlotte asked through chattering teeth.

Matt shook his head. From somewhere in the crowd, a woman materialized with a blanket. Matt wrapped it around Charlotte. Mr. Morris's shouting was getting closer.

"Take me home," Charlotte pleaded. "I want to go home."

Matt stood and swept her up into his arms. Despite the sun and the blanket, she was shivering. Matt turned toward home only to find his way blocked by the angry owner of the pool.

"Where do you think you're going?" he demanded.

"Home," was Matt's succinct reply.

"Look at my yard...my fence...my pool. Who's going to pay for the damages?"

"I'll call our insurance company from home. They'll be over this afternoon."

"Insurance companies," the man said. "Ha! I'll be lucky if they pay seventy cents on the dollar."

"Don't worry," Matt assured him. "Someone will pay." Yes, indeed, someone would pay. Maybe even in blood when Matt got ahold of him.

The man suddenly seemed to focus on Charlotte. "She's been driving crazy since she was sixteen. This was bound to happen sooner or later. I called the police. They're gonna take your license," the man threatened.

If he hadn't been carrying Charlotte, Matt would have hauled the man up by his collar.

"I was driving," he informed the man. "So you tell the police to look me up. Now get out of my way."

Something in the way Matt said it must have penetrated the man's anger, because he stepped aside and let them pass. Tommy was just running across the street as Matt reached the flattened gate.

"What happened?"

When Charlotte's shivering increased, Matt decided this was no time for long explanations. "Someone tampered with the brakes. Tell the police to check them. Can you do that?"

"Sure thing."

Matt only nodded before starting across the street, but he knew that he'd left things in good hands.

Charlotte was standing by the window, looking out over her own backyard when Matt entered her bedroom.

"Have the police left?" she asked without looking at him.

Matt stuffed his hands into the pockets of his khaki pants so that he wouldn't take her in his arms. It seemed now that he couldn't be anywhere near her without wanting to hold her.

"Finally," he said with a sigh. "Though they warned me there'd be more questions later."

"Later. I can take them later. But right now I don't think I could answer one more question."

Closing her eyes, Charlotte leaned her forehead on the window. Matt was glad to see some color back in her cheeks, though he wondered how much of it might be a reflection of the vibrant floor-length kimono she wore.

Still standing in the doorway, Matt surveyed the room. It was done all in white: whitewashed walls, white plantation shutters, white carpet, white mosquito netting draped artfully around her bed. Even the wicker furniture had white upholstery. It wasn't what he would have expected

Charlotte's bedroom to be like. The one spot of color was Charlotte in her robe of vivid pinks and purples. She was like the first splash of paint on a clean canvas.

She opened her eyes and turned to look at Matt. "I still have trouble believing any of my relatives could be trying to kill me."

"The police didn't have any trouble with it."

"Their line of work makes them cynical."

"Cynicism didn't cut the brake lines."

She closed her eyes again, and for a moment Matt thought she'd gone to sleep on her feet. "Are they still angry that we didn't call them when we first suspected something?"

"They'll get over it. Besides, they would have thought we were crazy."

"I feel that way now. Like I'm caught in some sort of nightmare." Straightening, she turned to face him. "For a few minutes, everything will seem normal. Then all of a sudden it'll hit me. Someone I love is trying to kill me. I'm so tired."

"You've had a shock," Matt said. But it wasn't the shock to the body that bothered him. It was the shock to her spirit. "Why don't you take a nap?"

"I think I will."

Nodding, Matt turned to leave.

"Matt," she said softly. "I'm sorry."

"For what?"

"For doubting you. For refusing to face facts. For endangering your life through my stupidity."

He was across the floor and had his hands on her shoulders so quickly that she didn't have time to step back.

"Don't apologize for being the trusting, warmhearted person you are." He gave her shoulders a little shake. "Don't ever apologize for your generous spirit. I'm the one at fault. I knew someone was after you, yet I didn't stop him."

"There you go again, trying to accept responsibility for my mistakes. I've told you before that you can't do that."

"Shut up," he murmured as he gave in to need and hauled her into his embrace. "Just shut up for a minute and let me hold you." It felt wonderful to have her in his arms. It was heaven having her soft body pressed to his. "Do you have any idea what it was like for me to see you at the bottom of that pool?"

"No," Charlotte whispered. She felt his lips brush the crown of her head and snuggled closer to him.

Matt took a deep, shuddering breath. "I don't want to talk about it."

Still secure in his embrace, Charlotte smiled. "You're the one who brought it up." It was easier to see the humor when she was in his arms.

"Do you know what I was thinking as we went into that pool?"

"I don't know about you, but I kept imagining the headlines. 'Man, Woman and Car Drown in Pool. Pictures on A5.'"

He tightened his embrace. "Don't make jokes."

"Okay," she agreed. She could hear the anger in his voice—and the fear. Because he kept his emotions bottled up inside too often, she asked, "What were you thinking?"

"That we were going to die and be buried as husband and wife without my ever having made love to you."

Chapter Thirteen

She struggled out of his embrace so that she could look into his eyes. He was serious. Dead serious.

She smiled. "It occurred to me, too."

"Now why does that make you smile?"

"Because I'd always thought my life was supposed to flash in front of me. Instead, all I could think of was what I hadn't done."

"Let me assure you that before the sun sets tonight, we will have done it all," he promised. "Or died trying."

Cupping her face in his hands, he angled her head so that his mouth could plunder hers. His kiss was hungry and urgent. He'd intended to be gentle, but her taste drove him wild, and her sweet moan made it impossible for him to remember anything but his deep, abiding hunger for her. Then his hands were in her hair, holding her still so that he could kiss her eyelids and her temple, so that he could trace the curve of her ear with his tongue and trail kisses down her throat.

When his teeth nipped the lobe of her ear, Charlotte forgot to breathe. When his mouth toyed with the place, where her pulse raced at the base of her neck, her bones turned to water. When his lips played along the swell of her breasts, she lost the ability to think rationally. There was only feeling and emotion. There was only Matt and the world of sensations he created—and a happiness she had never experienced before. She stepped closer to him, bringing her body against his, reveling in the way her soft curves accepted the hard planes and muscles of his.

Matt heard her laugh—it was a low, sensuous sound unlike anything he'd heard before. It told him, as nothing else could, that he was giving pleasure as well as receiving it. For the first time, it was more important to give than take. His hand slid down her spine, pulling her closer. Like the sky meeting the earth, she filled all the empty places within him. Empty spaces he had never acknowledged and now would never need to. How could he have known she would heal the scars when he hadn't realized he still carried them?

"I need you," he whispered as his lips sought hers again.

Charlotte wanted to tell him that she was his. Had been his for so long, but his mouth took hers and she was unable to say the words. Instead her hands slipped under his shirt to explore the heat and texture of his skin, to revel in the ripple of muscles and the broad sweep of his back. There was power here—and enduring peace. And madness, Charlotte realized when his hand cupped her breast. A madness that drove her to respond when she thought he had already touched the depth of her soul. A madness that had her frustrated with the cloth that kept her body from touching his.

He was impatient with the silk. It wasn't as warm or rich as her skin. With trembling fingers, he pushed the robe off one shoulder then the other, but it didn't slide to the floor as he'd expected. Instead it bared just enough skin to tantalize. He kissed her shoulder, nipped at her neck and nuzzled both the softness and the beaded center of her breast through the silk until all his patience had fled. Sweeping her into his arms, he carried her to the bed and laid her upon it. He pulled his shirt over his head and kicked off his shoes. The vivid colors of her kimono contrasted with the pristine white of the coverlet until, with a single motion, he untied the sash and pushed aside the splash of color.

Her skin was golden where the sun had kissed it, creamy white where the sun had been denied. He longed to taste the ivory sweetness. His hand cupped one breast, then the other. They were full and heavy, and the pouting nipples begged for his kiss. He eased down beside her on the bed and his lips replaced his hands. With tenderness he loved the dusky buds as his hands moved lower—exploring, delighting, demanding—until Charlotte could only call his name.

She moaned when he moved away from her. Whimpered when his mouth quit teasing and when his clever hands left off the magic they were working. She could barely open her eyes to watch him remove the last of his clothing, then he was with her again—his lips whispering words of passion and desire, his hands driving her beyond thought, his body mating with hers in a dance as ancient as the earth and as mysterious as spring.

She abandoned herself to the sensations, until she thought she would fly into a million pieces. She had forgotten that nerve endings could sing, that body and soul could become one, until the shuddering release of the flesh compelled the soul to take flight and the sweet languor that came after engendered a rapturous peace.

No, she hadn't forgotten these things, she realized as Matt kissed her with incredible tenderness. She had never experienced them. Never even known they were possible until Matt had shown her. Smiling, she clung to him as he rolled onto his back. With Matt, she would have it all. Nestling her head on his shoulder, she fell asleep.

It was late afternoon when she woke. The shutters had been turned to filter out the strong western sun and the sheet had been pulled up over her. She smiled, hugging to herself the knowledge that she had been changed in some elemental way. It wasn't anything she could put into words without sounding as if she were spouting bad poetry, but she knew how to share the knowledge.

She turned, ready to wake Matt with soft touches and hungry kisses, but the place where he had lain was empty. Still warm, she discovered when she touched the pillow, but empty nonetheless.

It was foolish to be hurt. He hadn't promised to stay with her, and she hadn't thought to ask for promises. No regrets, she told herself. She hadn't wanted Matt to have them and she wouldn't allow them in herself. If the moments they had shared were the only ones she was to have, they would be all the more precious. But, oh, she wanted more. She lay back on her pillow and acknowledged that love had made her greedy: she wanted forever. She was fighting tears when she heard the door open.

"Matt?" She turned to see who it was.

"Who else would be sneaking into your room at this hour of the afternoon?" Wearing jeans and a sweater, he came over to sit on the edge of the bed. The kiss he gave her swept away any thought of tears. "I'm glad you're not up yet."

She smiled up at him. "Oh? Why is that?"

"Because beautiful women who have barely escaped drowning need all the rest they can get."

"That sounds vaguely sexist."

"Never let it be said that I don't support equal rights." He kissed her again then pulled the sweater off over his head. "I woke up wanting you," he whispered.

"Why didn't you wake me?"

"I had to run an errand." He stood and pulled several foil packets from his pocket and dropped them onto the nightstand. "You aren't on the pill, are you?"

She didn't say anything, just looked up at him.

He sighed. "I didn't think so. Look, I'm sorry about earlier. I usually take my responsibilities more seriously than that. I, uh . . ." He raked a hand through his hair. "I guess I could blame it on the accident and the adrenaline and all, but the truth is that when I'm around you, I forget things."

That made her smile. "You make me sound like a walking case of amnesia."

"Amnesia isn't contagious." He flashed her an endearing smile. "You also make me tongue-tied."

"Why don't you quit talking, then." She flipped back the cover. "And let's see if bed rest will help that condition."

The room was in shadows when Charlotte reluctantly eased out of bed at five o'clock. The black-tie dinner wasn't until seven-thirty, so Matt could afford to sleep a little longer. She, however, needed to send Mrs. Nguyen to the cleaners to pick up her dress. If the housekeeper hurried, she might be back before Charlotte finished her shower. She found Mrs. Nguyen cleaning out the refrigerator.

"About time you got up. You're going to sleep your life away."

Charlotte tried not to smile. "I have it on good authority that a person should stay in bed when she's narrowly escaped death."

The housekeeper tossed some leftover chicken into the trash. "Humph. Who said a foolish thing like that?"

"Never mind," Charlotte said with a laugh. She was in too good a mood to be drawn into an argument with Mrs. Nguyen. "Will you pick up my dress at the dry cleaners? I need it tonight."

"Shouldn't wait till the last minute."

"I know. I should always pick it up twenty-four hours early," Charlotte dutifully repeated what the older woman had been saying for years. "But I didn't."

What looked like a full container of lunch meat hit the trash. "Humph. What dress is it?"

"Is there any cheese in there? I'm starving."

"No cheese."

"How about some peanut butter and crackers?"

Mrs. Nguyen set the jar on the counter and Charlotte went to the pantry for crackers.

"What dress do you want me to pick up?"

"My black one with the crisscross straps in the back." She stopped long enough to get a knife out of the drawer and a glass from the overhead cupboard. "Want to pass me the milk? Thanks."

"It's not at the cleaners."

"Sure it is," Charlotte said as she spread the peanut butter. "I took it in myself two days ago. The one with the beadwork on the sleeves."

"I know where that dress is," the older woman told her emphatically. "It's hanging in the guest room because I didn't want to wake an almost-drowned person from her nap. Mr. Oliver picked it up this afternoon when he went out on errands. Other things are going on around this house that I don't know about, but I know where the dress is."

Charlotte popped the last cracker into her mouth. It was time to head upstairs for a shower, but she knew from experience that it was best to take a few extra minutes to find out what was bothering her housekeeper.

"What things are going on that you don't know about?"

"Humph." She paused long enough to throw out a loaf of bread. "If I knew what was going on, then I would know what it's about."

Charlotte tried not to smile. "Quit throwing away perfectly good food and tell me what's wrong."

"Fire in the kitchen. Snake in the garage. Car in the neighbor's pool. That's what's going on. Can you explain those things to me?"

"Accidents," Charlotte said as quickly as she could.

The police had suggested that the fewer people who knew what was going on, the better. Charlotte felt that was especially true for Mrs. Nguyen, since she was likely to go out and buy a gun if she thought someone was trying to kill Charlotte—and that would be more dangerous than all the fires and snakes and bad brakes put together.

"Everything is going to be fine," she told the older woman. "I promise."

"You're smiling," Mrs. Nguyen said.

"I know."

The older woman smiled, too. "You should take more naps. There is still lots of time before the party. I heard that almost-drowned people should stay in bed a long time."

"Charlotte certainly is on her best behavior," Alice Kelsey told Matt.

The two attorneys were standing close to the dais in one of the smaller ballrooms of a landmark Beverly Hills hotel. Across the room, Charlotte was working her way from group to group with the expertise of a politician at election time.

"I heard there was an interesting development in the Gilbert case today," Alice continued, never taking her eyes off Charlotte.

"A matter of the second wife having married before— and neglecting to get a divorce. It will nullify Ron's last will."

"Why does that make you happy?"

"I like to see justice triumph once in a while."

"You're such an idealist." Alice was still watching Charlotte. "And you've married the ideal woman. She's being absolutely charming. What did you say to her?"

"I didn't say a thing." He snagged a glass of champagne from a passing waiter and resisted the urge to run his finger inside the stiff collar of his shirt. God, he hated these penguin suits. "She happens to possess a great deal of natural charm. I think it's safe to say that you haven't seen her under the best circumstances before tonight."

"That's true. Why Claude, how nice to see you," she said to one of the partners. "You remember Matt Oliver, don't you?"

Matt shook the older man's hand and said all the appropriate things, but his eyes kept straying to where his wife stood across the room. He hadn't realized that the back of her dress was so...backless. And she had used that shimmery powder again. He was certain every man in the room knew it, too. Even Mr. Russell and Mr. Winslow.

"And it's nice to see that you're being charming this evening, as well," Alice said once Claude had moved on to the next group of people.

"I'm always charming." Matt liked the way Charlotte's skirt swayed as she walked. And she was wearing those black high heels he'd seen in her room last week. They were even sexier than he'd imagined.

"Ha! You've been an absolute bear all week. If you had growled at one more secretary or glared at one more law clerk, I was going to sit you down and have a nice, long chat."

"I wasn't that bad." He dragged his gaze away from his wife and looked at Alice. "Was I?"

Alice rolled her eyes. "You were worse than that. Anyway, I'm glad to see that you and your wife have ironed out whatever problems you had. In fact, the whole office will be grateful."

"Anything for office morale," he murmured as his eyes sought Charlotte. "Any other advice you want to give me?" he asked as the band began to play.

"Make a point to dance with Mrs. Russell. Don't ask Mrs. Winslow to dance but be sure to compliment her on the dinner."

"Is that it?"

Alice smiled at him. "Try not to ogle your wife all evening."

"Since when is it bad form to ogle my own wife?"

"Not bad form, actually. You're just making all the other husbands look bad by comparison."

"Fine. Instead of ogling Charlotte, I think I'll go dance with her."

Depositing his glass on a table, Matt walked up behind his wife. Knowing that twenty-four hours ago the sight of her bare back would have driven him crazy, Matt took great pleasure in placing a kiss on her shoulder. He wasn't prepared for the effect her smile had on him. While he puzzled over that, he also admitted that her back was still driving him crazy. Only now, he knew that crazy was exactly what he wanted to be—as long as she'd be crazy with him.

"Gentlemen," he said to the four men gathered around her. "I hope you'll excuse us. I want to dance with my wife."

Charlotte laughed as he led her out onto the dance floor. It was a slow dance and she went willingly into his arms.

"Do you think you might have been a tad abrupt with those men?" Charlotte asked.

"Not at all. I have it on good authority that I'm charming tonight."

"Oh? Who told you that?"

He kissed her just below the ear and felt her shiver. "Alice. She also says you're charming."

"Just following instructions."

"Instructions? Whose instructions?"

"Alice's. She cornered me first thing and said she didn't have time to tell me who was important and who wasn't, so I should charm everyone."

"Oh, Lord."

"So I've been busily charming the pants off everyone."

"In that case, I demand that you cease and desist immediately."

She leaned back to look at him. "Why is that?"

"Because the only person you should charm the pants off is me."

"Don't worry. I have every intention of doing that as soon as we get home."

Matt stopped dancing and, still holding her hand, headed for the exit.

"Where are you going?"

"Home."

Charlotte laughed as she trotted along behind him. "Don't be ridiculous. There are still several people I haven't had a chance to charm."

"You've already hit the important ones."

"Mr. Russell and Mr. Winslow? How did you know?"

Matt stopped by the table long enough to pick up Charlotte's evening bag and drape her mink over her shoulders.

"They both made a point of telling me how lucky I am."

"Why would they do that?"

"Probably because neither one is so old or so happily married that he doesn't wish you'd at least try to charm the pants off him."

"I'm not getting out of bed today," Charlotte informed her husband when the alarm rang the next morning. "You can flush that clock down the toilet on your way to work."

"No, I can't." Matt reached over to shut off the alarm. "Because I'm not going to work, either."

Charlotte burrowed further into his arms. "That's ridiculous. I can do it because I'm the boss. What makes you think you can get away with it?"

Matt loved the way she snuggled up against him. Her breast was peeking out from under the cover, and her leg, which was nestled between his, was rubbing intimately against him. It would almost be worth losing his job over.

"It just so happens that both of the senior partners urged me to take time off for a honeymoon whenever I want." His hand came up to caress her breast. "And it just so happens that I want it right now."

"In a big way, if I'm any judge."

"Stop that," he told her as he brought her hand out from under the covers. "Before you have your wicked way with me, we've got to call our offices."

Charlotte raised up on one elbow. "You're serious about this?"

"Absolutely. I think everyone's entitled to a week's honeymoon."

"You call first. But I warn you I'm not going to Mammoth Lake or Cabo San Lucas."

He smiled. "Believe me, fishing is the last thing I have on my mind."

Three days later Matt woke without the aid of the alarm clock. Charlotte hadn't let him set it since Tuesday morning. Alarm clocks, she'd informed him loftily, had no place on a honeymoon; he had happily bowed to her superior knowledge. He only wished it was as simple to banish her worries.

There were shadows beneath her eyes now. She wasn't sleeping well, though she tried to hide the fact from him, and she wasn't eating well, though she tried to hide that from Mrs. N.

There hadn't been another attempt on her life, and for that Matt was grateful, but the police weren't any closer to an arrest, either. Their honeymoon was almost over; come Monday morning he and Charlotte would go off to their respective jobs, and she would be vulnerable once again. If Matt was certain of anything in this world, it was that the murderer was just biding his time.

Matt placed a gentle kiss on her brow. Only the smudges under her eyes kept him from waking her with hungry kisses. The three empty foil packets on the nightstand were mute proof that he'd selfishly awakened her during the night, and each time he'd been stunned that she'd come so willingly into his arms. This morning he'd have to settle for a cold shower.

Easing out of bed, he swept the foil packets into the trash. He wouldn't feel guilty about his needs, because those were the moments when the shadows were truly lifted from Charlotte's eyes. Only when they were engaged in the mind-numbing passion that still astounded him did she truly forget that someone she cared about wanted her dead. At first he'd told himself that was all he could do. And at first he'd been content to believe it.

But each time he took her—each time she gave so generously of her body and her sweetness—the connection between them became more intense, so that now he could feel both her fear and her despair. It would be a hard truth for anyone to accept, but for Charlotte, with her generous spirit and her inbred loyalty, it was even worse. And Matt knew that even though the traitor had failed four times, he was killing something vital inside her.

Charlotte was lying on her side, watching the door, when Matt came out. She'd awakened alone, but the sound of the shower had assured her she wasn't abandoned.

"Good morning," she said, and enjoyed the way his mouth curved into a smile. She'd almost learned to expect this heady feeling in the morning—the way her heart skipped a beat when he smiled, as well as her certainty that he looked more handsome in the morning when they'd made love the night before.

"You'd better hurry up if you expect to get downstairs before noon." He kissed her, then because one was never enough, she hooked her hands behind his neck and pulled his lips to hers again. "Of course, I've grown rather fond of Mrs. Nguyen's lecture on 'sleeping my life away,'" he said.

"Beast," she accused with a laugh. But she slipped into her robe and headed for the bathroom. She was almost to the door when she turned back around. "I was thinking while you were in the shower."

"Uh-oh."

"I've decided that lying around for a week has let your mind go to seed."

"What about my body?"

She looked down in time to see the bulge form in his pants. "Your body's in great shape," she said, and savored his laughter. "Since a mind is a terrible thing to waste, I'm going to let you help me make out a will this afternoon. I want to be sure that my things go to someone who'll take care of them."

Matt fumbled with the button on his shirt. "I'll call and make an appointment for you with Alice."

"Okay. But I want to do one in my own handwriting this afternoon."

"A holographic will?"

Charlotte nodded. "Will you help me?"

Matt gave what he hoped was a nonchalant shrug. "Of course."

But the minute the bathroom door was closed, he began to pace. That did it, he decided. He wasn't going to stand around while Charlotte made preparations to be killed.

It didn't matter that he'd tried for the past eighteen months to get her to make out a will. It was standard operating procedure to encourage anyone who came into a large inheritance to make provision for their own death.

Charlotte had resisted the entire time, saying she didn't intend to die right away.

Her refusal to be reasonable had infuriated him, but now, because someone was trying to kill her, she'd been forced to accept her own mortality. Well, he didn't want her to. He wanted her to keep that same indomitable spirit and verve for life. He wanted her to keep believing she was immortal. If that was irrational, then so be it.

Grabbing up the phone, he punched in the numbers for Bob Stone's office. Luckily the investigator was in.

"Have you got any new information?" Matt demanded immediately.

He heard Bob sigh. "No. And as far as I can tell, the police are at a standstill, too. The only thing we can do is wait for the murderer to make another move."

"Like hell we'll wait."

"I rather thought you'd feel that way, but I don't know what else to do."

"I have a plan."

"Matt, you've lost your objectivity."

"It's not just a good plan," Matt assured the private investigator. "It's a great one."

"I don't think you're in any position to judge. The minute a man falls in love, he loses the ability to think rationally."

Love? Had he fallen in love? he wondered. Aloud he said, "What about women?"

"They never had that ability."

Charlotte would call that blatantly sexist, but this was not the time to discuss Bob's chauvinistic tendencies. "Will you help me?"

"The police aren't going to like this."

"How do you know? You haven't even heard it yet."

Bob sighed. "I'm listening."

Chapter Fourteen

It was late Sunday when Matt pulled into the parking lot of the cheap hotel in the seediest part of Hollywood. A beat-up van with Miguel's Tortillas scrawled on the side was parked across the street. Bob Stone was inside with enough recording equipment to set up his own studio, and Matt was wearing a microphone that would enable the private investigator to record everything that Howie said.

So Uncle Howie was the one. Matt had suspected him all along...and yet, there'd been that threat he'd made the night of the Rutherford party. The one about Matt taking care of Charlotte or Howie would make him regret it. Something about it had rung true at the time.

The worst part was going to be telling Charlotte. Not just telling her but presenting her with the proof. He hoped she wouldn't hate him for what he was about to do. For what he'd done.

Matt had set up the Rutherford clan. While Charlotte kept an appointment with Alice on Friday, Matt had called all three of the Rutherford siblings. He'd accused each one of the murder attempts. They'd all denied it, of course, but he'd been adamant. He'd let each of them know he was aware of his or her financial difficulties. Then he'd offered each one the deal. If the murderer would let Charlotte live the six months necessary for Matt to inherit his wife's estate, then Matt would not only help arrange an "accidental" death for his wife, he'd split his inheritance with that person. As Matt had pointed out, half of everything was worth a lot more than one third of RP.

Then he'd sat back and waited for one of them to get back to him. It had taken Howie less than twenty-four hours to set up the meeting.

As Matt got out of the car and locked the door, he decided Howie had picked the perfect spot. It was easy to envision dirty deals being transacted in any one of the rooms here, though Howie had specified Room 35 at the back of the hotel. Matt hoped the car phone would still be in his Jaguar when the meeting was over. Hell, he hoped the car would still be here.

This was the part Matt was looking forward to. Once Howie had recorded his perfidy for the police to hear, Matt was going to get a little revenge. Bob had warned him that taking a bloodied pulp into the police station would cast doubts upon the confession, but Matt knew there were places on the body that could be hurt without leaving telltale signs. And he knew Howie Rutherford was soft enough that it wouldn't take long to make him regret what he'd done to his niece.

The part he dreaded was telling Charlotte. He'd left her sleeping peacefully after another morning of loving. The truth would hurt her, but the fact that she'd be safe again made it all worthwhile.

He guessed that he finally understood love. There'd been little enough of it in his life before Charlotte, but now he knew it meant doing what was best for a person even though you'd suffer. And there was no doubt that he'd suffer, because even Charlotte, with her generous spirit and forgiving heart, would hate him for what he was about to do. She'd begged him once before not to make her choose between him and her family. Now he was going to force her to take a stand.

Afterward, he would return to his place in Santa Monica, and they'd go through the motions of getting a divorce. He'd never hold her or laugh with her or make love to her again. But at least she'd be safe. And that would have to be enough for him.

Charlotte woke alone in a darkened room. Glancing at the clock, she discovered it was six-thirty already. She flipped on the bedside lamp and found a note from Matt. He'd gone out to run a few errands, the note said, and would be back soon. VASSAR was activated, so she should keep the doors and windows locked. Since there was no time on the note, she had no idea when he'd be home. The postscript said she should stay in bed until he returned. Bossy man!

Tossing the note aside, she went into the bathroom. The woman in the mirror looked awful, she decided. There were circles under her eyes, her hair looked limp and listless, and there was no energy in her walk. Matt deserved someone with a little more life. As far as that went, she deserved better, too.

An hour later a different woman emerged from the bathroom. Makeup, judiciously applied, had gone a long

way toward covering the circles, and a complete line of
hair-care products had put life back into her hair. Before
that, thirty minutes with a Jane Fonda workout tape had
started her blood pumping again.

Certain Matt would be home any minute, she went
downstairs to see what she could throw together for dinner. The refrigerator was practically empty after Mrs.
Nguyen's vigorous cleaning a few days before, and Charlotte had been reduced to checking the canned goods when
the doorbell rang. She deactivated VASSAR and went to
the door.

"Carver. How nice of you to drop by." Matt had made
her promise not to go out and hunt the man down, but
he'd said nothing about what she could do if the cad
walked willingly into her home.

"I hope you don't mind that I dropped in." Charlotte
saw that his hands were shaking. "I wanted to talk to
you."

"Come into the living room." Charlotte stood aside for
the little man and reminded herself that he had reason to
be nervous. But he had chosen to lie to Rhue, and she
wouldn't feel sorry for him.

Carver looked around. "Are we by any chance alone?"

"For the moment." She closed the front door as Carver
made his way inside. "Matt will be home soon, but we can
talk until then."

"Your housekeeper—is she here? Or her son?"

Carver's gaze swept the room as Charlotte settled on the
arm of the sofa. "They're at a wedding. Her niece's, I
think. There's just you and me...and the robot," she said
when she saw VASSAR's light glowing in the corner of the
room. She tried not to let her impatience show when the
older man turned his back on her to glance into the solar-

ium. "In fact, I'm glad you came by. I've been wanting to talk to you."

"Make it quick," he said as he turned back around. "We don't have much time." The gun he pointed at her made Charlotte realize he was serious.

"What—" She swallowed and tried again. "What are you doing?"

"What I should have done some time ago. Take care of you myself rather than depend on those bungling fools Wampum Willy sent."

"Wampum Willy?"

Carver laughed. It was a nasty sound that had nothing to do with pleasure. "I guess you might call Willy my banker. He's a loan shark," Carver explained when Charlotte said nothing. "I borrowed a great deal of money from him and now he wants it back. With interest."

Charlotte looked from Carver to the gun and back into Carver's beady little eyes again. He reminded her of the snake.

Charlotte suppressed a hysterical laugh that welled up inside her. She had to stay calm—and serious. When a man pointed a gun at you, it was serious business. But it was difficult to think of anything except the fact that her relatives weren't trying to kill her. This horrible little man with the gun wanted her dead, but that wasn't as bad as having someone she loved—someone she'd loved all her life—try to murder her.

"I'm a little confused here, Carver. I...um...if you need to borrow some money, why didn't you just say so?"

"That's cute," he said with a snicker. "Like you're willing to loan me a couple hundred thousand dollars. Yeah," he said when Charlotte felt her eyes go big and round. "That's a little more than you're prepared to offer."

"I'm willing to discuss it," Charlotte told him. And she was. She was also willing to discuss the national debt, the money needed to bail out the country's S and L's, or anything else Carver wanted to talk about. Because, she reasoned, as long as they were talking, he wouldn't be pulling the trigger on that gun.

"You keep that kind of money in the house?"

"No."

"How about jewelry?"

She looked down at her hands; the only jewelry she wore was the plain gold band. "I have some diamond earrings and a necklace. And a tennis bracelet. Altogether, it's probably worth forty or fifty thousand."

"Looks like we're going to have to play it this way then." He motioned toward the back of the house with the gun. "Let's go."

"Where are we going?"

Her question seemed to confuse him. "I don't know. The kitchen, I guess."

Charlotte stood but her legs felt like sponge. She wondered if she was going to be able to walk that far. "You're going to kill me, aren't you?"

The fact that he didn't answer told her she was right. She remembered how she'd resisted making out a will when Matt had asked her to after her father's death. She'd told him she didn't plan to die anytime soon. Matt had been right when he'd said that death was one thing you didn't get to plan. She stopped in the foyer and turned around. Carver looked nervous and almost as scared as she felt.

"If I'm going to die," she said quietly, "I'd at least like to know why."

"Your aunt gave me my walking papers last night, did you know that? No, I can see you didn't. She said we weren't 'suited to each other.' And after all the money I'd spent on her. I bought her pearls and clothes and even took her on a cruise. She was my sure bet.''

"I don't understand," Charlotte said.

"I borrowed the money to court her. I did a good job of it, too. The idea was to marry her, empty her bank accounts, and skip town after paying Willy back. Then I discovered that the old broad wasn't rich. I mean, she gets a decent amount of money each month, but she can't lay her hands on any big amount. Hell, she lives like a queen, but half the time she can't pay all her bills. That's where you come in, isn't it?''

Charlotte swallowed. "I cover whatever she can't pay for.''

"That's what had me fooled. That's why I figured there was money somewhere else. Then your father died and left Rhue a piece of that box company. I told Willy that if we could just hold out until she got her hands on that, I'd be able to pay him back. Then, when I figured things were going to break my way, you got married. So Willy decided that we'd have to kill you. Only Willy hired the biggest bunch of bungling idiots I've ever seen. And you wouldn't die.''

"You were behind the break-in at RP?''

"One of Willy's boys.''

"And the accident with the forklift?''

"Same guy. He was an idiot.''

"The exploding juicer?''

"I didn't like that. Thought it was too chancy. But after one of Willy's men worked me over, I agreed. Then we had to put one of the caterer's men out of commission so Willy's man could take his place. He was supposed to put some kind of plastic explosive in the thing. I still don't know what went wrong.''

"And the snake?''

Carver smiled. "That was my idea. I like snakes. I owned a boa constrictor once."

Charlotte swallowed the bile in her throat. "The brakes?"

"I really thought that one would get you. Get both of you. But it didn't, so I'm going to have to shoot you and make it look like a robbery."

"But I thought you said Rhue had broken off your engagement. What good is killing me going to do?"

"Your death is going to upset her." He smiled. "I mean, really upset her."

"I can think of other ways to upset her," Charlotte suggested. That had to be the ultimate irony—to have survived all those murder attempts and then get herself killed because Carver wanted revenge on her aunt.

"This time I have it all planned out. I can probably find enough stuff in the house to keep Willy off my back. That's the robbery angle. When Rhue learns about your death, I'll go comfort her. She'll be so grief stricken that she'll do whatever I say. We'll get married, I'll sell the box company and split. It'll work out great."

"You know you won't get away with this."

"That's what they always say on TV. In real life lots of guys get away with lots of things."

"But they already know that you don't own an import-export company."

"Who knows?"

"Matt and the private investigator he hired. They'll tell Aunt Rhue. She'll never marry you."

He motioned toward the back of the house with the gun. "I'll take my chances."

Charlotte didn't think her legs would support her much longer. "I'll give you money. Anything you want."

"What are you gonna do? Write me a check?"

Charlotte stumbled and fell into the little table by the stairs. The brass lamp fell off with a loud thud. She'd bent down to pick it up when the lights flickered.

"Leave it," Carver told her, but she already had it in her hand.

It was heavy. Solid brass. But she couldn't throw it as fast as he could shoot a bullet. Still, it was the only weapon she had. She pulled the plug out of the socket and sparks flew from one of those little black thingamajigs on the cord. A low whine came from the living room, then VASSAR rolled around the corner and into the foyer.

Carver took his eyes off Charlotte for just a second. It was all she needed. She hurled the brass lamp and ran for the breakfast room. The lights went out all over the house when Carver screamed. Praying she'd disabled him, she took advantage of the darkened house and ran for the back door. She heard a gunshot as the light fixture exploded in the breakfast room. Charlotte skidded around the corner into the kitchen just as every light in the house lit up. She knew she'd never reach the outside door with the lights on, so she detoured toward the dining room.

"I'll get you for that, you little bitch," Carver screamed. The house went dark.

Charlotte fought the urge to laugh. VASSAR was playing havoc with the lights just as it had done with the sound system at the party, and Tommy had said that loud noises were what confused it. That was something she knew that Carver didn't, just like she knew every nook and cranny in the house. Those were her only two weapons. She hoped they would be enough to keep Carver off guard so that she could escape.

The house was a square with all the rooms on the bottom floor opening onto the center foyer. She was in the dining room at the back of the house; she could even see the front door from where she stood, but she couldn't get to it without running the chance that Carver would see her dash across the black-and-white marble floor. She could easily escape into the backyard, but then she'd lose whatever advantage VASSAR and a darkened house gave her. Her only chance, as she saw it, was to lead Carver all the way around the house until she made her way back to the front door. Once out on the street, she had a chance of running to the neighbors or summoning help from a passing car.

Dropping to her hands and knees, she started to crawl across the dining room using the table as cover. She was halfway there when the phone rang and turned the lights back on. Charlotte let the phone ring one more time, then yanked on the nearby cord. It fell to the floor and was silent, and the house was plunged back into darkness. The sound of Carver in the kitchen had Charlotte rolling under the table. From her position amid the table and chair legs, she watched Carver's two highly polished wing-tip shoes step into the dining room.

With a muttered oath, Matt hung up the car phone. He'd been trying to reach Charlotte ever since the police had allowed him to leave, but the line remained busy. That was good, Matt told himself. That meant she was awake and feeling good enough for a long conversation with a friend. He was already on Los Feliz Boulevard and would be pulling into the driveway in less than five minutes. She'd be fine until then.

He couldn't help smiling over the fiasco he'd been part of this afternoon. He'd been astounded to discover all three of the Rutherfords in that run-down motel room, but he thought he'd recovered rather well. Then he'd pitched his idea to them as Bob had coached him. He'd used vague terms and tried to get them to fill in the details.

The Rutherfords, in turn, had seemed willing to cooperate but unable to finish a sentence. That should have been his big tip-off. Howie hadn't been that subtle in all the time Matt had dealt with him. Finally, too impatient to continue the little cat-and-mouse game, Matt had come right out and said that he was willing to help kill Charlotte if the Rutherfords would wait for six months.

That's when all hell had broken lose. First Howie had taken a swing at him that had missed by less than an inch; one tap on the jaw had taken care of him. Then Walter had come at him with a baseball bat he'd kept hidden under the dilapidated mattress. Matt had almost disarmed the second brother when Rhue ran at him with a hat pin that was at least six inches long. He'd discovered that he couldn't bring himself to hit a woman.

Matt had been grateful when the police broke down the door, at least until they'd read him his rights. That's when he'd discovered the Rutherfords had brought the police. However, as the only reasonable private citizen in the room, albeit the one in handcuffs, Matt had taken it upon himself to explain the situation to the officers. He had been well into the story by the time Bob Stone arrived. The police had not been amused, though they'd all been turned loose after a stern lecture on letting the police handle things. He could hardly wait to tell Charlotte; she'd get a laugh out of it.

Matt sobered when he remembered that the police had been left without suspects for the attempts on Charlotte's life. But that was a problem he'd deal with tomorrow. Right now, he was looking forward to spending the evening at home.

When he turned the corner and got his first look at the house, Matt knew that he wouldn't get his wish tonight. There'd be no quiet evening at home with Charlotte. No shared laughter over his misadventures this afternoon, no slow lovemaking into the early hours of the morning.

As he watched, the house lit up and then went totally dark. It happened again before he turned into the driveway. He passed a group of joggers standing on the corner and Mr. Morris, who was leaning against the new portion of his fence. Matt muttered several vivid oaths. VASSAR was obviously on the loose again.

Turning into the driveway, Matt cut the engine and sat for a moment, dreaming of drop-kicking the robot into the pool and watching it rust. Reluctantly he got out of the car and headed for the kitchen door.

"Charlotte," he called when he stepped into the house. Like magic the lights came on.

"Welcome home," Carver said.

Matt started to smile. Then he saw the gun in the man's hand.

Charlotte was upstairs in the master bedroom when she heard the car pull into the driveway. It wasn't where she intended to be, but Carver had cut her off from the front door and so she'd been forced to go to Plan B.

Admittedly Plan B was a little fuzzier than A, but it had something to do with VASSAR and the remote control in the bedroom. She was working out the details when she heard Matt's car. Before she could get the window open to warn him, Matt was in the house and the lights were back on.

Placing his hands on his head, Matt did as Carver instructed and walked into the dining room. The little man

had the gun jabbed in his back and was only a step behind. Matt might have taken the chance on disarming him
if he'd known what had happened to Charlotte. But not
knowing if she was in the house—or even alive—kept Matt
from making any quick moves.

"What have you done with Charlotte?" he asked once
Carver told him to stop. If something had happened to her
while he was out playing cops and robbers... It didn't bear
thinking about.

"She's in the house."

"Where?"

"That's a very good question. One you're going to help
answer. Call her," Carver instructed.

Matt shook his head. "No."

"Fool."

Charlotte stood quite still and stared at the remote control in her hand. She'd heard just enough of what had been
said to realize that Carver had Matt at gunpoint. The
question was, what could she and VASSAR do to help
Matt escape? She was still puzzling over it when she heard
the gunshot. The house went dark.

"Matt," she screamed. The lights came on before she
reached the bedroom door.

"No," she heard Matt shout.

The house plunged back into darkness and she stopped
in her tracks, waiting to hear something else... some indication whether Matt was dead or alive...anything to tell
her if her life was worth fighting for.

Matt hadn't been prepared for the shot. One minute the
gun had been jabbed in his ribs and the next it had been
pointed at the buffet. The sound of Charlotte screaming
his name had kept him from action just long enough for

Carver to jab the gun back in his side. The one word he'd bellowed had been a warning for Charlotte to stay away, as much as anger at his own inability to take advantage of the incident. Carver smiled up at him.

"Call to her," Carver said.

"Like hell," Matt muttered, and saw the little man's eyes narrow in anger.

"She's worried, you know," Carver explained in a frighteningly reasonable tone. "She thinks I've shot you. If you don't call to her she'll probably think you're dying. Then she'll do something stupid like try to save you."

"Stay where you are," Matt shouted. "I'm okay." The lights flickered with each syllable then remained on when he'd finished. He was relieved that she kept silent. The one word she'd screamed had echoed through the big house so that he hadn't been able to discern her location. If he hadn't, then neither had Carver. At the moment, that was the only thing in their favor.

Charlotte hadn't realized she was holding her breath until she heard Matt's voice. He was okay for the moment. She gulped in air greedily and said a prayer of thanksgiving. While she was at it, she begged for inspiration.

"This little game of ours has gone on long enough," she heard Carver shout. The lights flickered off and on as he spoke, so that she felt as if she were fighting for her life in the middle of a laser show. "Your husband and I are going to walk to the front door. I want you to join us before I count to thirty or the next bullet goes through him. One. Two..."

She might be scared but she wasn't stupid, Charlotte told herself. If she thought for one minute that turning herself over to Carver would result in Matt's freedom, she wouldn't hesitate. But she knew that the minute she started down the stairs Carver would shoot Matt and then gun her down before she could escape. Their only hope lay in fighting their way out of this. And her only weapon was a maladjusted robot.

She knew Matt and the gunman were in the dining room almost directly under her, which meant they'd be passing under the walkway outside the bedroom. But Carver hadn't said anything about coming down the stairs. He'd only said to join them at the front door. That meant he thought she was somewhere on the first floor. If she could keep him thinking that, there was a chance she could drop a surprise on him when he passed beneath her.

Praying that VASSAR wasn't within sight of the two men, she pressed the buttons that would send the little robot hurtling forward and backward several times. She was delighted to hear numerous pieces of furniture topple in the solarium and living room. Grabbing the heavy vase off the dresser, she stationed herself directly over the passage from the dining room to the foyer. She had barely hefted her weapon into position when Matt came into view.

"Eighteen," she heard Carver say. "Nineteen..."

From the sound of his voice, she guessed that Carver was no more than two steps behind Matt. Telling herself that in life, as in business, timing is everything, she released the vase and prayed for a direct hit.

Chapter Fifteen

Matt heard a noise overhead and glanced up to see an Oriental vase hurtling downward. With the lights flickering off and on as Carver counted, the whole thing seemed like an old-time movie. But he was prepared for the vase to land somewhere near Carver, and, more importantly, he was ready to take advantage of this opportunity.

Even as the vase was shattering, Matt spun around and knocked the gun from his hand. The little man was no match for him in size or muscle, and Matt had him up against the wall with his hand around his throat before Charlotte was down the stairs. Though there was some satisfaction in listening to the gurgling sound Carver made trying to suck in air through a flattened windpipe, Matt turned him loose as soon as Charlotte asked him to. Carver slid to the floor, gasping for air as Matt picked the gun up from the floor.

"Well, don't just stand there. Call the police," Matt commanded.

"Don't you think you should point the gun at him or something?"

"He's not going anywhere for a while," Matt assured her, though he wished Carver would try so that he could have the satisfaction of smashing his fist into the man's gut. The little weasel should have to pay for what he'd put Charlotte through.

By the time the police, Bob Stone, Howie, Walter and Rhue had invaded her house, Charlotte had a raging headache. She didn't mind the police traipsing in and out of her house or the lateness of the hour or the noise or the crowd of neighbors gathered outside. What really bothered her was the way Matt had retreated back into his shell. It was as though they were strangers, as though they'd never made love or slept in each other's arms. And that frightened her more than anything else.

She thought once about walking over to him and asking him to put his arms around her, but she was afraid he'd just look at her in that distant but polite way he was now. Instead, she massaged her temples and wished everyone would go away.

Matt realized she was nursing a headache long before Charlotte gave in to the need to rub it away. What she should do was tell everyone, including the police, to go away and leave her alone. If it was up to him, that's what he'd do. But this wasn't his house and it wasn't his responsibility. He was on borrowed time now; once this mess was cleared up, he'd go pack his stuff and leave. So he'd go along with however Charlotte wanted to handle this. That's what he told himself.

But when Howie started asking if there was anything in the house to eat, he gave the two brothers succinct directions to a restaurant on Los Feliz Boulevard. And when the police kept going over the same details, he informed them that Charlotte would come down and give a statement the next day. He even went outside and told the neighbors to go tromp all over someone else's pansies. He wondered who was going to help take care of Charlotte from now on, then reminded himself that she'd taken care of herself before he'd come along. He didn't know how, but she had.

Finally only Rhue and Bob Stone remained. He didn't mind giving Bob the boot—after all, he was sure the man was charging him for every minute of his time. But knowing Rhue's penchant for tears, he decided to let Charlotte handle her.

"You're sure you'll be all right?" he heard Charlotte ask her aunt. That figured. Charlotte was the one who'd been shot at and terrorized, but she was worried about Rhue.

"I'll be fine, darling. I'm just thankful that you're all right. I don't understand how I could have been so blind." The older woman rose and smiled up at Bob Stone, who, with a solicitous murmur, draped a sweater over her shoulders.

"But Aunty, I hate to think of you out by yourself at this hour."

"Don't worry about your aunt," the private investigator assured Charlotte. "I'll see that she gets home safely."

Matt decided he sounded like an out-of-work Shakespearean actor. Some women, he knew, liked that type of man. He decided Rhue was one of them from the way she fluttered her eyelashes. Matt wondered what type of man Charlotte preferred.

"They make a cute couple, don't you think?" Charlotte asked as they waved the two older people off.

"At least you don't have to worry about him being after her for her money. He knows exactly what her financial situation is."

"Don't be so cynical. I think it would be nice if, after all the grief Carver caused, Bob turned out to be Aunt Rhue's Mr. Right."

"Not very likely," Matt muttered.

"Why is that?"

"Your aunt grew up with money and education while Bob grew up..." He knew things about Bob's background that would make her hair curl. "Let's just say that Bob wouldn't fit into her world."

"I don't think that love takes those things into consideration. The heart sees a person as he is now."

"Yeah, sure. For about the first six months. Then a woman like your aunt starts to notice that the guy's a little rough around the edges and she starts wondering what they have in common. Other than the obvious."

He looked her up and down so that Charlotte had no doubt what he was talking about. If he was being rougher than necessary, he told himself, it was because he wanted her to convince him he was wrong. He wanted her to tell him that it didn't matter how he'd grown up or that there was still the kind of violence in him that could make him squeeze Carver's windpipe until the man turned blue in the face.

But she didn't say any of those things, she just started gathering up the coffee mugs and taking them to the kitchen. He grabbed one that she'd missed and followed her to the back of the house. He might as well give her all the good news now. Then he could be on his way and leave her to get on with her life.

"I spoke to Howie and Walter tonight. They've agreed to withdraw their objections to the settlement of your father's will."

"That's . . . wonderful."

"You don't sound so thrilled."

That's because you'll be leaving, she thought. Because I've fallen in love with you, you insufferable man, and as soon as everything is settled you'll be gone. Actually, he was already gone. Retreated behind that wall of anger.

But she only said, "I think I'm a little numb after everything that's happened. Tell me again in the morning, and I'm sure I'll be more enthusiastic."

"Yeah." He set the coffee mug in the sink. "I'll call you at work and remind you."

"Just remind me over breakfast."

"I won't be here for breakfast. Since your relatives aren't a problem any longer, I'm heading home as soon as I can pack my stuff."

"Now? Tonight?" When he only nodded she asked, "Why?"

Because I can't stay in the same house with you without making love to you, he thought. Because it was bad enough that I couldn't keep my hands off you before, but now it would be unconscionable. Because if you keep looking at me like that I'm going to forget my pride and beg you to give our marriage a real chance.

And if he did that, she might agree—out of a warped sense of obligation or gratitude or something equally generous. And because, in the end, all those differences she said didn't matter, would matter, and then she'd hate him.

He shrugged. "There doesn't seem to be much sense in dragging out the inevitable."

When all she said was, "Oh," he turned on his heel and started upstairs.

Charlotte couldn't believe it could end like this. She couldn't believe that everything they'd said, everything they'd done, could be forgotten so quickly. She couldn't believe that she was standing here rinsing out coffee mugs when her heart was cracking into little tiny pieces. Damn the man! How dare he make her love him and then walk out like nothing had happened? Where was his honor? Where was that overactive sense of responsibility?

She dried her hands on the towel. She had a thing or two to tell him. He wasn't getting out of here without facing the fact that he'd made her fall in love with him. Or without realizing that he was throwing away the best thing that had happened to him. She could accept the fact that he didn't love her, but he did want her. And she was willing to bet that if he gave her a chance, she could make him happy.

She could just imagine his reaction if she told him that. He'd tell her it wasn't logical. That they'd married so that she could inherit RP and now that that was done, there was no reason to continue with the marriage. She didn't think he'd consider the fact that she loved him to be the basis of a lifetime commitment.

By the time she reached the upstairs landing, Charlotte had her strategy all mapped out. She was going to appeal to him on a rational, reasonable level. No talk of love. No mention of her breaking heart. Just good, plain logic.

He was stuffing clothes into boxes when she reached the bedroom.

"You know, there aren't that many hours of the night left. It seems to me that it would be more sensible to wait and pack tomorrow."

He wasn't going to look at her. If he looked at her, he'd weaken. "I'm already packing."

She rescued his glasses from the bottom of the box just before he pitched his shoes in on top of them, then rummaged through the other boxes until she found his glasses case. "I suppose this divorce business is going to be expensive and time-consuming."

What did it matter how much it cost or how long it took, when his heart was bleeding all over the place? "I'll see that we put our best divorce attorney on it."

"I hope it won't take much of my actual time. My calendar is pretty full for the next six months."

"I'll have my attorney call yours."

"Fine," she murmured. But don't think you can get rid of me that easily. "And I'll have to make out a new will."

"You just started one with Alice."

She smiled. "True. But in that one I left everything to the Nguyens and my husband."

"You did what?" he demanded. He turned to glare at her. That was a mistake. It was hard to think straight when she looked at him with her big green eyes, when she licked her soft lips, when she held her head just so, as if she were waiting for him to kiss her. "That was a damn stupid thing to do."

"At the time, if you'll remember, we thought my relatives were trying to murder me. Besides, now that we won't be married any longer, I want you to handle the estate."

"Like hell," he muttered.

"I'm sorry. I didn't catch that."

"I said Alice is a competent attorney. Why not keep her?"

"I've gotten used to you," she said sweetly.

He groaned. He'd gotten used to her, too. He'd gotten used to waking up with her, to listening to her laugh, to making her moan with pleasure at night. She was going to be a damn hard habit to break.

"I'm sure you had two of these shoes when you arrived," Charlotte said as she pulled out one unmated loafer. "Do you have any idea where the other one is? It's not like you to be so untidy."

No, it wasn't like him. He usually had everything neatly matched. Nothing was like it used to be. And it never would be again. "It's around somewhere."

"You know, it's really too bad this marriage thing didn't work out for us. I was reading an interesting article the other day. It said that married men live longer."

He slanted her an angry look. *This marriage thing?* How could she refer to the most wonderful time of his life as "this marriage thing?"

"I hear those statistics are invalid. The years only *seem* longer when you're married."

Charlotte tried not to laugh. She loved it when he got mad and huffy, because then she knew she was getting to him. "The article also said married men are happier."

"Happiness isn't measurable." Unless a man could feel the contentment when he walked in the door. Unless he could wake up at night and feel her body next to him and want her with an impact that was so intense, so mind-boggling that nothing else mattered. Unless the idea of living without her made him want to punch something.

"It also said married men are less likely to go bald."

"Baldness doesn't run in my family."

He picked up two boxes and carried them down the stairs. Charlotte watched him from the landing but refused to help.

When he came back for another load, she said, "I just thought there might be more benefits to staying married than to getting a divorce."

"This isn't some employment contract we're discussing. It's a marriage. People don't get married because it'll add years to their lives. They don't stay married because of the benefits. People get married because they're in love!'' he shouted.

Picking up the last of his stuff, he started down the stairs. He hesitated at the door, wondering if he should turn around and say something polite. Then he decided it was best this way. Maybe the anger would help him forget he loved her. Maybe the shouting would help him forget the way she'd melted in his arms. He grabbed hold of the door handle and turned it, but the door wouldn't open. He turned to look at her. She was walking down the steps, and she had VASSAR's remote control in her hand.

He glared at her. ''What do you think you're doing?''

''Keeping you from making the worst mistake of your life.''

''How's that?''

''If you walk out that door, you're throwing away happiness and several years of your life—not to mention a full head of hair.''

''I can live with that.''

''I can't.''

Setting the box down, he started up the steps. ''Give me the controls.''

Charlotte didn't answer. Instead she laid the small device on the stair and stepped on it. She didn't have to be an electronics genius to know that no one would be unlocking any doors with that.

''Why'd you do that?''

''Because I love you.''

He looked from her to the shattered control and back into her eyes again. He wanted to believe her. God, how he wanted to believe, but he shook his head. ''No, you don't. There are things about me you don't know. About how I grew up and what I've done.''

She started down the steps toward him. "I know that you're logical and neat to a fault."

"Not when you're around."

She kept coming toward him. "And that you have this super-man complex that makes you think you can straighten out the world."

"That shows what you know. I wouldn't be caught dead in tights."

She stopped on the bottom step. Their eyes were level. "And that you have this anger in you that you'd like to forget, but you can't because it's part of the good, honorable man you are."

"How do you know about that?"

She smiled. "Because I love that part of you, too."

He swept her into a fierce embrace. "Oh, God, how I love you. The thought of living without you was hell."

"Good. Don't ever think of it again," she told him as she turned her face up to his for a kiss that assured her he'd never let her go. Laying her head on his shoulder, she asked, "Why were you leaving, then?"

"For your own good."

"I knew it! That's the one bad habit I'm going to insist that you break."

"It might take years."

"I'm willing to give you a lifetime."

He kissed her again, just to be sure she was really in his arms. "I want us to get married."

"We are."

"No, this time I want to do it right. We'll invite your family and our friends. Aunt Rhue can even organize the reception. If that's not love," he informed her, "I don't know what is."

"Okay."

"I want to grow old with you and sit in the backyard watching our grandkids play."

"We'll need to have kids first."

He smiled. "I'm willing. But first I want a honeymoon."

"A honeymoon? Before the wedding? Have you always had this problem with logic?"

"Only around you." He swept her into his arms and started up the stairs. "You're the woman who taught me that logic is highly overrated."

* * * * *

Ahoy, Readers!

Debbie Macomber is back at the helm with

NAVY BRAT

Navy brat Erin McNamara planned to pass adulthood joyfully embracing the landlubber's life—even if it meant steering clear of Lt. Commander Brandon Davis, the navy man who set her heart racing at twenty knots per minute! But Brandon was equally determined not to give up his *seafaring* ways. And although the outlook was stormy, he simply had to navigate irrepressible Erin into becoming his navy bride!

This April, drop anchor with NAVY BRAT (Special Edition #662), Debbie Macomber's follow-up to NAVY WIFE (Special Edition #494) and NAVY BLUES (Special Edition #518)—and set your sights on future navy stories—only in *Silhouette Special Edition!*

Available *in April* at your favorite retail outlet, or order your copy by sending your name, address, zip or postal code, along with a check or money order for $3.25 (please do not send cash), plus 75¢ postage and handling ($1.00 in Canada), payable to Silhouette Reader Service to:

In the U.S.	In Canada
3010 Walden Ave.,	P.O. Box 609,
P.O. Box 1396,	Fort Erie, Ontario
Buffalo, NY 14269-1396	L2A 5X3

Please specify book title with your order.
Canadian residents add applicable federal and provincial taxes.

NAVY-1

Take 4 bestselling love stories FREE

Plus get a FREE surprise gift!

Special Limited-time Offer

Silhouette Reader Service®

Mail to

In the U.S.
3010 Walden Avenue
P.O. Box 1867
Buffalo, N.Y. 14269-1867

In Canada
P.O. Box 609
Fort Erie, Ontario
L2A 5X3

YES! Please send me 4 free Silhouette Special Edition® novels and my free surprise gift. Then send me 6 brand-new novels every month, which I will receive months before they appear in bookstores. Bill me at the low price of $2.74* each—a savings of 51¢ apiece off cover prices. There are no shipping, handling or other hidden costs. I understand that accepting the books and gift places me under no obligation ever to buy any books. I can always return a shipment and cancel at any time. Even if I never buy another book from Silhouette, the 4 free books and the surprise gift are mine to keep forever.

*Offer slightly different in Canada—$2.74 per book plus 69¢ per shipment for delivery. Sales tax applicable in N.Y. Canadian residents add applicable federal and provincial taxes.

235 BPA R1YY (US)   335 BPA 8178 (CAN)

Name _____ (PLEASE PRINT) _____

Address _____ Apt. No. _____

City _____ State/Prov. _____ Zip/Postal Code _____

This offer is limited to one order per household and not valid to present Silhouette Special Edition® subscribers. Terms and prices are subject to change.

SPED-BPA1DR   © 1990 Harlequin Enterprises Limited

COMING SOON FROM SILHOUETTE BOOKS

ONCE MORE WITH FEELING

SONG OF THE WEST

by the BESTSELLING AUTHOR of
over SIXTY novels,

Two of your favorite love stories from an award-winning author in one special collector's edition.

Don't miss the opportunity to relive the romance!

Available in May at your favorite retail outlet.

NR-1